FOSTERING
DEATH

THE JESSE DAMON SERIES

FOSTERING DEATH

KM ROCKWOOD

A Jesse Damon Crime Novel

WILDSIDE PRESS

For Pat Staten,
who always had a book
tucked under the seat of her forklift
to read during downtime on the overnight shift

Published by Wildside Press LLC
www.wildsidepress.com

CHAPTER 1

"She didn't have to die." Mr. Coleman, aged considerably in the twenty years since I'd last seen him, lifted a crisp handkerchief to dab his eyes. Blue veins snaked over the back of his trembling hand. "Especially like that." His voice was thin.

A plump lady in a big hat took his other hand and patted it gently. "Your wife will get her reward in heaven. She believed in the Lord. And she helped so many unfortunate children!"

Trying to be as invisible as possible, I eased myself back among the flower arrangements on easels, choking on the cloying scent of chrysanthemums. I rubbed my freshly shaved face with my rough hand. Maybe I shouldn't have come here.

"The mortician did a good job," the lady said. "She could be asleep. Quite natural."

Mr. Coleman glanced into the coffin, then quickly looked away.

Straight at me.

His already pale face went paler.

"What are you doing here?" he asked, his reedy voice rising.

Other conversations ceased as all eyes turned toward me.

I'd been right. I shouldn't have come.

He looked me over, head to foot. "And you couldn't even dress properly."

Inwardly, I winced. I clutched my jacket to my chest, folded so its worn black lining showed instead of the garish red plaid. I'd worn my darkest flannel shirt and clean jeans. The work boots were the only footwear I owned.

"When you wrote that letter to her from prison, didn't I write back to tell you she never wanted to hear from you again?"

"Yes, sir. I never tried to write her again."

"What made you think you'd be welcome here?"

I had been among the dozens of foster children who'd passed through the Colemans' house over the years. Mrs. Coleman was the closest thing to a mother I'd ever known. I said, "I'm sorry, sir. I didn't mean no disrespect. She meant a lot to me."

His quavering voice grew even louder. "I find that hard to believe. You were a huge disappointment to her. She looked on you almost as her own, keeping you for all those years. She thought she *saw* something in you. But she was wrong, wasn't she?"

I had no answer for that. I inched toward the door.

"She cried after she read about you in the newspaper. Did you know that?"

"No, sir," I said. "I'm sorry."

"Sorry doesn't quite cut it, does it?" Fury blazed in his pale eyes. "Since when do they let killers out of prison, anyhow?"

Everyone was staring at me. I didn't think this was a good time to start explaining about parole.

Two burly men in somber suits were bearing down on me. I turned and strode out of the viewing room to the entry hall.

As I skirted a stand by the door, the lady standing next to it chirped, "Don't forget to sign the visitor's book!" and tried to hand me a slim gold pen.

I ignored her and kept on going, out the front door and down the granite steps, which were getting slippery from the falling sleet.

Angry at myself, I swiped my face with my sleeve. For the first time in years, I couldn't will away the tears that stung my eyes.

I stumbled at the bottom of the steps and turned into the alley next to the funeral home, anxious to get away from everyone. A few feet down, I stopped and took a shuddering breath. After the overheated air in the funeral home, the fresh air felt good as I gulped it into my lungs. Maybe it would help clear my head.

How could I have been stupid enough to have come here? What did I think was going to happen? That I'd find a connection with my past, and we'd all link arms and sing "Kumbaya" together? All I'd managed to do was upset Mr. Coleman when he could least afford more grief. And make myself feel crummy in the process.

I shivered and shifted the jacket in my hands, trying to unfold it.

"Well, look who's here, Detective Montgomery. Jesse Damon," a voice said behind me.

"Interesting indeed, Detective Belkins. I have to admit I hadn't expected to see him here," came the answer.

"Didn't sound like he was particularly welcome."

Detectives from the local police force. Of course they'd recognized me. Since my release from prison, Belkins especially had taken it upon himself to make sure I knew I was being watched.

With the cuff of my shirt, I swiped at my eyes again. I wasn't going to let them know I'd been crying.

Belkins tapped me on the shoulder. Hard. "You know the routine, Damon. Drop the jacket and assume the position."

I tossed my jacket onto the damp asphalt, trying to avoid the slushy puddles. I spread my feet and leaned on the rough brick wall of the funeral home, bracing on my hands.

"Anything on you we should know about?" Montgomery asked as he stepped up behind me. "Weapons, drugs—anything you want to tell us about?"

"No, sir." I had more sense than to have anything I shouldn't be carrying. I wasn't about to violate parole over something stupid like that.

Quick professional hands frisked me, removing the wallet and key ring with its single key from my jeans pocket, skimming over my clothes, under my arms, and between my legs.

Montgomery's strong dark hand reached up and grabbed my wrist, pulling my hand behind my back and turning the palm out. I felt the familiar cold bite of handcuffs. He repeated the motion with my other hand, tightening them enough to hurt. I knew Belkins would have put them on even tighter.

"Turn around. Slowly," Montgomery said.

I turned around, trying to shake the dark curly hair out of my eyes.

Montgomery was pulling fur-lined leather gloves over his manicured hands. My wallet and keychain lay on the pavement next to my jacket.

Both of the detectives were dressed warmly. Belkins wore a squashed fedora on his head, melting sleet dripping from the brim. His teeth clenched an unlit cigar.

Montgomery stood a head above him, his mahogany face handsome above his spotless tan trench coat, a jaunty hat perched on his shaven head. I wondered how he managed to look unrumpled and dry standing out in this sleet.

"Damon knows his place, doesn't he? Knows there's no point objecting." Belkins chomped on the cigar. His watery blue eyes squinted to mere slits above his bulbous red nose.

Montgomery frowned at him and turned back to me. "You're still on parole, aren't you, Jesse?" he said, his voice deceptively friendly.

"Yes, sir." They knew the answer to that. They also knew that if I was on parole they didn't need a warrant to detain me or bring me in for questioning. Not even reasonable cause for suspicion.

Belkins reached over and jerked up the leg of my jeans. "No black box?" he asked. "When'd you get off home detention?"

"Little while ago, sir."

He shook his head. "Don't know what your PO was thinking."

I saw no point in trying to answer that.

"What are you doing here?" Montgomery asked.

"Mrs. Coleman was my foster mother. Just wanted to pay my last respects."

"Don't think that was a particularly good idea." Montgomery adjusted the scarlet muffler a bit tighter around his neck.

Shivering as melting sleet dripped off my hair and down the back of my shirt, I shook my head.

"How did you know where the viewing was being held?" he asked.

"I saw a funeral notice," I said. "In the newspaper. At the library."

Belkins raised his bushy eyebrows. "The library. Did you know he could read, Montgomery?"

"Oh, Jesse's nobody's dummy." Montgomery rocked back on his well-shod heels. "Does some stupid things, sometimes, but he's smart enough."

"Not smart enough to mind his own business." Belkins took the cigar out of his mouth and peered at me. "Do you know how she died?"

I hadn't thought much about it. She wasn't young, and all the years I'd known her, she'd never really been in good health. All I'd read in the paper was when the viewing and funeral would be. "Not really," I said.

Montgomery just stared at me, his dark eyes giving me no hint to what was going on in his mind.

I forced myself not to fidget. It had to have been a natural death. Or maybe an accident.

Who would want to kill Mrs. Coleman?

Belkins looked like he thought he knew someone who would. Me.

"Somebody kill her?" I blurted out. Instantly, I regretted saying anything. I made a mental note to get to the library and check out the newspapers for the past few days, see if I could find anything out.

Assuming, of course, I didn't get locked up right away.

"You tell me," Montgomery said, his eyes boring into my face. I looked down at my boots.

"Refresh my memory, Damon," Belkins said, staring at the unlit end of the cigar. "How long were you in prison?"

"Just under twenty years."

"And what was the conviction?"

He knew all this. He just wanted to make me say it. "Murder. Conspiracy. Possession of a handgun during commission of a felony."

"And you pled guilty?"

"An Alford plea." That plea—not admitting guilt but conceding that the state had enough evidence for a conviction—had been a problem from the start. Parole boards and counselors like to hear convicts express remorse. Hard to do when not admitting guilt.

"That's right. Wouldn't take responsibility, eh?" Belkins stuck the cigar back in his mouth. "Then or now."

Montgomery changed the subject. "Still working night shift at Quality Steel Fabrications, Jesse?"

"Yes, sir."

"Still driving a forklift?" Montgomery tugged his collar a bit more snugly around his neck.

"Yes, sir."

"When I check with them, will they tell me you've been missing a lot of work?"

"No, sir. I been there every night." As if I could afford to take a night off. Between paying for the rent on my little basement apartment and the monitoring expenses for parole, I didn't have much money to spare.

Belkins adjusted his hat, shielding his face better from the sleet. "I say we haul him downtown and see what we can find out. No sense standing out in the cold here."

"I want to see who else comes to the viewing," Montgomery said.

"We can get someone to take him in and hold him until we're done here."

Montgomery eyed me. His gloved fingers stroked the cleft in his chiseled chin.

Out of the corner of my eye, I saw people leaving the funeral home and turning down the alley. They stopped when they saw us and retreated. I felt the drip of melting sleet running from my wet hair down the neck of my shirt become a rivulet. The shirt was already drenched, so I guess it didn't really matter.

"It's my anniversary," Montgomery said. "Cecile and I have reservations for dinner. She won't be happy if I tell her I'm working late."

A mean smile played on Belkins' lips. "I got no plans for tonight. I can see what I can get out of him."

My gut tightened. Belkins wouldn't be particular about the methods he used for interrogation. I didn't really want to face him alone. Montgomery was young and hungry. He wouldn't want anything on his record that might stand between him and a promotion. Much better for me if he were present.

But there wasn't a damn thing I could do if they decided to run me in.

"We know where he lives and where he works," Montgomery said. "We can always pick him up. Or ask his PO to hold him when he reports in. He's not going anywhere."

"True." Belkins continued to grin at me. "He knows he'll be locked up for the rest of his life if he takes off. Which is where he belongs."

"Besides, you know he's not likely to tell us much anyhow." Montgomery checked his watch.

"I bet I could get him to tell me something." Belkins' grin turned into a leer.

Montgomery glanced over at him. "Does us no good to get information we can't use in court."

Belkins shrugged.

Montgomery grabbed me by the elbow and spun me around. He unlocked the handcuffs.

It took an effort, but I didn't rub my numb wrists. I knew better than to move until they told me to. I stood, looking at my wallet and keychain as they lay where the brick wall met the cracked asphalt of the alley. The slush puddle was swallowing them rapidly.

Montgomery finally said, "You can go. For now."

Another group of people stepped out of the funeral home and straggled across the entry to the alley.

I leaned down, scooping up my wallet and keychain. Then I picked my jacket up from the wet pavement and turned down the alley, away from everyone. I took a tentative step, expecting Belkins to change his mind and tell me to stop.

"And don't even think of going to the church funeral service," Montgomery called after me. "That poor old man's been through enough."

He was right about that. I kept my gaze straight ahead and kept going. I didn't know where the alley went. With my luck it would dead-end at the garage. I'd climb a fence to avoid walking back past them if it came to that. Or hide behind a dumpster until the alley was clear again.

What did they throw in dumpsters out behind funeral homes, anyhow?

I turned at the corner of the building and saw an opening between the garage and another building. I walked toward it, hoping it was a through walkway. It was. I didn't let myself glance back until I was halfway down it.

No one was in sight. The detectives weren't following me. I unfolded my jacket and put it on. It was damp, but at least it blocked the needles of sleet that were driving into my shirt. I pulled the watch cap out of the pocket and pulled it over my head. Wool holds body heat even when it's wet, although I wasn't sure my body was producing any heat to speak of.

I emerged on the street behind the funeral home and saw a patrol car idling by the corner. The driver eyed me as I turned in the opposite direction and walked away.

After a few blocks, I thought I heard the sound of a car close to the curb following me, but between the wind and the sound of the sleet hitting the sidewalk, it might be just my overactive imagination hearing things. The area between my shoulder blades, the place where "IN-MATE" would be stenciled in white letters on an orange prison jumpsuit, itched. Word was it was positioned so the tower guards would have a target to aim for in an escape attempt.

I wished I'd taken the opportunity back in the alley to check to see if anything I didn't know about was in my pants pockets. I didn't doubt Belkins might slip me some crystal meth or something if he thought he could get away with it, but it had been Montgomery who had frisked me, and he'd be too professional for that kind of nonsense. I hoped.

Shoving my hands into the jacket pockets, I ducked my head into the wind. I wasn't about to give anybody watching the satisfaction of seeing me check my pants pocket. Or even look back to see it somebody really was following me. One good thing about the sleet—my face was so wet it hid any tears.

When I turned the corner to head toward the aging building where I rented a basement apartment, the patrol car was sitting in the alley. They must have swung around the block. Or maybe it was another car.

Had a car been following me? Entirely my imagination? Without breaking my stride, I glanced back.

A battered, blue pickup truck was creeping along by the curb, lights out. What was that all about? I couldn't see a cop, undercover or otherwise, being caught dead in a pickup in that bad shape.

I looked back at the patrol car. It was pulled up in the dead-end alley that the single window of my basement window looked out on. Its nose hung over the sidewalk. I'd have to pass it to get to the stairs that led down from the sidewalk to my front door. As I approached, the cop in the passenger seat, a woman with her hair pulled back in a severe bun, rolled down the window. She stared at me.

I didn't stop or make eye contact, but I did take my hands out of my pockets and let them hang by my sides. No point giving anyone an excuse to go for a Taser. I'd never been tased myself, but I'd seen it done, and it didn't look pleasant. I had no desire to experience it firsthand.

Resisting an urge to wipe my eyes again, I concentrated on keeping my breathing regular. I'd keep walking if they didn't say anything to me.

If Montgomery had slipped something into my pocket and told them to search me, they'd stop me.

Unless they were waiting for me to go in so they could search the apartment. Not that they'd need reasonable suspicion for that, either. The parole papers I'd signed gave permission for warrantless searches any time.

Biting my lip, I reminded myself that parole was well worth all the restrictions that came with it. My apartment might be a dingy single room with the kitchenette in one corner and a tiny bathroom off another, but as long as I paid the rent, it was mine. And the key that opened the door was in my own pocket, not hung on some correctional officer's belt.

The cop made no move to open the car door. Another advantage to the weather. She wasn't going to get out of the warm, dry car unless she had to.

As I approached the top of the stairs, I listened for someone to shout, "Stop!" But no one did.

I slipped my hands back into my pockets and hunched down into my jacket. The sleet looked like it might be changing to snow. I didn't look back. That would only make me look nervous. And guilty.

The cops were going to keep a close eye on me. It went with the territory. Cops don't like parolees. They would be sure I was up to something. They were waiting for—what? Something I said or did that they thought tied me to Mrs. Coleman's death. And anything else they could incidentally pin on me.

That meant the detectives investigating her death would probably put a lot of their efforts into trying to show that I'd killed her. Unfortunately, that meant they might not investigate what had actually happened.

Montgomery might be my best bet. If I could find out anything useful, he would listen. And look into it. Solving a homicide would be a big deal. And a detective bucking for a promotion didn't want to be part of a team that made an arrest that ended in an acquittal. Or worse, in a conviction that was reversed on appeal.

I did have one advantage over any official investigation. I *knew* I hadn't killed Mrs. Coleman.

Salt crunched underfoot as I approached the outdoor stairs down to my apartment. The janitor had spread it to keep ice from forming.

I heard the heavy *thunk* of a vehicle's door slamming.

CHAPTER 2

"Jesse!"

I froze. That whiny voice didn't sound like it was coming from a cop. Resting my hand on the railing of the stairs down to my front door, I glanced over my shoulder.

The blue pickup stood at the curb, engine running and lights out.

"Jesse. You got to help me score."

Aaron. A kid from the packing line at work. A kid who was going to get fired from a good job because he kept missing work. A kid who was into crystal meth and whatever else he could get his hands on. A kid who might well have turned police informant to save his own ass. That might explain why he hadn't been fired yet for all the absences from work. Also why it didn't bother him to be stopping me to ask about drugs in front of the cops sitting in an alley a few hundred yards away.

I turned to face him. "I don't 'got' to do nothing." I reached for my key, ready to continue down the stairs and into my apartment.

"You're right, you're right." Aaron's bloodshot eyes watched my hand reach into my pocket, and he flinched. Then he grinned and sniffed, pulling out a small packet of tissues and wiping his nose. He stuffed the tissues, including the one he'd just used, back into the pocket of his jacket.

I looked at the jacket with a tinge of envy. It was an expensive jacket, down-filled and undoubtedly very warm. I shivered in my damp wool hunting jacket from Goodwill.

"I was just hoping you would," he said. "I got to score. Bad."

"You know better than that."

Aaron's eyes were filled with the genuine anguish of a jonesing addict. "What am I gonna do?"

"I told you before. Call Narcotics Anonymous. They'll help you."

"They'd tell me I got to stop using."

"They'd be right."

Aaron rubbed his arm. "It's freezing out here. Let's go into your place so we can talk."

"Let's not. We got nothing to talk about."

Aaron nodded. "You're not gonna say anything that's gonna get you in trouble. I get that. You're smart."

"If I was smart, I wouldn't be standing here talking to you at all," I said.

"I'm getting desperate."

"You told me you could run down to Park Heights in Baltimore and pick up anything you wanted."

Aaron's face fell. "I tried that. Cost me a whole tank of gas. They sold me a little crystal meth and said that was all they had. So I got a couple of rocks that they said was crack. But it was just little white pebbles."

In spite of myself, I laughed. "Real rocks, huh?"

Aaron shook his head. "Expensive ones, too. I got to do something." He reached into his jacket pocket.

What did he have? I tensed and half-raised my fist.

He pulled out a wad of bills and shoved them toward me. "You don't have to handle nothing. Just tell your contacts they can trust me. I can pay. Plenty more where that came from."

Which, I suspected, was seed money from the vice squad.

I stepped back and put my hands behind me. Last thing I needed was for the cops to see me take money from Aaron. Especially if the serial numbers had been photocopied.

"Don't you see that patrol car right there?" I nodded toward it.

Aaron glanced toward the alley. He seemed surprised. "Where the hell'd that come from?"

I just shook my head.

"You should let me into your apartment," he said. "Then nobody could see what we're doing."

"Nothing for anybody to see. And I bet you got something on you that could get me in real trouble."

"Nope." Aaron scratched the three-day stubble on his chin. "If I had anything, I would've used it."

"How about all that money? Where'd that come from? You could buy anything you wanted. Who told you to come to me?"

Anger flared in Aaron's eyes. "Are you calling me a snitch?"

"You said it; I didn't."

Aaron's voice started to rise to a shout. "You think you're tough, don't you? You think you can treat me like dirt and get away with it."

I turned away. I wasn't going to dignify that stupidity with an answer.

He pulled the tissue out of his pocket, wiped his nose again and grabbed my jacket with his other hand, still clutching the money.

Mindful of the patrol car, I forced my hands to remain motionless. At this distance, the cops in the patrol car probably couldn't hear what we were saying. Unless Aaron was wired. But they could see. I didn't want to look like I was threatening him. If I made a move to push him away, would they come to his rescue? Or just write a report to be resurrected later when they could use it?

The interior light in the cab of the pickup by the curb came on. I glanced over; the door was open a crack. What kind of backup had he brought along?

"Aaron!" a plaintive young voice called.

He loosened his grip on my jacket. "What?"

"You told Mom you'd pick me up, and we'd come straight home. That was hours ago."

I backed up a step. "You brought a *kid* with you when you're trying to score?"

Aaron shrugged. "My mom'll only give me gas money if I do stuff for her, like pick up my kid brother if she's at work."

Disgusted, I said again, "And you brought him along when you're trying to score?"

"Hey, I left him in the truck. He's too little to know what's going on. He'll be fine."

"You got no idea what you're playing with, do you?" I shook my head. "Did you take him down to Park Heights with you, too?" I didn't want to think about what could happen to a little kid if he got in the way of a deal that went down wrong.

No cop would knowingly send an informant out to make a buy with a kid in the truck. So maybe this really wasn't a set-up. Or the cops didn't realize that he'd be idiot enough to bring the kid along.

Aaron pulled another wad of bills out of his pants pocket and added it to those in his hand. "Come on," he said. "I know you got something. Either sell me some or tell me where to go to get some."

"You really gonna give me some of that money just for telling you where to go?"

Aaron sniffed. "I trust you, Jesse."

My eyes narrowed, I stared at him. Kid in the truck or no kid, this *had* to be a setup. If I took any money, even if I didn't supply anything, I'd be up against an intent to distribute conspiracy charge. "Only one person you can even begin to trust," I said.

"Who?"

"You're standing right there in his boots."

"Me?"

"I'm not sure even that's a good idea. But for sure you can't trust nobody else. Including me."

Aaron stood up a bit straighter and stared down the steps to my apartment. "I know how much you make. You live in a crummy basement room. You got to pay all those parole fees and court costs. Extra money would come in handy. You gonna help me or not?" He held up the bills again and waved them in front of me.

"Not." I took a step back.

Aaron's face twisted in anger. "You know, I could make your life pretty miserable. Get you fired from the job."

He probably could—I didn't think it would be that hard. But I just said, "Try it. I don't think you've got much credibility with anybody at work anymore."

"I could tell that girlfriend of yours some things."

Ouch. This was a sensitive area. I took a deep breath. "I don't have a girlfriend."

"Sure you do. Kelly? From work? You know she's been putting out in the warehouse to anybody who'll pay her. I been with her myself."

My chest tightened. Kelly wasn't my girlfriend, but I'd certainly like her to be. She treated me just like a regular person, not like a paroled murderer.

She was just divorced, with two kids to think about, so she spent most of her non-work time with them. I realized neither one of us was in a position to make any kind of commitment, and I think she did, too.

A couple of times she'd invited me over to her house for supper. I'd help out with the cooking and cleaning up, then sit down with the kids and their homework. Or just watch TV with them. Give Kelly a little time to herself and hope she didn't open a bottle. It almost felt like I was part of a family, and I was achingly aware that I could become overly dependent on the warm feeling it gave me.

After the kids were asleep, sometimes we went to bed ourselves. If she hadn't drunk too much. I didn't drink. I wasn't about to take a chance on violating my parole over something as stupid as drinking alcohol.

Kelly had introduced me to sex, and no matter what she did or what anybody else said about her, I would be eternally grateful to her for that.

But if she reached the point where she might be looking for a steady boyfriend, if she ever did, what could I offer her? A future of uncertainty, stepping carefully and never sure I wasn't about to be picked up and sent back to prison to serve out my backup time? That was no way for a woman to live. Especially a woman with children. She deserved better than that.

Aaron was standing there, swaying slightly and still holding out the money. I knew he was lying about her putting out in the warehouse. Her job almost never took her back there, and I was in and out all shift long. She could be seeing other men, but it wasn't during work hours. I'd never asked her about other men.

Really none of my business. I shouldn't care.

So why was that sour taste rising in my throat? I felt like I might vomit.

Without me paying much attention, Aaron was babbling on. Since he hadn't gotten a rise out of me with the job or Kelly, he'd changed topics.

"You can't tell me you're not using," he said, giving my arm a shove.

"Don't touch me," I warned.

"Your nose is running, and your eyes are red. You've been snorting something, haven't you?"

I stirred myself to answer. "Maybe I just got a cold." I wasn't about to tell him I'd been crying.

"Riiiight." He stuffed the money back in his jacket pocket. "I know you could turn me on to a few contacts. Wouldn't do you no harm."

I just stood there, trying to keep an eye on the cops as well as Aaron. The sleet was changing to snow, which didn't make any noise as it hit the ground. I wished he'd lower his voice. Although if he was wired, they were listening to every word we said anyhow.

"You're gonna be sorry," he said, turning toward the patrol car and away from his brother in the truck. "I could tell them things about you. Get you locked up again."

My muscles tightened, and my mind started to go blank. Raising my clenched fists, I took a short step toward him.

Aaron flinched back.

A light in the patrol car winked on. I stopped, took a deep breath, and made myself drop my arms to my sides and back up a step toward the stairwell. This wasn't prison. The consequence for giving Aaron a little of what he deserved wouldn't be a month in disciplinary segregation, it would be street charges for assault. Possibly on a police informant, and in front of two officers. Not smart.

Aaron wiped his nose one last time, threw the tissue on the sidewalk, and scuttled over to his truck, climbing in and slamming the door. It lurched forward. I watched the taillights until it turned the corner. The patrol car just sat there.

I shivered and started toward the stairs. If the cops were going to burst in and search my place, there wasn't a damn thing I could do about it.

Beyond the stairwell, a sign above the entry to the first floor store front hung by one corner, banging in the wind. The sign was pretty new. Just recently, the abandoned pizza parlor had been rented out to a store-front church. Seemed more like a cult, really. They'd made a big deal about dedicating their new hand-lettered sign. It read, "All-Seeing Tabernacle of Inaccurate Conception." Underneath, in smaller letters, it said, "Seek Impotent Wisdom—A Pure Mind in a Pure Body."

That seemed pretty strange to me, but then the church members were pretty strange themselves. From what I could see, they were all male, and I figured they must have embraced celibacy in their quest for enlightenment. Or whatever they were seeking. They must have been pretty proud of it, and pretty weird, to announce it to the world like that.

As I watched, a gust of wind caught the sign and sent it tumbling to the pavement. I picked it up—it was surprisingly heavy for its size—and propped it against the brick wall in the sheltered entryway. It might be a weird sign, but they'd gone to the trouble of painting it and hanging it, and it'd be a shame to have it ruined, lying face down on the wet sidewalk.

I glanced back at the patrol car. The interior light was still on. The cop in the passenger seat brought the radio transmitter to her mouth.

They would sit there for as long as they wanted to. Nothing I could do.

The wind picked up, and snow blew harder as I finally started down the steps to my apartment. My feet crunched on the salt. I pulled out my key.

I didn't think I'd ever get over the sense of satisfaction that came with holding the key in my own hand and unlocking the door myself.

A movement in the dim corner of the landing at the bottom of the stairs caught my eye. Half-frozen slush was beginning to pool around the drain in the cracked concrete. I peered more closely.

A small figure was huddled in the corner, somewhat out of the sleet. A cat. I eased my hand toward it. The cat cringed back further, but didn't hiss, and it didn't try to get past me. I scooped it up and looked at it.

It was wet and bedraggled, but it wore a red collar heavy with gaudy rhinestones and gems, and it wasn't starving. If anything, it was fat. Had to be somebody's cat. I carried it up the stairs to put it on the sidewalk. Going up on the salt couldn't be good for its paws.

The patrol car ripped out of the alley, its light bar flashing. As it careened down the street, the siren rose into a scream.

They had something better to do than tear my place apart. At least for tonight.

The cat clung to my jacket. I let it snuggle against me until the lights and siren had faded. Then I put it on the sidewalk, giving it a little shove. "Go home," I told it. "This is no weather to be out in."

The cat stood in the dim light from the entrance to the temple. Its fur was a mixture of blacks, reds, and tans. It stood on the sidewalk, now getting even more thoroughly soaked and stared back at me with startling amber eyes. Its fur flattened against its body, ears and tail drooping.

"Go home," I repeated. Like it could understand me.

The cat just stood there.

I went back down the stairs, into my apartment and shut the door firmly behind me. My clothes were soaked, and I was freezing. I took my boots off, loosening the laces and pulling out the tongues. I set them under the radiator to dry. I had to wear them to work tonight. At least I had dry socks I could put on. Maybe turning the jacket inside out and putting it on the back of a chair in front of the radiator would dry it out some by the time I had to leave. Stripping off the wet flannel and T-shirt, I replaced them with dry ones.

A cup of instant coffee sounded good, but I was due at work at midnight, and I needed to get any sleep I could. With my stomach still tied in a knot and all the thoughts racing around in my head, it was going to be hard enough to doze off as it was without putting any caffeine into my system.

My jeans were more than damp. I tossed them onto the seat of the chair with the jacket. I did have a dry pair for work. Then I sat on the edge of the bed to change into dry socks.

The bed that came with the furnished apartment might be lumpy but it sure beat the thin foam mattress with a slippery fire proof cover I had in prison. And instead of one skimpy blanket, I had a pile of bedding I could snuggle down into. When I got covered up and warm, I could relax and maybe fall asleep.

I thought of the cat, staring at me reproachfully as it huddled in the snow. And here I was, settling down comfortably.

Surely it would go home. The owners would be glad it came back and let it right in.

Unless it was lost. And if it wasn't lost, what was it doing there outside my door in the first place?

It was just a cat.

But all I would be able to think of was the cat, out in the cold, and I'd never get to sleep. Not if there was something I could do about it.

Cursing my own stupidity, I switched on the outdoor light in the stairwell and opened the door.

The damn cat was back in the same corner, now wetter and more miserable-appearing than before. It looked at me and opened its mouth in a pathetic meow.

With a sigh, I stepped out into the cold and reached for the cat. Again, it didn't hiss or try to move away. My foot landed in the slush. The new sock was now completely soaked. Sleet stung my naked legs.

I brought the cat inside and shut the door. It looked up at me and meowed again. It might be chubby, but when had it eaten last?

I was planning to make tuna sandwiches to take for lunch at work tonight. I supposed I could spare a bit for a cat. I put the cat down and grabbed the can opener and the can of tuna. I put a little of it in a bowl and put it in front of the cat.

It gobbled the tuna down and looked up hopefully.

I put some more tuna in the bowl.

The cat downed it and looked up again.

Oh, well. I could make peanut butter sandwiches for lunch. I emptied the rest of the can into the bowl. The cat ate it.

I looked around. I didn't have anything faintly resembling a litter pan or cat litter. But I couldn't put the damn thing out again until the weather got better. I'd bought a newspaper so I could cut Mrs. Coleman's obituary out of it. I retrieved the rest of it from the trash and tore it into little pieces, putting it in a box that I lined with a trash bag. I lifted the cat into it and moved its paw in a digging motion. It got the idea right away and peed, then covered the spot with shredded newspaper. That didn't mask the smell all that well. Great.

And of course it would need somewhere to sleep. I'd gone to the Laundromat that morning, wanting to be sure my jeans and shirt were clean to wear to the funeral home. I hadn't put the clothes away yet, so I opened a drawer in my decrepit dresser and dumped the clean clothes in there. Then I put a soft towel in the bottom of the laundry basket and shoved the whole arrangement out of the way so I wouldn't step on it, half under the foot of the bed, near the radiator. When I lifted the cat into the basket, it settled right down, purring.

At least it appreciated my efforts.

Changing to yet another pair of dry socks, I checked the alarm and climbed into bed.

* * * *

When the alarm shrilled, I was heavily asleep. I reached over and slammed it off. A warm lump was nestled up against my neck and shoulder.

The cat.

Reaching over, I stroked it. It nuzzled my hand.

In bed, I was warm and comfortable. The air in the apartment was cold—the heat went off around nine p.m. I could feel the chill on my arm.

I knew better than to lie there after I'd turned off the alarm. I struggled up, trying not to disturb the cat too much. It didn't have to go work a midnight to eight shift at a factory. It sat up on the bed anyhow, watching me.

My boots weren't quite dry, but that couldn't be helped. I pulled on another pair of socks, these ones wool, over the ones already on my feet. I finished dressing and packed my lunch—peanut butter sandwiches and a Thermos of instant coffee. Not the best lunch in the world, but come four a.m., I'd be glad I had it.

The cat was still sitting on the bed, now scratching at its ridiculous collar. I unbuckled it and hefted it in my hand. It was heavy. Who would put it on a poor cat? I tossed it onto the dresser and gave the cat a scratch on its chin.

"Sorry. I got no more tuna. Or cat food. I'll see what I can get on my way home from work." Like it could understand me and I could really afford to spend money on cat food and litter.

Stupid. The last thing I needed was a pet. What would happen to it if I got locked up again? Besides, it obviously had a home. Look at that collar. Someone would be searching for it. I should keep an eye out for posters for a lost cat.

As I tugged on my jacket and watch cap, the cat wound around my feet and followed me toward the door. I held the door open in case it had had enough of me and my apartment and wanted to go home. But it got one look at the chilly night and jumped back up on the bed, sitting and staring at me.

"Well, I got to go," I told it, feeling foolish for talking to a cat.

"Meow," the cat answered.

In spite of myself, I grinned and gave it a final ruffle behind the ears before I left.

As I passed the alley, a flicker of light caught my eye.

A door to the Tabernacle was propped open and one of the members, dressed in the characteristic saffron robes which could offer little protection against the chill night air, sat on a cinderblock next to the dumpster. Next to him sat a kid, maybe about nine or ten years old. The kid was wearing regular clothes. The light flickered again, and the man lit a cigarette. Or a joint. The security light shone down on him, shadowing his features.

I knew the cult had some pretty strict guidelines, and I doubted smoking anything was acceptable.

And what was a kid doing there?

None of my business, really.

The man lifted his head and looked in my direction, but didn't say anything.

I shrugged mentally and hurried on to work.

CHAPTER 3

The heavy scent of oil and hot steel filled the air of the factory. Sparks flew and presses thundered as I punched my time card and gathered my hard hat and gloves. Most of my coworkers milled around the time clock, waiting for our foreman, John, to hand out assignments. Since I already knew I was going to be driving a forklift, I put my lunchbox on a table in front of the vending machines and headed for the charging station, where the electric lifts were plugged in to recharge their batteries.

Kelly was there ahead of me, going over the pre-shift checklist for the large lift she would be driving. Next to it was the smaller lift that was assigned to me. On a hook in the wall near it hung a clipboard with the grimy stub of a pencil tied to it by an equally grimy bit of string. I grabbed the clipboard and started going over the smudged list.

When I got done, Kelly was fussing with her waist-length dark hair, sweeping it into a tight ponytail which she pulled over her shoulder and tucked under the hoodie she was wearing. I tried to tear my gaze away from her magnificent chest, but I must have looked a moment too long.

She laughed. "Keep your mind on your work, buddy. Not to mention your eyes."

I grinned and looked at her face. "You wanna go out for breakfast when we get off work?" I had an emergency twenty stashed in my wallet. I could certainly justify this as an "emergency." Especially if we ended up back at her place.

She shook her head. "I got an appointment with a lawyer after work today. How about tomorrow? You can come over my place, and we can fix breakfast there."

Much better. She knew how tight money could be, and if we were already at her place, we'd be that much closer to her welcoming bed.

Our foreman John rounded the corner, clutching his clipboard with all the information he'd need for the shift, like what jobs were to be run and what shipments needed to be loaded.

He consulted it now, raising his bushy white eyebrows. He tilted his hard hat back a bit. "Can you two stay a bit over when the shift ends?" he asked.

Kelly frowned. "I got an appointment at nine fifteen."

"It'll just be a few minutes," John assured her. "And you'll get overtime for it."

Kelly would get overtime, but I might not. I had another two weeks to go before I'd been employed three months and would join the union. Without union protection, I certainly wasn't going to insist on overtime. I knew John would try to authorize it and slip it through, but it might not be approved.

"Okay," Kelly said. "But not more than half an hour."

"More like two tenths," John said.

I would be staying regardless. I wasn't about to jeopardize this job over a few minutes, whether I got paid for it or not.

The whistle blew, signaling the machine operators to take over from the previous shift workers.

Kelly climbed into the seat of her lift, checked her ponytail to make sure it was securely out of the way, and headed off to the shipping room where she'd spend most of the night loading and unloading trucks.

Starting my lift, I drove toward the warehouse to fetch the first load of dozens to bring parts to the shop floor. The night proceeded uneventfully.

When the shift ended, Kelly and I ran through the post-shift checklist and went to hang around the time clock, waiting for John to finish going over the shift notes with the eight to four foreman.

"You still on for tomorrow after we get off work?" Kelly asked.

I grinned and cast an admiring look over her full figure. It curved in all the right places. My hands itched to reach over and pull her up against me. She certainly wouldn't appreciate it here at work, so I didn't.

"You bet." I glanced around. That was all I was going to say with all these people around.

She smiled back. "The kids'll be in school," she reminded me. "And we'll need a shower after work…"

I bit my lower lip and nodded. I felt heat spreading throughout my body.

Kelly was the only woman I'd ever slept with. An experience I was more than ready to repeat whenever the opportunity offered.

My throat felt tight, and I wasn't sure I would be able to talk. I managed to get out, "Want me to pick up anything?"

She shook her head. "Maybe we could go out to lunch or something."

"Okay. Or wait till the kids get home and take them to McDonald's for supper."

"It'd have to be an early supper. They're going to their Dad's for the weekend."

Did that open up the opportunity for us to spend the entire weekend together? I took a deep breath and tried to refocus on the sounds and smells of the shop around us, not on Kelly's proximity to me.

A worried thought wormed its way into my mind. Kelly's ex wasn't exactly a model parent. I asked, "After he got drunk and left them in the car for hours last time he had them overnight, the judge is letting him take them for the whole weekend?"

Kelly shrugged. "He agreed to leave them at his mother's if he goes out. And his lawyer argued he should have another chance to prove himself a fit parent."

"Does that mean he's still trying to get custody?"

"Yeah. But he prob'ly won't have much of a chance at least until next school year."

If it were my kids, I'd be more concerned about it than Kelly seemed to be. But she'd been going through this since the divorce, so she had a much better handle on it than I did.

John appeared and handed the clipboard over to the next shift foreman. He turned to us.

"We're getting a new inventory/dispatch procedure," he said. "Everybody who needs to use it is supposed to be trained. It's going to be you two who are impacted most, so I got permission to give you a brief overview this morning."

"When's it going to be implemented?" I asked.

John sighed, his eyebrows meeting over his nose. "That's the thing. Tomorrow."

Kelly frowned. "As in midnight tonight?"

John nodded. "As in midnight tonight."

I scratched the stubble in my cheek. I hadn't shaved since before Mrs. Coleman's viewing. Maybe it was just as well Kelly hadn't taken me up on the invitation to breakfast. "It's certainly not my place to decide this stuff," I said, "but why on a Friday? Seems like Monday would make more sense. Especially if a lot of people need to be trained."

"They want to have a test run on Friday, so they have the weekend to iron out any problems that arise," John said. "And as for the training— they had sessions for the other shifts, but they forgot about us. As usual."

Kelly shook her head. "And we're supposed to be the first ones to make the change."

"That's right."

"What's different?" I asked.

"It's an automated system. For now, they're just switching the procedure with the finished products. They intend, though, to have parts inventory on it eventually. That'll effect you, Jesse, more than Kelly."

I glanced at Kelly. She was chewing her knuckle, her eyes dark.

"So what do we have to do?" I asked.

"Come on over to shipping." John led the way down the hallway, past the pounding machinery. He didn't say anything more until we got in the relative quiet in the cavernous open area that housed shipping and receiving. Kelly's territory.

"See this here computer?" he said, waving his hand at a monitor, keyboard, and printer on a make-shift shelf outside the dispatcher's office, below a hook with a clipboard stuffed with packing lists. "Up till now, when a truck pulled in to be loaded, Kelly would go to the clipboard and pull the paperwork that matched the shipment number. Check the packing list against the crates on skids waiting to be loaded. If the other shifts had done their jobs right, the shipments would be assembled and waiting. If they hadn't gotten everything together, I'd tell you, Jesse, and you'd take the packing list and pull what was needed from the warehouse. Follow me so far?"

I nodded.

"But now, you type in the shipment number. Then the packing list prints out. Kelly, you take it and match it to the waiting loads. Once again, if the loads aren't ready, you'll tell me, and I'll have Jesse get on it."

I glanced over at Kelly. She was sucking on the knuckle now, looking concerned.

"Let me show you." John punched in a series of numbers on the keyboard. "This is a test list. There isn't a real shipment; it's just a test one they put in there for us to practice on."

The printer whirred to life. Several sheets of paper shot out from the top of it and launched themselves into the air. We watched as a breeze from an open loading bay door blew them across the floor, swirled them around, and deposited one on a lighting fixture above our heads.

John shook his head. "I guess you'll have to hold onto them as they come out."

"How come they're so many pages?" I asked. "Only used to be one page. Just a list."

"They got a lot more information on them," John shouted back at us as he chased the remaining pages across the shipping room, stomping on two of them and watching helplessly as another floated through the open truck bay and into the yard.

He brought the pages he had back and frowned at them. "See?" he said. "These have all kinds of stuff on them—prices, inventory numbers. They look like they can be used as a bill of lading as well as a packing list. Let me get a new copy."

Holding his hand ready to catch the paper as it came out of the printer, he punched in the number again. This time he grabbed each piece as it came out. Then he handed them to Kelly.

She shuffled the pages and frowned. "Where's the information I need?" she asked.

"Somewhere in there." John took the papers back and read the first one. "It can't be that hard to find," he said, continuing to scan them. "Ah. Here. On the third page." He pointed and showed them to Kelly.

I peered over her shoulder. Instead of being a simple list of quantities and product numbers, the new paperwork had lots of stuff written on it. "Until we get used to this, it's gonna take us a lot longer to figure out what we need to be doing," I warned.

John sighed. "Probably. You'll just have to do the best you can. And in a month or so, they're saying they'll put another computer and printer in the warehouse, and Jesse'll have to put it in whenever he takes parts out or puts finished products away. It's supposed to make it easier for the office to know what we've got on hand and what we might need to order."

Easier for the office and more difficult for us peons to deal with. Forget us in the shop who actually do the work I thought, but I didn't say anything. John gave us the printout and told us we could go.

We punched out and left the plant together.

"Six tenths of an hour overtime," I said to Kelly, putting my hand on her shoulder. "Not a fortune, but something. Hope I get it, too."

She shook my hand off. "I got to get going," she mumbled.

I took a closer look at her. Were those tears forming in her eyes? "What's the matter?" I asked.

"Nothing. I just got to get to the lawyer's office. And now I won't have time to change my clothes or take a quick shower." She hurried toward the parking lot.

Puzzled at her abrupt departure, I stood and watched her go. If the appointment had anything to do with custody problems with the kids, though, I guess she had a right to be distressed. I turned and walked toward my apartment.

I stopped at the Dollar Discount store on the way home. I picked up two cans of off-brand tuna fish, a bag of cat food and a bag of cat litter. I hesitated over a half-gallon of milk. Milk was a luxury I'd been resisting, but didn't cats like milk? I thought I'd remembered hearing somewhere that milk wasn't good for cats, but that didn't seem right. In the end, I got it. I could always use it myself if the stupid cat didn't. Since I was buying milk, I picked up a box of generic corn flakes, too.

That took care of most of my emergency twenty. I'd have to replace it tomorrow when I got paid.

The streets were cold and eerily quiet as I walked home. Dark clouds hung overhead, promising more sleet and snow. My jacket was still damp and the weak morning light held no warmth.

The janitor at my building had been busy. The sidewalks were clear and the stairs, both those up to the darkened Tabernacle door and down to my apartment, were covered with a fresh layer of salt and slushy puddles. The fallen sign still sat in the shelter of the entryway where I'd propped it last night. It didn't look any the worse for wear.

As I stepped into my apartment, I could hear soft chanting coming from upstairs. I'd been afraid that the Brethren, as they called themselves, would be noisy overhead during the daytime, which is when I needed to sleep. But they were surprisingly quiet. The only sound that ever reached me was chanting, like now. If anything, it was soothing. And the increased occupancy of the building, presumably resulting in increased rent, had made a real difference in the janitor's efforts at maintenance, including snow removal.

I stopped in the doorway and looked around my single room domain. It wasn't exactly luxurious accommodations, but it sure beat a prison cell. And it was all mine—I didn't have to share it with whatever cell buddy was arbitrarily assigned.

The odor of soiled newspaper cat litter reached my nose, but the cat wasn't in sight. It's not like there were that many places for even a cat to hide. I emptied the newspapers onto a garbage bag and closed it, refilling the box with real cat litter. Then I filled one of my bowls with cat food and the other one with milk, calling softly.

No response. I didn't see how the cat could have gotten out.

The laundry basket I'd fixed up last night was shoved further under the bed. I reached down and pulled it out.

Sure enough, there was the cat, lying there and purring, looking up at me. With two tiny kittens snuggled up against it, nursing.

I guess it was a she.

She looked so contented and proud of her little family I couldn't help but smile. I rubbed her head and then gently pushed the basket back under the bed.

The weather would be no excuse for missing my ten o'clock appointment with my parole officer. I fixed myself a cup of instant coffee, adding a little of the precious milk. I went to pour myself a bowl of cornflakes when I realized both my bowls were being used for the cat. I should have priced bowls at the store while I was there. Maybe I could get one or two more. After I got paid.

The cat didn't seem interested in eating right now, so I retrieved the milk bowl from the floor and poured cereal into it.

I took a quick shower—I didn't want to show up at the parole office smelling of machine oil and sweat. I checked on the cat family again, but they seemed to be doing fine, so I figured the best thing to do would be to leave them alone. I didn't have any idea what I could do if they were having problems anyhow.

The parole office was in the basement of the county complex, underneath the police station and connected to the jail. Convenient. I set out into the worsening weather.

No one was in the basement waiting room of the parole office when I got there. The room was overheated, and I stripped off my jacket. Moisture condensed on the grimy windows high on the walls, distorting what little daylight tried to pierce the gloomy interior. A musty smell hung in the air.

A sign-in board sat on a ledge on the closed half-door that led back to the inner sanctum of the offices. I signed in, chose a cracked plastic chair with its back against the wall, wiped the seat with my jacket so it was dry enough to sit on, and plunked myself down. No telling how long it would be before someone showed up, but it didn't make much difference. I'd have to wait. I closed my eyes and tried to rest.

A click of high heels on the wooden floor of the hallway behind the half-door told me a staff member had arrived to check the sign-in sheet. Without turning my head, I glanced over at the doorway. A shapely young woman, her impossibly blond hair piled high on her head, picked up the sheet and studied it. She looked around the empty room as if it were full of people and she was having trouble picking out who she wanted.

"Jesse Damon?" she finally asked.

"Yes, ma'am." I got to my feet and grabbed my jacket.

"Mr. Ramirez called in. He's stuck—a big tree down on his street."

Did that mean I'd have to come back again? All I said was, "Yes, ma'am."

"But…" She glanced down the hallway behind her. "You got your fee?"

"Yes, ma'am." I pulled my wallet out of my pocket.

"The secretary can take that. Come back to her office." She unlatched the door and held it open for me.

Her musky perfume lingered as I stepped past her. I preceded her down the hallway. Safer for staff not to let a parolee walk behind them.

She directed me to a cramped office with a big desk. An empty cushioned chair was behind the desk, an empty folding chair in front of it.

"Sit down." She indicated the rickety folding chair. Another security precaution. A seated parolee presented less of a safety risk than a standing one.

I sat.

Another woman hurried in, looking flushed and nervous. She was heavy set and sweat beaded her forehead under her carefully coiffed red hair. "Sorry to keep you waiting," she said as she eased herself into the chair behind the desk. That was so unusual, issuing an apology for keeping me waiting, that I had trouble coming up with an appropriate response.

She didn't close the door behind her.

"No problem," I finally said.

"You have your fee?" she asked. I pulled two twenty dollar bills out of my wallet and handed them over. When I'd first been released, I'd been on home detention, and the fee was double, to cover the cost of the monitoring. Paying only half of that was a relief and let me indulge in little extras, like savings. Or cat food and litter.

She held each bill up to the light, looking for the embedded strip that would assure her it wasn't counterfeit. Then she turned to her computer and typed something in. The printer whirred to life.

"Your receipt," she said, pulling a paper out of the printer and handing it to me.

"Thank you." I sat, waiting for her to tell me what to do next.

She looked over my shoulder, out into hallway. Her brittle face relaxed, and she sat back in her chair.

"Someone wants to see you," she said.

I turned to see two burly policemen, one with his hand on the butt of his service gun in the unsnapped holster, the other holding a pair of handcuffs.

CHAPTER 4

I sat on a worn wooden bench in the detention center, right next to the sign that read "No Weapons Beyond This Point." I'd been relieved of my belt and boots. I hoped they kept track of the boots. They were steel-toed and expensive. I could never afford another pair.

Although if I got locked up, I wouldn't be allowed steel-toed boots anyhow.

What about the cat and her kittens? I couldn't leave them locked in an empty apartment until my rent ran out and the landlord came to check it out.

If they booked me, I'd tell them I needed to talk to a lieutenant, and hope I got a sympathetic one who would call the humane society. Not the best situation for the little family, but it would sure beat starving to death. And maybe whoever had lost their cat would find her.

Looking for a more comfortable position, I shifted on the hard bench. My hands were cuffed securely to a waist chain that wound through an eyebolt set in the wall over my head. Leg irons bit into my ankles. There was no point saying anything. Nobody cared about my comfort.

I avoided looking at anyone or anything. I had to fight to keep from jerking my feet back every time heavy boots came within inches of my gray woolen socks.

If I were in a holding cell, I'd be getting a lunch of some sort. Very unlikely out here.

Leaning my head against the cinderblock wall behind me, I closed my eyes and tried to rest. No way of knowing the next chance I might get to sleep.

The first time I was arrested, I was sure things would work themselves out, and I wouldn't be held for long. A day. A few months. A year at the most. It'd turned into twenty long years.

Here I was, shackled and detained again. This time, I had no illusions. If I was sent back to prison, I'd be there for years. Most likely for the rest of my life. Nothing for me to do but wait for someone else to decide what happened to me next. I could think of several possibilities, most of them not good.

A pair of boots stopped in front of me. I didn't open my eyes.

"Damon. Stand up."

I rose unsteadily to my feet.

"A couple of detectives want to talk to you."

Had to be Belkins and Montgomery. At least it didn't sound like Belkins would be there by himself.

The guard unlocked the waist chain and yanked it free of the eyebolt. He slapped it around my waist and snicked the lock down.

Grabbing my elbow, he escorted me up a steep staircase. I've never gotten used to climbing stairs in leg irons, and I almost fell. At the top of the stairs we went down a long dim hallway to an interrogation room with a battered table flanked by two worn but sturdy chairs and a harsh overhead light.

I knew the routine. Sit and wait. Possibly for hours. No doubt in my mind that the dark piece of glass in the wall was a one-way window. If I got out of the chair, someone would be in immediately, and I might end up shackled to the chair. I would have no way to tell how much time passed. An unsettling feeling. That was the whole point of the arrangement. I waited.

Yesterday I hadn't gotten enough sleep. And I'd worked all night. I was pretty tired, and if I looked like I was falling asleep, they might hurry things up without making my situation any worse. I let my head drop and closed my eyes.

Sure enough, the door opened. I didn't turn to look at who was coming in, but the sour scent of stale cigar and the odor of someone who was just slightly overdue for a shower and change of clothing suggested that Belkins had entered. Underneath that smell I could detect Montgomery's fresh aftershave and his minty mouthwash.

Belkins stopped behind me. Montgomery came around, perching himself on the edge of the table, his legs crossed. His elegantly shod foot swung gently in a mesmerizing arc. The glare from the overhead light winked off a large green stone set in a ring on his right hand. Unblinking, he stared straight into my face. I kept my eyes downcast.

Neither one of them said anything. Good interrogators know that most people can't stand a silence for long and will fill in the emptiness with talk. Often unwise talk.

Even though I was familiar with the technique, I sometimes found myself saying more than I should. I knew I had to answer questions if I didn't want to be reported to Mr. Ramirez in the parole office as uncooperative. That didn't mean I had to start the conversation.

The silence grew uncomfortably.

Belkins broke first. He slapped me on the back of the head. "Say something, damn it."

Montgomery shifted his gaze to Belkins and frowned. "Watch it, Belkins. We're recording this."

"So erase the first bit." Belkins jabbed my shoulder. Hard. "And why're you letting him know we're recording?"

"I imagine Jesse's well aware that we're recording." Montgomery smiled. "Aren't you, Jesse?"

A direct question. I had to answer. "Yes, sir."

"So what do you think we want to talk to you about, Jesse?"

I shook my head. "I'm not really sure."

"Guess."

"Mrs. Coleman?"

"See. He's no dummy. Are you, Jesse?"

I shrugged.

Montgomery leaned forward, bringing his face close to mine. The smell of his minty breath grew stronger as he asked, "So, Jesse, how do you think Mrs. Coleman died?"

I didn't want to venture an answer, but I had to give the impression I was cooperating. Otherwise I'd spend the rest of the afternoon in this interrogation room, and probably most of the night in a holding cell. It wasn't what they were looking for, but I said, "The obit just said she'd died suddenly, at home. She wasn't young." I glanced up at Montgomery's chiseled dark features.

"True." Montgomery's bottomless brown eyes bored into mine. I shifted my gaze to avoid his. "But she was in pretty good health, especially for someone her age," he said.

My stomach churned. "An accident?" After the brief session with the detectives outside the funeral home, I was pretty sure it wasn't an accident.

"She fell. Down the basement stairs at her home. Broke her neck." Montgomery leaned forward, his dark chiseled features immobile, inches away from me.

With limited success, I tried to keep my face equally expressionless. I thought of the steep, dark stairs that ended at the concrete floor of the basement. "How'd that happen?" I asked.

"How do you think?" Montgomery asked.

"Anybody can fall." A sob caught at the back of my throat as I thought of Mrs. Coleman tumbling down the stairs. With an effort, I took a deep breath and choked it back.

Montgomery leaned back. "True. Do you think she just fell?"

I shrugged.

"Or do you think she was pushed, Jesse? Or thrown?"

My stomach knotted. "I hope not," I said.

"What about if she was hit over the head?" Belkins chomped on his unlit cigar. "Before she went down the stairs."

"Maybe she hit her head when she fell?" I said.

"That's not what the coroner says," Montgomery said. "He says she suffered the head injury first. Then she went down the stairs."

Maybe at least she'd been unconscious and had been spared the fear and pain of falling down the stairs.

"And that if she hadn't broken her neck in the fall, she'd of died from the blows to her head," Belkins said.

"Somebody was stupid enough to hope the coroner would think all the injuries came from the fall," Montgomery said. "I'd expect you to be smarter than that. If you had time to plan the whole thing out. So maybe you didn't mean to kill her. It just happened. And you panicked."

I swallowed hard. "I didn't kill her. I haven't been near the Colemans' house since I was released."

Montgomery leaned back and raised his eyebrows. "Really? So then who do you think would have hit Mrs. Coleman over the head, Jesse? And why?"

Whatever I told them, they'd twist around and use against me. But I had to say something. How much should I tell them? "She used to keep money in the house," I blurted out. Didn't take but a second for me to realize it was stupid for me to let them know I was aware of that. "Maybe she still did. Did anyone check?"

Montgomery looked down at his manicured fingernails. "Why would she keep money in the house?"

"She didn't believe in credit cards. And she always said you never knew when you might need money. Especially with emergency foster kids arriving at all hours of the day and night."

"How much would she have had?"

"A couple hundred dollars, at least," I said.

"And where did she keep it?"

"Back when I lived there, she kept it in twenties and fifties stuffed into the thesaurus on the bookshelf. In the office."

Montgomery brushed imaginary lint from the front of his blazer. "In the thesaurus?"

"Yeah. She said hardly anybody ever looks in a thesaurus. Not like a dictionary or something."

"He knows about the money," Belkins said.

My guts lurched. I'd been saying entirely too much.

Montgomery nodded. "The money's gone."

"I'm sure Damon could use a few hundred bucks," Belkins said.

"Pretty much anybody could use a few hundred bucks." Montgomery folded his arms over his chest.

"But most people would earn their money." Belkins shifted behind me. I braced for another blow to the back of my head. It didn't come.

Montgomery got up and paced a few steps. "Tough way to die. Hit over the head by somebody she probably knew. Somebody she must have let into the house."

I stared at a dark stain on the surface of the battered table. Blood? "She didn't deserve that," I said.

"Nobody deserves that," Belkins said. "But Mrs. Coleman died like that. A nice, defenseless old lady. Who took in kids who needed a home. And trusted the wrong person."

No one I knew would ever have described Mrs. Coleman as "defenseless." Obviously he had never met her when she was alive. But I kept my mouth shut.

"And somebody killed her," Belkins continued.

"Somebody who thought killing an old lady was an okay thing to do. An old lady who spent her life taking in stray kids. Stray kids like you." Montgomery said.

I didn't trust myself to say anything. It might come out as a sob.

"Way we figure it," Belkins said, "it *had* to be somebody who knew her. Somebody she let in."

Montgomery sat down and leaned forward again. "Somebody who didn't mind killing."

I shivered and took a quick look up.

"You've killed before," Belkins said.

As the prison saying goes, don't deny, don't defend. Just makes things harder.

"I've heard that the first kill is the hardest," Montgomery said, his dark face thoughtful.

"All the combat veterans say that," Belkins added.

Montgomery leaned forward again. "You agree with that, Jesse?"

It wouldn't do any good to point out that I hadn't actually killed anyone. My murder conviction said otherwise. I just shook my head.

We sat in silence for what seemed like forever, but was probably only a few minutes. Belkins put his hand on the back of the chair I was sitting in. "You were in foster care with the Colemans for a couple of years, weren't you? And it's pretty obvious from the funeral home that Mr. Coleman isn't a fan of yours. You want to explain why?"

I shifted in my seat. "I guess Mrs. Coleman was pretty upset when I picked up that conviction. She felt like I let her down."

"And was she right?"

"Yeah. She'd hoped I'd go on to college. Make something of myself." Another sob rose from deep my chest, but I managed to turn it into a cough. Mrs. Coleman had believed in me. Nobody else ever had. Not even me.

Belkins snorted and turned away. "That certainly didn't happen."

Like I needed a reminder.

"What would you say if I told you someone saw you outside the Colemans' house the afternoon she was killed?" Montgomery said.

They had to be making this up. "I'd say they were lying."

"You think a neighbor's going to lie about something like that?"

Not good to suggest a prosecution witness was lying. "Or made a mistake."

"That jacket of yours is pretty distinctive," Montgomery said.

I was uncomfortably aware of that. When I'd been released from prison, I'd bought the cheapest warm jacket I could find in the Goodwill shop. A black and red buffalo plaid hunter's jacket with big patch pockets. It was old and very noticeable, but not all that unique.

Montgomery got up and paced across the floor. "Too bad for you that you work nights. We'll be asking about you there, but they can't provide an alibi, since Mrs. Coleman was killed during the day."

I was sure they'd already been asking questions at work, but they were right about that not helping much.

"I say we ask his PO to lock him up," Belkins said. "Hold him for a violation hearing."

Montgomery stopped and stroked his chin. "What will that accomplish?"

"Get a killer off the street," Belkins said. "No parole board would ever cut him loose again if he's violated. Killers kill. We might save a few innocent lives."

"We need to get a conviction in this case. Not just an arrest." Montgomery wanted the kudos that went with solving a high profile case. It would help in his quest for promotion.

Belkins was burned out and didn't care as long as he could make it to his retirement date. And he didn't like murderers loose on the streets. Especially me. "As long as we know who did it and he's locked up, who cares?"

"I say we cut him loose. We might find out more keeping an eye on him than he's ever going to tell us." Montgomery resumed his pacing.

They were seriously playing with me, I reminded myself. If someone could definitely place me near the Colemans' house the afternoon she was killed, we wouldn't be sitting here. I'd be in a cell right now, waiting for a parole revocation hearing. I tightened my jaw and willed myself not to let any expression show on my face.

If they had any idea how close I was to breaking down in tears, they'd up the ante for sure. Press on while they had the advantage.

"How about we ask the PO to put him back on the ankle monitor?" Belkins suggested. "If he's on home detention, he won't have nearly so much chance of getting involved in things he shouldn't."

Montgomery nodded approvingly. "That way he still works and doesn't cost the taxpayers as much, he's limited in how much time he has to get into nefarious activities, and we can keep an eye on him better. I'll call his PO."

He sounded like a campaigning politician. I wondered if he had his sights set on more than a promotion within the police department. Home detention was better than being locked up, I thought. And I'd have to pay the extra monitoring fee. It would also severely restrict what I could do with my hours outside of work. That, of course, was the point.

CHAPTER 5

Aaron was leaning against the railing around the steps to my basement apartment, eating what looked like a piece of pizza and drinking from a bottle in a bag. Probably beer. Or whiskey. He had a joint tucked behind his ear.

As if my day hadn't been bad enough. Aaron was one of the last people I wanted to deal with right now.

I visually scouted out the area. I didn't see any patrol cars. No one was standing around, studying the nondescript contents of any of the surrounding store windows. None of the cars parked along the street seemed to be occupied by anyone pretending to nap or read a newspaper. A brown box truck was parked halfway down the block. Maybe it had some surveillance equipment in it. Maybe Aaron was wired.

Come to think of it, I'd seen that truck parked around here a lot lately.

"What are you doing here?" I demanded.

His eyes took a few minutes to focus, blinking rapidly. He seemed surprised to see me. "Jesse?" he said.

"Yeah. What are you doing here?"

He shoved the rest of the pizza into his mouth, chewed a few times, and swallowed. "Just hanging out," he said, a string of cheese hanging from the corner of his mouth. "Want a piece of pizza?"

I didn't see a pizza box anywhere. "No, thanks," I said.

He shrugged and reached into the voluminous kangaroo pocket of the hoodie he wore under his jacket and pulled out another piece. It was more than a little mangled. And covered with lint.

I couldn't help but ask, "How much pizza you got in that pocket, anyhow?"

He blinked a few more times. The pupils of his eyes were dilated. He was high on something. "A whole pizza. What's that—eight pieces?" he said. "I had to wait until it cooled down a little before I stuck it in my pocket. Zee really likes pizza. So I brought him some."

No accounting for taste. But even if the pizza had started out pretty good, I didn't think being carried in the pocket of Aaron's grimy sweatshirt could help. "So who's Zee? And where is he?" I asked.

Aaron looked around. "I dunno. Haven't seen him."

"So what are you going to do with the rest of the pizza?"

"Eat it, I guess. I think I got the munchies." He giggled. "You want a piece?"

"You already asked me that. No, thanks."

He crammed the next piece in his mouth, took a swig of the contents of his bottle in the bag, and gestured toward me with it. "Want a drink?"

"No, thanks." I had visions of serious bodily fluids smeared all over the mouth of the bottle, not to mention swimming around in whatever was in the bottle. I'd have to be dying of thirst before I'd share Aaron's drink. He was pretty skinny, his skin was bad, and he itched. He probably used drugs any way he could, including intravenously. I couldn't imagine he'd be any more fastidious about sharing the rig he stuck in his arm than he was about his jacket or his food. A recipe for AIDS.

"Look," I said. "Why do you spend so much time hanging out around here? There ain't a whole lot going on around here. Most of the stores are out of business. Even the liquor store's shut down. Just me and the old folks who live on the second floor are around. Except for the nutcases who come to the Tabernacle."

Aaron scratched the side of his neck. Hard. He drew blood.

"Don't nobody bother me here," he said. He got a crafty look in his eyes. "Maybe you'll get some oxys for me? Or meth? I can pay good money for it."

"If you got money, you can get whatever you want. You don't need me."

His mouth sank into a sulky pout. "I got to go to Baltimore to get anything like the meth you got. Down on Park Heights. It's a long way. The gas is expensive, and besides, they cheat me."

City drug dealers cheating a naïve redneck who came down looking for a deal, pockets full of money? Big surprise there. I grinned, remembering his woeful tale of the white pebbles they'd sold him as crack.

If this was being recorded, I needed to clear up the bit about him ever getting meth from me.

"You never got meth from me. Or anything else. I'm clean. I plan to stay clean. Tell that to whoever's putting you up to hanging around asking me for drugs. The answer is—and always will be—NO!"

Aaron blinked rapidly again. "You don't have to yell."

I took a deep breath. I needed to keep control of myself. "Look," I said more calmly. "I'm on parole. I'm not getting involved in drugs. They won't do you any good, either. You plan to hold onto that job?"

"Of course," Aaron said. "I been in the last day or so."

"I noticed."

He smiled and licked his dry lips. "But I don't think I got to worry too much."

"You got a doctor's note or something?" I asked.

"I don't need no doctor's note. But I can get one if I need it."

I supposed he could, if the police were using him as an informant. Since I'd been working at Quality Steel, the cops had broken up a scheme a few of the employees had set up, hiding drugs and fake IDs in shipments. One of the people involved had been an executive. I was pretty sure that if they wanted to continue the investigation the management would cooperate. Even if it meant leaving a loose cannon like Aaron in a job. At least, on the packing line, he wasn't likely to get anybody hurt.

I stepped past Aaron and started down the stairs. "I got to get some sleep," I said. "I got to go to work tonight."

"Okay." Aaron took a long drink from his bottle. "I'll just hang out here for a little while more."

"What for?" I asked.

"In case somebody shows up."

"Who would show up?"

Aaron shrugged and pulled another piece of pizza out of his pocket. He raised his eyes to look straight into mine and grinned. "Just somebody'll make sure I get what I need. And that you get what you deserve."

I gave him a hard look and headed for my apartment.

He grabbed me by the shoulder.

"Jesse. Wait a minute."

I swung around, my fists clenched. Aaron backed off, stumbling over his untied bootlaces. "Hey, man. No offense. But I got something to tell you. Something you'd want to hear. But you got to give me something back for telling you."

I looked around. Still no cops that I could see. And the brown truck was driving away. I grabbed Aaron by the neck of his jacket and hauled him toward the alley. We needed to be out of sight, but I wasn't about to let him into my apartment.

The bag with the bottle crashed to the sidewalk.

Aaron lost his footing, and the jacket started to slip in my hand. I shoved my other hand into his chest, lifting him up, and repositioned my grip on his shirt collar, pushing him ahead of me into the alley.

I slammed him up against the dirty brick wall. His head bounced against it, but he didn't seem to notice. My forearm pressed into his neck. He tried to balance on the tips of his toes, but it was my arm that kept him from collapsing into a heap on the dirty pavement.

Aaron's bloodshot eyes opened wide. His rancid breath came ragged in my face.

"What the hell do you want?" I hissed. Using my other hand, I frisked him for a wire and patted his clothes for a recorder of some sort. I found nothing but a few empty plastic baggies and his wallet. Not even keys. I didn't stick my hand onto the pocket with the pizza.

But I had no idea what kind of tiny new transmitting or recording devices they might have hidden on him.

Aaron's mouth gaped open and closed a few times. Spittle dripped from his lips. He made a choking sound.

I eased up a little on his throat.

"Why are you here?" I asked.

He blinked rapidly. "I was waiting for Zee," he gasped.

I pressed a little harder.

"And I wanted to talk to you…"

"Talk away," I said. "Then get your sorry ass away from here and stay away."

"I ain't done nothing."

"Showing up at my place is doing something," I said.

"What do you mean?"

"Did the cops put you up to this?"

"What do you mean?" he asked again.

"The other day. You showed up here. There were two cops sitting in a patrol car in the alley, watching. You want me to believe you weren't trying to set me up?"

His eyes widened. "Cops?" he asked.

I just stared at him.

"Yeah." He coughed. "I remember. But they didn't have anything to do with me."

"Then why didn't you just take off?" I asked.

"I wanted to go into your place," he said, trying to raise his hand to his dripping nose. He couldn't get it past my arm. "Then they couldn't see what we were doing."

"We weren't doing nothing."

"Yeah, I guess."

"So why are you here now?" I increased the pressure on his throat. He made that choking noise again.

"Just trying to score."

"I don't buy that," I said, ignoring his strangled noises. "I done told you, I got nothing to give you."

"Not give," he said, his eyes watering. "Sell."

"Yeah? If I did have something, which I don't, I wouldn't sell it to you. I don't need money that bad." I might like money as much as the next person, but I liked my freedom much better.

"Not for money," he said.

"Then what?"

"Information."

"What could you possibly tell me that I'd want to know?"

"About the old lady."

That gave me pause. "What old lady?"

"The one whose funeral you went to."

How the hell did he know about that? I hadn't gone to the actual funeral, but that didn't make a difference. "What do you know about her?" I asked.

"You gonna let me score if I tell you?"

"No. But I might not kill you."

Aaron tensed up even more, if that was possible. I pressed harder.

"You wouldn't do that. They'd send you back to prison." His voice was raspy.

"No place I ain't been before," I said. "And it might be worth it. But first they'd have to catch me."

Aaron coughed, and his eyes filled with tears. "Please, Jesse."

I eased up a bit. "What do you know?"

"Nothing, really."

I increased the pressure again.

"Okay. Just something I heard." He coughed again.

"What did you hear?"

"This guy I get stuff from sometimes. He had a lot of money. Said he got it from his mother. That she owed him." He paused.

I leaned on my arm. "And…?"

Aaron coughed. "He said she wouldn't give him no more. And he was screwing this girl who was there helping her. A housekeeper or something. When she wouldn't give them no more money, they roughed her up a little. But she fell down the stairs. She maybe died."

"He roughed her up?"

"He says Rose, or whatever her name is, was the one who hit her."

"Rose?"

"The housekeeper. See, Rose isn't legal. He thinks maybe she's letting him screw her so maybe he'll marry her. Then she can file for a green card."

"When did you hear this?"

"Last week sometime. Or the week before. I dunno exactly."

"What's this guy's name?" I asked.

"I just know him as Zee. I dunno his real name."

"What does he look like?"

Aaron tried to shake his head, but I held him too tight. "Just a guy. He don't use meth, so he don't look too bad."

"What does he use?"

"Mostly oxys. He says he could get them from the old lady. But he can't no more."

"Why is that?"

"Because she's dead. But he's got a big stash somewhere. When things cool down, he'll get them. Or maybe send me for them. Give me a cut."

"So where's this stash?"

"I dunno. But he says it's worth a lot."

It would be, I thought. But only if the two of them didn't take all of them themselves.

"Where does he hang out?"

"Here."

"Where's 'here'?"

"He hangs out with the weirdos in the temple."

"Is he one of the members?"

"I guess. Sometimes he wears those yellow robe thingies."

Who but a member would be dressed like that? "What does he look like?"

"Just a guy."

Not a whole lot of help. "White or black?"

"White."

"What color hair?"

"Brownish."

"Big?"

"Taller than me, but even skinnier."

"You ain't telling me a damn thing worth anything. I bet this guy don't even exist. You're just making it all up."

A cunning look crept into Aaron's bloodshot eyes. "He knows about you."

"What do you mean, he knows about me?"

"He knows you're on parole. For murder. He says maybe you'll end up going down for the old lady's death."

"Why does he say that?" I leaned hard on my arm.

"I dunno, Jesse. I swear." Aaron coughed, and his hands clawed at my arm.

"Tell me what you do know. Or it'll be *your* death I'm going down for. And it'll be worth it."

"I can't breathe," he gasped.

I took some of the pressure off. "Talk."

"Just that Zee said the old lady owed him."

"Why would she owe him?"

"*I* don't know. He said the old lady gave him money sometimes."

I leaned a little harder. "Why would she give Zee money?"

"Please, Jesse." Tears came to Aaron's bleary eyes. "He said he needed money. He was supposed to pay child support. He needed a lawyer to try to get his kid to live with him. And he was using whatever money he got to cop drugs."

That I could believe.

A gust of wind picked up some newspaper from the asphalt and blew it against the wall. Sharp needles of sleet drilled into the back of my neck.

I eased up and let Aaron plant his feet firmly on the ground. He straightened his jacket and pulled a crumpled tissue from his pocket. "You could've hurt me, Jesse."

Looking at him in disgust, I shoved my hands in my pockets, as much to keep them from punching Aaron in the face as to get them out of the cold. "I still got the same thing to say to you. Go to an NA meeting. Ask them to help you get your act together."

"I don't need no help."

"Yeah? What are you gonna do when you lose your job?"

Aaron's lip curled. "Ain't gonna lose it. That ain't such a good job, anyhow. I can get another one."

It was a calculated risk, but I turned my back on Aaron and retreated to my apartment. I needed to get some sleep before I had to go to work. Then I had to clean the cat pan and set out enough food in case I stayed the night at Kelly's. Like I hoped.

CHAPTER 6

When I left for work that night, the sleet had stopped and light from a few brittle stars glittered on the ice-covered sidewalks. I hunched into my jacket and headed into the wind.

A snow plow rumbled by. Its blade made no dent on the frozen streets, but it dumped cinders in its wake, which would give traction. I backed up against a crumbling brick wall to avoid being cindered myself as it passed.

Inside the plant, a much smaller than usual group of workers huddled around the picnic tables waiting for John to hand out assignments. The roads were treacherous. Would they cancel most of the production shift? A few of the operations, like the plating line, took a good six or eight hours to set up and tear down, so some people would be assigned to those jobs. Any union member who clocked in would be paid for four hours.

Since I wasn't in the union yet, they didn't have to pay me for anything I didn't work. If most production was canceled, they wouldn't need two lift operators on the shift, and of course Kelly had seniority and would get the nod. But I could operate the platers. Maybe they'd put me on that.

The workers from the shift that was ending looked at our diminished numbers uneasily. How bad were the roads? The parking lot outside was filled with older American-made pickup trucks, most of them rear wheel drive. Notoriously unreliable on icy roads.

John came out with his clipboard and counted heads. He began issuing jobs, most of them on the continuous operating lines. I held my breath while he assigned the four platers to other workers, two of them people who had never run them before. My heart sank. I couldn't really afford to miss a shift's pay, but it wasn't something I could control.

Finally he turned to me. "We're not running much production tonight," he said. "And the roads are bad. I don't think we'll get too many trucks in. Do you think you can handle what needs to be done on both jobs, if I keep track of where you're needed next?"

"Yeah. But how about Kelly? She's got seniority."

He raised those busy eyebrows and looked down at me from his six-foot-six height. "She called in," he said.

"Oh." Kelly needed the money as much as I did. Was she sick? Or one of the kids? Maybe the babysitter couldn't make it because of the weather.

Regardless, I was working tonight.

John was right about the light traffic. Only one truck pulled in, and when I got it unloaded, the driver called his dispatcher and said he was going to catch some shuteye in the cab right there in the loading bay.

When John told me to take my last break of the shift, I headed to the men's room. Aaron, who had inexplicably shown up for work and was on his usual place on the packing line, was sitting at the break table with Clay, a plater operator. Cardboard cups of what the vending machine passed off as coffee sat next to them. In this corner of the plant, the thunder of the machinery was muted, and when Aaron raised his voice, I could hear him clearly.

"Well, look who's snuck off from work," he said loudly, rubbing the spot on his neck that was probably still sore from my arm pressing against it. "If it ain't the shift snitch himself."

Clay glanced in my direction. "What do you mean, snitch?"

"You don't know?" Aaron took a sip of the muddy dark liquid in his cup. "Jesse, there, he's on parole."

Clay gave him a pained look. "I know that. Everybody knows that. Half the new hires on the production staff are on parole. The company gets some kind of a tax break for hiring ex-cons."

"Yeah. But Jesse's got a murder conviction."

"Don't matter to me, long as he don't murder me," Clay said.

Aaron rubbed his neck. "Jesse's got years of back-up time. He's trying to get in good with the parole people, so he snitches out anybody he can. That's why they got him driving the lift. So he can go anywhere he wants to without anybody thinking twice about it."

Clay scratched his head under his hard hat. "He thinks he can get in good with his parole officer by telling him things that happen here at work?"

"Well…" Aaron had the decency to look confused. "He reports most stuff to the company management, to get in good with them. And any criminal stuff he tells his PO."

"And just what is he finding out and reporting?"

"Anybody who's swiping any of the materials or supplies from the plant."

Clay raised his eyebrows. "Sheet metal and wire? Steel shelving? I can't imagine anybody making off with enough of anything here to make a difference. It's heavy. How would you get it out? And how would you sell it?"

"Scrap."

"You're telling me," Clay said, a puzzled look on his face, "that somebody's making off with enough steel from here to sell for scrap? Without anybody noticing? And if they did, where would they sell it? I know for a fact that there's been a lot of copper pipes and wiring stolen around the city in the last few years. All the junkyards have to keep records of what they buy. They even ask for a photo ID now when you're selling scrap."

Aaron set his mouth stubbornly. "He's supposed to report anything. Like anybody drinking or smoking or dealing drugs."

Shaking his head, Clay grabbed his paper cup and squashed it in his hand. It wasn't quite empty, and a muddy stream dribbled down his arm. "Why would he do that? If he wanted to stay out of prison, I'd think he'd stay as far away from that crap as he could."

"You'd think," Aaron said. "But I know for a fact that he's using himself. Can't kick the habit. Long as he rolls over on the rest of us, they don't violate him."

"But they let him drive a forklift?" Clay tossed the cup into the trash barrel standing next to the table. "Suppose he's high on something at work? They won't tolerate that. Especially in a driver. Don't make sense to me."

"Don't have to make sense." Aaron drained the last of his coffee.

Clay turned his thick head on its bull-like neck and looked in my direction. "I don't do nothing but a little hit of weed every once in a while. He'd just better mind his own business as far as I'm concerned."

I decided pretending I didn't hear them was the approach, so I ignored them and pushed open the door to the men's room.

They were gone by the time I came out.

That was about what I would expect from Aaron. I'd be willing to bet *he* was the snitch. And I supposed he'd be pissed with me after the little incident in the alley.

When the eight a.m. whistle blew, ending the shift, it took me a few minutes extra to hook the lift up to its charger.

When I went to pick up my lunchbox from the table, it was gone.

People usually just left their lunch on the tables near the time clock. A few decrepit vending machines dispensed stale snacks, cans of off-brand soda, and the muddy liquid that purported to be coffee. Most of the production staff knocked off for lunch at the same time and ate there. Those of us who got our breaks at different times usually ate at a table out by shipping, where the noise and fumes from the machinery wasn't as bad.

I *knew* I'd put my lunchbox on the table out here after I'd finished eating.

It could have gotten knocked on the floor or something. I looked under the tables and then carefully scanned the collection of lunch boxes and bags the day shift had left on the tables.

It wasn't there.

John came by, zipping up his jacket. "Looking for something, Jesse?" he asked.

"My lunchbox."

"Sure you left it there?"

"Yeah."

"Clay had an extra lunchbox on his way out. He said he found it back on the table in shipping. Think you could have left it there?"

"Maybe." But I was sure I hadn't.

"I told him to put it in the lost-and-found box."

"Where's that?" If Clay'd taken my lunchbox, I doubted I'd find it there. Or anywhere. Unless he'd put some of the potassium cyanide from the plating room in the Thermos or something.

"It's in the timekeeper's office. There's a slot under the window for small stuff. But a lunchbox wouldn't fit, so I unlocked the door so Clay could put it in there. I'm sure the timekeeper's in there now, though, so you can just go ask her if you could take a look."

"Thanks."

The timekeeper wouldn't let me into her office, but when I told her what I was looking for, she came up with my lunchbox and opened the door just wide enough to pass it out to me.

I had a feeling that if John hadn't seen Clay leaving with it, my lunchbox would never have ended up there. But I was going to wash it out really well before I put anything in it again. And see if, in the future, I couldn't stash it in the plating room office instead of leaving it out on the table.

Weak morning sun washed across the sidewalk as I stepped outside and pondered what to do. Yesterday Kelly had invited me over to her place today, but she hadn't shown up for work. Was she okay? I badly wanted to go check up on her. Would that just make her mad at me?

If she didn't want to see me, I could just turn around and leave, I decided, heading in the opposite direction from my apartment. Kelly lived in a residential section of town, in a big old stone house she was trying to keep after her divorce. I knew it was a struggle. She loved the house and said she didn't want to uproot the kids. They went to the best school in town, and if she moved, they might have to switch schools.

A patrol car eased down the street, slowing down. Was it following me?

I pulled my hood up over the watch cap and shoved my hands in my pockets. At least there wasn't any snow falling. Or worse, freezing rain. I tucked my head into the wind and set out across town, avoiding the little knots of kids waiting for buses, their vigilant guardians nearby. The road crews must have made considerable progress clearing the roads if school was starting on time.

By the time I got to Kelly's house, the school buses had picked up all their passengers, and the parents had gone inside or left for work. I glanced behind me but saw no sign of the patrol car.

The walk and steps up to Kelly's front porch glistened with ice. A haphazard path, a single snow shovel scoop wide, meandered along the sidewalk in front of the house. The driveway was passable, but no tire tracks showed on the newest dusting of snow.

I thought about going around to the back door, which Kelly usually used. But that seemed pretty familiar, and I wasn't sure what kind of reception I was going to get, so maybe the front door would be better.

The front steps were slick, so I was careful until I got to the front porch. I pushed the doorbell. Its muffled chimes sounded inside the house, but otherwise it was silent. No lights appeared to be on.

I debated going over to the front window and peering in. I tried the doorknob. It turned in my hand.

Suppose Kelly or the kids were sick? Suppose the old furnace had belched carbon monoxide and they were all lying unconscious? Suppose her ex had gone berserk and killed them all?

Suppose I went in without being invited and got picked up for breaking and entering?

The door opened, solving that problem. Chris, Kelly's eight year old son, stood there. He was half-dressed, and his hair was uncombed.

"What are you doing home?" I asked. "Aren't you supposed to be in school?"

"I guess," he said. "But Brianna won't get dressed, and I can't leave her alone."

"Alone?" I was alarmed. "Where's your mom? And the babysitter?"

He shrugged. "The babysitter couldn't make it last night. Mom stayed home."

"Where is she now?"

"Upstairs. Asleep."

"You mean she didn't get up to help you and Brianna get ready for school?"

He shrugged again. "Nope. I mean, I can fix us breakfast and stuff, but I can't *make* Brianna get ready for school. She's only in first grade, you know. And she hates school. She says she's never going again."

First graders shouldn't hate school. Something was wrong. From what I had seen of her, I suspected poor Brianna had some kind of learning disability. Kelly didn't want to hear that, though, especially from me. When I'd brought it up, she told me they were her kids, not mine, and I should mind my own business. She was right—they were her kids.

"Can you see if you can get Mom up?" Chris asked, opening the door wider.

"I guess I can try," I said, hoping an invitation from an eight year old would count if someone did call the police.

The house was chilly. I knew Kelly kept the heat down to try to save money.

Brianna sat in her pajamas on the living room floor, a half-empty bowl of cereal next to her. A small spill of milk puddled on the hardwood floor.

"Why don't you two finish getting ready for school?" I said, heading to the kitchen to get a paper towel to wipe up the milk before it ruined the finish on the floor.

"I'm supposed to bring in a permission slip for a trip," Brianna said, not moving. "Today's the last day. If I don't bring it in signed, today, I'll have to stay back with the kindergarten kids when everybody else goes. And it costs money." She sniffed and wiped her nose with the back of her hand.

"Where is it?" I asked.

"On the dining room table. Where I left it for Mom."

A small mountain of papers and mail, opened and unopened, sat on the dining room table. I started to sift through it.

Brianna appeared beside me, her feet bare on the cold floor. "The paper's blue," she said, reaching into the stack and pulling out a paper.

A field trip to a children's museum next week. Sure enough, the last day for the permission slip to be in was today. It cost five dollars.

I pulled out my wallet. I hadn't stopped at the bank with my paycheck, and I didn't have a whole lot of ready cash, but I suspected that Kelly, after not working last night, would have even less. I took out a five and paper clipped it to the permission slip.

Chris came in, holding a long stick with some round balls hanging from it. "This is my science project," he said. "We were supposed to write a report on the solar system or make a project. We could make a poster or a model and bring it in. I made a model, but it doesn't have a sun. I made that in school. The rough draft was supposed to be turned in yesterday, but the teacher said I could bring it today."

"Rough draft?"

"Yeah. You know, the trial version. Then we make a good one."

The project was flimsy and misshapen. It was pretty obvious he hadn't had much adult help with it. But he'd done it, and the next version might be better. "You got something to wrap that in?" I asked. "If we take it outside, I wouldn't want it to get wet or broken."

"We could use a beach towel," he suggested.

"You go get a beach towel. Then get dressed."

He looked at Brianna's permission slip with the money clipped to it. "Do you think I could get ice cream at lunch today?" he asked.

"How much?"

"Seventy-five cents."

I pulled out my meager supply of pocket change and counted out six dimes and three nickels.

Brianna was sifting through the remaining papers on the dining room table. "What's this?" she asked, holding one up. "It looks important, and when it came, Mom got mad."

I took it from her. It *was* important. A notice of a custody hearing for the kids. I scanned down the page. It was for a week from Monday. At ten o'clock at the courthouse.

The kids weren't in school. For sure the court would ask for a report from the school. How would this look?

"You go get ready for school, too," I told Brianna.

Putting the paper by itself on the table, I went upstairs to Kelly's bedroom. The hallway was dark. An empty Southern Comfort bottle lay on the floor outside the closed door. I knocked.

Kelly's sleepy voice came from inside. "What now?" she asked. "Can't you get your own breakfast?"

"Kelly, it's me. Jesse."

"Jesse? What are you doing here? Go away."

"Kelly, the kids need to get to school."

"What?" I heard her feet hit the floor. The door opened a crack.

A sour odor of alcohol and unwashed clothes seeped out the opening.

"The kids are late. And you have a notice here about a custody hearing in a little over a week. It won't look good if they're missing school today."

The door opened wider. Kelly looked like she'd been in a train wreck. "What am I gonna do?" she wailed.

Like I should know. But I tried. "Take a quick shower. Get dressed. Drop the kids off at school."

She nodded, then put her hand on her forehead. "I feel sick," she said.

I looked at the bottle by my foot and then at her. No time to mince words. "Hung over?" I asked.

Kelly's shoulders drooped. "I guess."

"I'll see if I can't find some instant coffee," I said. "Take an aspirin. But get ready. The kids are late as it is."

In the kitchen, I heated a mug of water in the microwave and packed lunches of peanut butter and jelly sandwiches, juice boxes, and apples. I could hear water in the sink running upstairs. The kids drifted in. I sent Chris to comb his hair and helped Brianna with her boots.

Kelly appeared in the doorway. She was wearing jeans and a sweat shirt. Her long dark hair was brushed and pulled back into a ponytail that hung down her back. Her face was covered in uneven red blotches. Her eyes were bloodshot and bleary.

I mixed the instant coffee into a mug and handed it to Kelly. She frowned at it, but she took a drink.

"Sign this," I said, shoving Brianna's permission slip and a pen at her. She signed it.

"Where are your car keys?" I asked. She reached for them on a hook by the back door.

"Give me your project, Chris." I took it from him, leaving his hands free to struggle with his backpack.

We all looked pretty pathetic. But staying here and feeling sorry for ourselves wasn't going to help any of us. "All set? Let's go."

We trooped out the back door to the garage. The kids climbed in the back seat of the old station wagon.

"You drive," Kelly said, holding out the keys. "My head's killing me, and I can't see straight."

"You know I don't got a driver's license," I said. "I can't drive."

"You can drive," she said. "You drive a forklift all night at work. It's not that different."

"I'm not going to take the chance on violating my parole with something stupid like driving without a license. You'll have to drive."

Begrudgingly, she climbed into the driver's seat and started the car. I closed the back door behind the kids and got in the passenger seat.

CHAPTER 7

The kids had enough sense to keep quiet as Kelly drove.

At the school, she parked in a visitor's parking space in the lot. "Go ahead, kids," she said. "You're not that late."

"Somebody needs to sign us in," Chris said, his voice trembling.

"I can't let them see me like this," Kelly protested. "Jesse, can you take them in?"

"Does it have to be your mom who signs you in?" I asked Chris.

"The babysitter does it sometimes," he said.

"Okay. Let's give it a try."

We got out of the car. Kelly closed her eyes and rested her head on the steering wheel. I took each kid by the hand, and we walked across the parking lot to the front entrance of the school. It was a series of huge glass doors with a camera mounted on a light post to scan the area. What kind of security did they have for schools these days?

"How do we get in?" I asked Chris.

He looked at me like I was crazy. "We walk in the front door," he said. "But we got to go to the office because we're late."

We went to the office.

The waxed floors in the long hallway gleamed in the sunlight. The office was behind a windowed wall. The glass was clear and shiny. A faint smell of school pizza trickled my nose.

Put me in mind of my life with the Colemans, when I went to a well-run and polished school like this one. After my father got out of prison and took me back, I went to a chaotic inner city school where the floors were filthy, the walls cracked and worn, and whatever windows weren't boarded over were streaked with grime.

A few well-dressed people were waiting at the front desk. I stood back patiently, wishing I'd had time to shower and change out of my dirty work clothes. I was pretty sure I smelled of oil and sweat.

At least the kids were well dressed and smelled fresh.

One of the ladies—her desk plaque said "Mrs. Rivers"—leaned forward and looked at me, frowning. "May I help you?"

I stepped forward. "I hope so, ma'am. I brought Brianna and Christopher Mathias to school. I'm sorry they're late."

Her eyes narrowed disapprovingly. "Are you the children's father?"

"No, ma'am."

"Jesse's my Mom's boyfriend," Brianna offered.

Mrs. Rivers sniffed. "Really." She handed me a clipboard and a pen, saying, "Please fill this out."

"What's that?" I asked.

"The children are late. You need to sign them in."

Carefully, I wrote their names on two spaces, then put my name in the next column. I looked at the clock and wrote in the time. 9:57.

She handed little slips of orange paper over to the kids. "Give the late pass to your teacher," she told them.

"Should we go to our lockers first?" Chris asked her.

"Yes. Go to your lockers. Do you have lunch money?" She looked at me meaningfully.

"Jesse made our lunch," Brianna offered. "I got Very Berry Juice."

The kids went out into the hall and turned a corner.

I started to follow them.

"Just a minute, Mr...." Mrs. Rivers looked at her clipboard. "Damon."

I tried to look innocent, which I have found could be surprisingly difficult. "Yes?"

"I need to know the reason the children are nearly an hour late."

I didn't want to get Kelly in trouble. What should I say? "Their mother's sick," I said. Being hung over is a kind of sickness.

Mrs. Rivers glanced at one of the women who was in the office, nodding to her. This woman stepped forward and held out her hand. "I'm Mrs. O'Neill, the PPW assigned to this school."

"The what?" I asked.

"PPW. Pupil personnel worker. It's my job to help the students when they're having difficulties or miss a lot of school."

"Kind of like a truant officer?" I asked, hastily rubbing my hand on my pants leg before I shook her hand. I hoped mine wasn't covered with too much dirt or oil.

"That's part of my job. But I'm here to try to help, not to get people in trouble."

That didn't sound hugely accurate to me—in my experience, everyone who works for the government is just waiting for people to mess up. But this wasn't really my concern. I was just trying to help Kelly out by getting the kids to school.

"I take it Mrs. Mathias isn't available right now to speak to me."

I thought of Kelly, sitting in the car, head on the steering wheel, asleep. She'd probably have a reverse imprint of the Ford logo on her forehead.

"No, ma'am." No point in saying she was just outside. "That's why she asked me to bring the kids in."

"I see. Will you ask Mrs. Mathias to call me and make an appointment?" She handed me a business card.

I stared at it for a minute. No one had ever given me a business card before.

"Yes, ma'am. I sure will," I said, pocketing the card and going back out to the car.

Kelly wasn't asleep. She was crying. Great blubbery sobs, her chest heaving and her nose running.

"I've really messed up, haven't I?" she asked, reaching for a crushed box of tissues on the floor of the back seat.

I looked at her, not sure how to respond.

She had messed up. But not so much she couldn't get it back together. This was someone who'd been kind to me when she didn't have to be, who'd treated me like a regular person when she knew I was a convicted murderer on parole. Someone I cared about. Not to mention the only woman I'd ever slept with.

"Nothing that can't be fixed," I said. "If you want to." That, of course, was the key. Kelly had to want to. Nobody else could do it for her.

She blew her nose noisily and hiccupped. She wiped her eyes with the sleeve of her sweatshirt.

I'm not good at comforting gestures, but she looked so forlorn. Awkwardly, I reached my arm around her shoulders and drew her as close as the center console of the car would let me. I expected her to shrug my arm off and reach for the key in the ignition.

But she leaned toward me, her face collapsing into my shoulder. The sobbing resumed in earnest. Her breath smelled of morning-after sour whiskey.

I gave her shoulders a squeeze and kissed the top of her head. I didn't know what else to do. The gearshift must be digging into her side something fierce, but she didn't seem to notice.

Finally she sat up and took another tissue. "You really think I can turn it around?"

I almost said, "You're asking me?" I hadn't exactly made a huge success of my life so far. Being determined not to go back to prison was about the outer limit of my goals.

"If you want to," I finally said. "Probably not gonna be easy, but you can do it if you set your mind to it. And get some help."

"Help?"

"Like AA."

She pulled away from me and turned the key in the ignition.

"Will you come over the house for a while?" she asked, not looking at me. "I could really use a friend right now."

"Sure." Maybe she'd feel better, and we could get something going here.

When we got back to her kitchen, I made two mugs of instant coffee and put some slightly stale bread in the toaster. "You'll feel better if you get some food in your stomach."

Kelly sat at the table, stirring her coffee and looking miserable. "You think I'm in trouble at work?" she asked.

"Probably not. John said you'd called in." I thought of all the time Aaron had missed, and he still had a job. Of course, the police had probably asked the company to keep him on until he provided them with the information they wanted, and they picked some people up. Like me.

But it was a union shop. The first couple of absences would result in warnings. There were a set number of incidents before someone would actually be fired. I doubted Kelly had reached that point yet.

She seemed to be reading my mind. "I got one warning. Last year. And I promised them I'd do better."

"You can check with Victor Sunday night. He's the shop steward. He'll know for sure."

Kelly wrinkled her nose as she nibbled at her toast, but she ate it. She was still sniffling. "How did the kids seem?" she asked.

Sugarcoating the truth wouldn't do anyone any good. "Worried. And scared."

"How can I be doing this to them?" she wailed, tears spilling down her cheeks.

"By putting yourself in front of them," I said bluntly. "They can't do a damn thing about it. They just have to take what you dish out."

She turned on me, her eyes flashing. "And I suppose you could do a better job with kids?"

I didn't take the bait. "I don't have kids. But you do. And you been messing up. I been a kid—one who ended up in foster care because my mother died, and my father went to prison. I don't want to see any kid put in a position like that if somebody can help it."

Kelly dissolved in tears again. "They wouldn't put them in foster care, would they?"

"If you and your ex are both boozers who can't provide a decent home, yes, they can put the kids in foster care. And you won't have an easy time getting them back. You think you feel bad now? Wait until you have to see them by appointment in the social services building. And they cry when you have to leave."

She dabbed at her eyes with a tissue. "You're not very sympathetic."

"Sympathy won't do no good. Not for you or the kids. You got to make up your mind what you're going to do. Then you got to do it. Me feeling sorry for you, or you feeling sorry for yourself, ain't gonna cut it."

She nodded. "I guess you're right. What do I need to do first?"

I looked at her bleary eyes and smelled her stale next-morning breath.

"Go take a shower. Get some sleep. Then as soon as you get up, call AA. Find out when the next meeting you can make is, and go."

While she was in the shower, I picked up the bottles, glasses, and tissues that surrounded her bed. I found clean sheets and tidied up the bed.

She came out of the bathroom with her hair wrapped up in a towel. She had on a worn terry robe. When she stepped into the room, she stopped and looked at the bed. She glanced up at me. "I don't feel real good," she said softly. "But if you want to…"

I shook my head. For one thing, she needed to get some sleep. For another, I didn't find her especially appealing right now. "Just get some sleep."

She climbed into the bed. I smoothed the quilt over her shoulders and up under her chin.

"Will you be here when I wake up?" she asked.

"If you'd like," I said.

"I'd like."

I was tired. I lay down on the sofa in the living room and fell asleep.

When the kids got off the bus from school, I got up and let Kelly sleep. The way her schedule worked out, I bet she never got quite enough sleep during the week.

I insisted they unpack their book bags and get to work on their homework.

"It's only Friday. We have all weekend. Why do we have to do our homework now?" Brianna dumped the contents of her book bag, crumpled papers, old pencils, crumbs and all, out on the dining room table.

"Then it'll be done & you won't have to worry about it anymore," I said as I went for a wastebasket and began sorting things from the pile.

Chris grumbled, but he got out his books and started in on his homework.

"Ask if you have any questions," I said. "I don't know all of it, but if I can help, I will."

"Thanks," he said, "This is math. I can do that myself."

"Good." I'm not so sure I could help with the math.

Brianna was drawing pictures of stick people and cats on her paper.

"What are you supposed to be doing, Brianna?" I asked.

"Lists," she said.

"Lists?" That wasn't an assignment I was familiar with.

"Yeah. You know. Lists of things that go together."

"How do you mean?"

She looked at me as if I were a total idiot. "Yellow things. Green things. Things that walk on four legs. Flowers."

I started to say that was too easy for homework for a kid her age, but then I remembered she was having lots of difficulties in school. "How's the reading coming?" I asked.

She pressed her lips tight together and closed her eyes. "It's hard."

"It's supposed to be hard. You have to work at it. Do you have any reading homework?"

"The lists are reading homework."

"Then we'd better get to it," I said. "Do you get to choose what things to use to make the list?"

"Yes." She continued to doodle.

"How many have to be in each list?"

"Five."

"What's the first list we should make?"

"I was going to do 'green.' I thought of lots of things, but I'm not sure how to spell it."

"Spell what?"

"Spell 'green.'"

"G—R—E—E—N."

She looked up in surprise. "You can spell?" she asked.

"Yeah. I'm pretty good at it." I'd helped a lot of fellow inmates read and write letters. And I'd spent the best part of twenty years reading. I wasn't a perfect speller, but I was pretty good.

"I thought only teachers could spell."

"Nope. Lots of people can. And you can always look up a word you don't know how to spell."

Chris raised his head from his work. "I always wondered about that. If you can't spell a word, how are you going to find it in the dictionary?"

I thought about that. Smart kid. "I think a lot of people use computer spell check programs these days instead of a dictionary."

"Do you know how to use a computer?" he asked.

"Not really," I said, thinking of the new computer system at work. "A lot of stuff I don't know how to use. Computers. Cell phones. Video players." A lot had been introduced in the twenty years I was in prison. I had a lot of catching up to do.

Brianna took a new sheet of paper and placed it in front of her. "Could you spell that again?"

I did, and she carefully wrote the letters.

"What did you think of that's green?" I asked.

"Frog. But I don't know how to spell that."

"How do you think?" I asked.

"Fa-fa-fa. Does it start with an F?"

"Very good."

"Rrrrr…Is that an R?"

"Yep. Way to go."

She beamed and sounded out the O sound.

"The vowels are hard," I told her.

"Yeah. Is it an O?"

"You're really good at this."

She had no trouble with the G.

We added grass, peas, shamrocks and the glass "stone" in her bracelet.

I thought about the green jewel in Montgomery's ring, which I bet wasn't glass. It would really cut up someone's face if he punched them with that hand. My hand strayed up and fingered where Belkins had smacked me.

I fixed hot dogs and beans for supper. Chris and I debated the merits of waking Kelly up for dinner, but he thought that hot dogs and beans could always be reheated easily enough, and might not be worth getting up for in the first place.

The hot dogs weren't the world's cheapest chicken dogs, and I thoroughly enjoyed mine, but I saw his point. It was no gourmet meal.

Now that I had a little more money, maybe I could add hot dogs to my food rotation. And frozen pizza. But I wouldn't keep any of it in my pocket.

"Isn't your dad supposed to come get you for the weekend?" I asked.

Chris turned away and stared at the dark window. "He was supposed to pick us up from school."

"And you didn't wait for him?"

"He was supposed to get us before the buses came. He didn't come, so I told Brianna we had to get on the bus. 'Cause if he never came, we'd be stuck at school."

"Has that happened before?"

"Yeah."

I shoved my chair back from the table. "You wanna watch TV while I clean up?"

Brianna looked at me wistfully. "Could we play Candy Land instead?"

"I guess."

Chris thought for a minute. "And would you play a game of checkers with me?"

"Sure. But first I have to do the dishes."

When I'd finished, they had the Candy Land game set up on the dining room table. We played that, and then Chris beat me at checkers.

"Brianna gets to play the winner," I said, moving over so she could set up her checkers.

"She's not very good," Chris said. "She hardly knows how to play."

"Then it'll be good practice for her. And you can explain if she has any problems."

Some of the stuff from Brianna's book bag still lay in a heap. I finished sorting it, smoothing out the papers.

Many of them were school work, connecting pictures and words. I cringed to think that Brianna was almost through first grade and still working on things like that.

A few were notes that seemed to require answers.

I frowned and smoothed one out.

It was a letter saying that Brianna wasn't doing well in school. No surprise there. The teacher requested a conference. Three weeks ago. And there was a request to test her for special education services. Suspected learning disability. Made sense to me.

"Did your mom ever see these papers?" I asked her.

Brianna shrugged.

"They need to be signed and sent back to school. And your mom needs to go in and talk to the people at school."

Tears brimmed in her eyes. "I don't want her to go in and talk to them. They'll just tell her how dumb I am."

"But you're not dumb. You're a smart little girl."

"I can't read," she said, setting her mouth stubbornly.

"That don't mean you're dumb," I said. "Lots of people have trouble learning to read. Even lots of smart people."

"They'll put me in Reading Resource," she said. "Only the dumb kids go there."

"Not true. People who are having trouble reading go there. Dumb ones and smart ones. They help you learn to read better. So you won't be behind most people in your class. And then you won't feel so dumb anymore."

"Really? Did you ever know anybody who learned to read in Reading Resource?"

"Yep. Lots of people. Some of them just as smart as you are."

She looked up at me, tears in her eyes. "You don't know what it's like to be six years old and in first grade. And not to be able to read."

"Mom!" Chris cried.

Kelly, wrapped in her bathrobe, was making her way down the stairs. Her hair was combed, and she didn't look perfect, but she was much better than before. She smelled of bath powder and soap.

I longed to gather her in my arms, kiss her fragrant neck, and take her back upstairs.

"We saved you supper, Mom," Chris said.

Maybe after the kids got to bed.

"So your dad didn't pick you up from school?" she asked.

"Nope."

She shook her head but didn't say much as I brought her food to the kitchen table. The unfinished checker game lay spread out in the dining room. Kelly only picked at her food.

I put on a pot of coffee. Brianna began shoveling things back into her backpack.

Kelly sat at the table, her eyes clouded. She still didn't seem to feel well. I decided my prospects for a tumble in her comfy bed later tonight were not good. Disappointing, but I could deal with that.

I had set aside the papers that needed to be signed for school. When she was done packing her backpack, Brianna brought them to Kelly.

I filled our coffee mugs and sat down next to Kelly. "Those are important," I said. "You really ought to read them over. And get in touch with the school if you have any questions."

Kelly's nostrils flared. "Oh, and I guess you know better than me what's important with the kids' school."

Surprised, I tried to backpedal. "No, no. It's just that they're from the special education department at the school. Brianna is having trouble with her reading. They might be able to help."

Kelly stood up, knocking over her mug. Coffee splashed over the table surface and dripped onto the floor. "There's nothing wrong with Brianna. She just isn't that good a reader, is all."

"Reading's important," I said.

"I'll decide what's important with my kids," she said.

"Okay." I tried to defuse the situation. "I was just afraid you hadn't seen the papers, is all."

"I'll thank you to mind your own business."

I glanced at the kids. Chris clutched his homework so hard he was wrinkling it. He stared at it. Brianna's eyes were filling with tears. She was stuffing the rest of the papers into her backpack.

"Look, I'm sorry. You do a good job with the kids. They couldn't ask for a better mother." Unless they could find one who didn't drink. But I didn't say that.

Kelly drew her robe more tightly around her. "Thanks for fixing the dinner," she said. "I suppose the kids told you it was a better dinner than I'd have fixed."

The kids looked at me with pleading eyes. "No. They didn't say anything like that at all. We wanted to fix dinner for you. The kids worked hard at it. And I was just trying to help."

"Yeah? Well, go help someone else."

With a last sorrowful look at the kids, I got up and got my jacket. "Sorry if I stepped in where I don't belong," I said. "I'll be going now."

Kelly didn't turn to face me.

"See you at work Sunday night," I said, and let myself out the back door.

CHAPTER 8

Saturday morning dawned bright and chilly. I woke up in my own bed instead of Kelly's across town where I'd hoped to be.

I looked at the phone that hung on the wall across the room. Would it be a good idea to call her and see how she and the kids were doing?

No. I knew better than that. Chances were pretty good she'd hit the bottle again last night. With her mercurial mood swings and irrational anger at everybody but herself, she was showing many of the signs of an alcohol abuser descending into the depths of despair. Not much I could do but try to be there to help pick up the pieces when she began to claw her way back out. If she did.

I wondered if the kids' father had ever come to get them.

The day stretched ahead of me.

I couldn't waste a day like this. For one thing, if Belkins had his way, I'd be back on home detention after my next parole meeting, which was Thursday. I should get outside and walk in the sunlight.

And I should see if I could find out something about how Mrs. Coleman had died. Anything at all.

Montgomery has suggested I'd been seen around the Colemans' house. I hadn't been there since a social worker had picked me up and delivered me to my father in the slums of Baltimore years ago. Maybe I should go take a look around. I should be able to do that without calling attention to myself or bothering Mr. Coleman.

The Coleman house was across town and out in the hills a little, in what today would be called a subdivision, but when I was a kid was just a "neighborhood." I made sure the cat had plenty of food and water, admired her kittens for her, and set out. I wore a heavy sweater under my oversized hoodie. Not as warm as my jacket, maybe, but much less noticeable.

It didn't take me even an hour to get there. When I'd been a kid, the walk downtown had seemed to take forever.

My feet found their own way down the once-familiar sidewalks, past street signs and the bus stop. I turned into the dead-end street where I had spent the best part of my childhood. The best part of my life, really.

The house itself looked much the same, with its deep front porch and gravel driveway that ran back to the detached single car garage. The yews in the front were overgrown, hiding the windows, and the dogwood tree which had been a stick with a few leaves when Mr. Coleman and I had planted it now spread over the entire front yard. This time of year, its branches were bare.

No one was in sight. A few dead leaves skittered across the pavement, landing in a slushy puddle near a broken curb next to the driveway.

I walked past the house, trying to look casual as I peered at it. I couldn't make out much except that it was older and more worn but reasonably well-kept.

What exactly had I intended to do when I got here? I knew going up and knocking on the front door wouldn't be a good idea. Mr. Coleman would call the police if he saw me. I couldn't blame him.

I decided to walk around the block, see if I could see the backyard between the houses. The houses, all built around the same time, had been staggered on their lots to provide maximum privacy.

The neighborhood was quiet. Much quieter than I remembered it. It was Saturday, so the children wouldn't be in school. People don't seem to send their children out to play the way they did when I was a kid. The original inhabitants who remained, like Mr. Coleman, would be elderly and would probably not have kids in the house.

The street behind was equally deserted. I tried to judge the distance from the corner. When I figured I was behind Mr. Coleman's house, I hesitated. The side yard between the two houses was overgrown, but there was no fence. One house had a glassed-in porch that ran down the length of the house. No curtains covered the windows, and I couldn't see any sign that anyone was around. The few small windows of the other house had their shades closely drawn.

I stepped off the sidewalk and pushed my way among the bushes between the houses.

My guess had been right. I could just see Coleman's backyard. The swing set I remembered was gone. The back of the garage was freshly painted. On its side, the paint was chipped and peeling. It looked as if someone had started repainting and quit partway through. The sticker bushes that lined the path to the garage were much bigger than I'd remembered, and their thorns looked even more wicked than they had when I had run into them as a kid.

A row of lilacs divided the properties. I recalled their heady aroma in the spring when they bloomed. I inhaled deeply, as if the winter-bare branches could give off the scent.

A slight movement on the path in Coleman's yard caught my eye. Whatever it was hadn't moved much, but it was big. Person-sized. I ducked down.

What was the matter with me? Here I was trespassing. Mr. Coleman had specifically told me to stay away. And Detective Montgomery had re-enforced that. If I got caught, my parole officer would certainly have something to say about it. I was sure I wouldn't be happy with what he said.

From my crouched position, I continued to stare through the branches at the place where I'd seen the movement. I was about to decide my overactive imagination had interpreted some windblown vegetation as something more substantial when I caught a staggering motion near the garage.

Peering through the bare lilacs and over the sticker bushes, I tried to make out what it was. A person. But not a person moving normally, more like somebody stumbling, pitching sideways, and reaching out a hand to brace on the garage wall.

Gingerly, I pushed my way through the vegetation and almost into the yard.

It was Mr. Coleman. He was dressed in a plaid shirt and dark pants. No jacket. I shivered. He looked down. I followed his gaze. A cane was lying on the ground, its handle facing away from him.

As I watched, he struggled to reach the cane. And tumbled to the ground.

He just lay there. He needed help.

Maybe I could go find a pay phone and call 9-1-1. But even if I got to the corner store, which might or might not still be there, so many public phones had been removed since then. Most people had cell phones now. I didn't, of course, but everyone else seemed to have one.

Or I could knock on one of the doors around and see if someone couldn't go help.

Then I'd have to answer awkward questions about what I was doing around here. And why I just didn't go help him myself.

The only thing that was clear was that I couldn't just go and leave him.

I stepped out from the lilacs and made my way around the sticker bushes, approaching Mr. Coleman from behind. I went down on one knee next to him, reaching for the cane and bringing it to where he could reach it.

He looked at me, his eyes fierce. He took the cane and tried to use it to sit up. He fell forward again.

"Are you hurt?" I asked. "Maybe you should stay there while I go in the house and call an ambulance."

"No ambulance," he said gruffly. "I'm fine. Help me up."

I placed my hands under his armpits and brought him to a sitting position. He seemed to understand what I was trying to do. He pulled his legs under him, planted the cane solidly on the flagstones and lurched upward.

With my hands still under his armpits, I supported his weight as he rose unsteadily to his feet.

When he was upright, I backed off. He hadn't gotten a good look at me. Maybe I could take off before he fully recognized me.

Mr. Coleman stood swaying slightly, looking around himself in confusion. "What happened?" he asked.

"You fell," I said, hoping my voice wouldn't give away my identity and trigger his anger.

"It's cold out here. I need to get back into the house." He turned and stumbled toward the back steps, almost losing his balance again.

I had to at least get him into the house. And maybe find someone to call. So far he hadn't realized who I was. He seemed to be in a daze. Maybe he'd hit his head when he fell.

Taking him by the elbow, I held him upright. We made slow progress toward the door.

The stairs were difficult, but we made it. I opened the back door, and he hobbled to a chair by the kitchen table.

The kitchen was chilly. I went back and shut the door. Mr. Coleman wasn't dressed for the cold. He was shivering. I went to the front hallway to get a sweater from the closet and grabbed an afghan from the couch as I passed by the living room.

Inside the house was pretty much like I remembered it, too. I swallowed hard to get rid of the lump that was rising in my throat.

I helped him put on the sweater and put the afghan over his lap. He smoothed it with a hand that felt icy when it brushed mine.

"Shall I fix you some hot coffee?" I asked.

"Tea," he answered, closing his eyes. "With plenty of milk."

I put a mug in the microwave and searched the cabinets for tea bags. I pulled the milk jug out of the refrigerator and shook it. It sounded funny, chunky. I opened it to sniff, but I didn't have to bring it anywhere near my nose to tell it was sour.

"The milk's turned," I told him. I'd seen the jar of honey in the cabinet and a bottle of lemon juice on the refrigerator door. They didn't go bad with tea. "How about some lemon and honey in it instead?"

He nodded without opening his eyes.

I was chilled through, too. "Do you mind if I join you?" I asked.

"Be my guest," he said, his eyes still closed.

I fixed two mugs of tea and put one in front of Mr. Coleman.

Even with the door shut, it seemed cold in the kitchen. I went to the living room to check the thermostat. It was set at a reasonable seventy-two, but the temperature registered fifty-nine. No wonder it felt cold.

"Something wrong with your heat, Mr. Coleman?" I asked.

He raised his clouded eyes. "It's not working."

That much I'd figured out. "Do you know why it's not working?" I asked.

"No." He took another sip of his tea.

"You still heat with gas?" I asked.

"Yes."

"Do you still have that service contract with the gas company?"

"I think so."

The phone still hung on the wall next to the back door. I opened the drawer that used to hold the phone book. There it was. I found the gas company's number and punched in the numbers.

Phones weren't something I'd had a great deal of experience with. The Colemans hadn't allowed their foster children to use the phone. My dad never had one. Prison inmates without anyone to call have no use for them. Now everybody seemed to have these cell phones glued to their ears all the time.

The gas company answered with recorded instructions. I delved through a confusing array of automated messages, but finally got through to a live person. I asked about having a repairman out as soon as possible.

"Dennis Coleman? At 539 Whispering Pines?" a disembodied voice said.

"Yes, that's right," I agreed.

"Service discontinued due to lack of payment," the voice said.

Lack of payment? The Colemans weren't rich, but I couldn't believe they couldn't afford their gas bill. I said, "I thought you didn't do discon-nections in the winter time."

"We don't if the customer contacts us and works something out. In this case, no one responded to the shutoff notices. A representative vis-ited the residence, but no one answered the door. His note says that it appeared to be unoccupied. No foreclosure notice posted, though."

"Well, it's very much occupied. And it's pretty cold in here. How do I go about getting service restored?"

"You can talk to a service representative about setting up a payment plan or applying for assistance. But you'd have to wait until Monday to do that."

"How about if the bill got paid? Could I do that today? Wouldn't that be easier?"

"Well, of course the easiest way would be to pay the bill. The office is open until five this afternoon on a limited basis. They can take the payment."

I winced. "How much to get it reconnected?"

"One thousand five hundred and twenty-nine dollars."

No way could I come up with that kind of money. I wondered if Mr. Coleman had that much. Probably. "How long does it take to get it turned back on after you get the money?" I asked.

"We've got an emergency crew on duty. If we get the payment by three this afternoon, we can have it turned on by five. Assuming the crew isn't out on another emergency."

Great. Now I just needed $1,529.

I hung up and turned to Mr. Coleman. Mr. Coleman ought to have money somewhere, although maybe not much in cash. Montgomery had indicated that the money Mrs. Coleman kept in the thesaurus had been taken.

"What happens to your social security checks?" I asked him.

"I don't get checks." He drew the afghan closer around his spare waist and took a sip of his tea.

"You have to get social security," I said. "You worked all those years."

"Yes. We…I have direct deposit."

"Into a bank account?"

"Into the checking account. To pay the bills." He tipped the mug so he could see the bottom, then lifted it to his lips again.

"When was the last time you ate?" I asked him.

"This morning."

"Breakfast?"

"I guess."

"What did you have?"

"Maybe it was yesterday."

I had to get him something to eat. I opened the freezer. It was stocked with freezer-burned roasts and several boxes of frozen pizza. Seemed like an odd choice for an elderly couple. But it would be easy to fix, and maybe he really liked pizza.

"You want me to fix a frozen pizza for you?"

His face wrinkled. "I hate those things. They stink up the whole kitchen."

No frozen pizza, then. I wondered why they were in the freezer. In a cabinet, I found a can of soup. This time I didn't ask him. I just dumped it into a big bowl and stuck it in the microwave.

When it was warm, I put the soup and a spoon in front of Mr. Coleman on the table.

"I'm not hungry," he said.

"Try to eat some anyhow," I said, rummaging around until I found a package of saltines.

Obediently, he picked up the spoon and scooped up some of the soup. His hand trembled, but he got most of the spoonful to his mouth. His face cleared, and he continued to eat until the bowl was empty. He took the saltines I'd laid out and gobbled them down. Then he looked up hopefully.

I thought of all the stories I'd heard about released prison inmates who got deathly sick to their stomachs after they had their first non-prison meal. Hadn't been a problem for me—most of my meals for the first few weeks had been ramen noodles and peanut butter sandwiches—but I thought it was probably because they weren't used to eating regular food, especially in unlimited amounts. If Mr. Coleman hadn't been eating much, I didn't want to make him sick.

"Let that settle before you have anything else," I said. "Now, where's your checkbook?"

"In the office."

I went to the tiny room off the living room Mrs. Coleman had called the office. When I'd lived there, it had always been locked. My memory of it was of a starkly neat space with a large desk and file cabinets lining the wall.

The door to the office wasn't closed, and the space was no longer starkly neat. The file cabinet drawers hung open. The files sat in untidy piles on all available surfaces and the floor.

Did Mr. Coleman still have the big book-type checkbook I remembered? Or did he use one of those little ones that are about the size of a wallet?

The piles on the desk seemed like a good place to start.

Sifting through a pile of unopened mail, I found a few envelopes from the gas company. Two of them had large notes on the outside in red. The cutoff notices.

I found a bank statement that hadn't been opened. I hesitated for a minute, wondering if it was my place to look at it, but how else was I going to find out if there was enough in the checking account to pay the gas bill?

The statement said Mr. Coleman had over ten thousand dollars.

Now I just had to locate the checkbook. And get Mr. Coleman to write a check that I could take to the gas company office.

As I shifted a stack of files and envelopes, several large manila envelopes fell off the pile. One spewed its contents across the floor. Old papers and photographs.

I stooped down to pick them up and tried to sort them out. Some of them were pictures of a young woman, very thin but unmistakably Mrs. Coleman. She'd never been thin while I knew her.

In a few, she posed with a man who didn't look like Mr. Coleman.

The thought of Mrs. Coleman with another man was strange. Well, why not? The Colemans had been married for a long time, but lots of people had relationships before they married. What would make me think she should have been any different?

In one picture, Mrs. Coleman was thick-waisted, more the way I remembered her. But her arms were stick-thin.

Then came a few baby pictures. The Colemans didn't have any children. I'd once overheard Mrs. Coleman saying that she couldn't have any. Maybe some relative's kid, although by the time I lived there, they didn't seem to have any relatives, either.

A birth certificate. A boy, born more than fifty years ago to a Mildred Mayford. No father was listed.

Mrs. Coleman's first name had been Mildred.

My heart froze. Had Mrs. Coleman had a child out of wedlock?

These days, that wasn't a big deal, but back then, it would have been devastating.

I rifled quickly through the remaining papers. A copy of a release for adoption, dated the same day as the birth certificate. Signed by Mildred Mayford, in a strong hand using the proper Palmer penmanship I remembered Mrs. Coleman having.

A crash came from the kitchen. I hurriedly shoved everything back into one of the manila envelopes and put it under a stack of old papers. I opened a file drawer—everything had been removed from it—and dropped the stack into it.

"What was that crash, Mr. Coleman?" I asked as I went back to the kitchen.

He stood precariously, leaning on his cane and the table. The chair lay on its back on the floor and the afghan was bunched next to it. "What crash?" he asked.

I picked up the chair and draped the afghan over its back. "I'm still looking for the checkbook. Do you have any idea where in the office it is?"

Mr. Coleman scratched his ear. "In the center desk drawer, probably. That's where it belongs."

I gave him a few more saltines and made sure he was seated again before I went back into the office. Opening the center drawer, I shoved a few things aside. There it was. So simple. Why hadn't I asked him more directly before?

I carried it out to the kitchen. Mr. Coleman was standing up again, holding onto the chair back and teetering. Taking a pen from near the phone, I said, "Sit down again for a minute, Mr. Coleman. We need to write a check to the gas company."

He sat down again. Taking the latest bill I could find, I filled in the information, and put $1,529 in the amount lines.

I gave him the pen. "Sign this," I told him.

He gripped the pen tightly and leaned hard on the check as he wrote something that I suppose was his signature.

He pressed down so hard the pen tore the check. And the one under it.

I tore those two out of the book and ripped them up. Then I made out the next one for the gas company again. "Try not to press so hard," I said.

This time he signed it without ripping the paper.

I took it out of the book, folded it up and put it in my pocket. If I left pretty soon, I could get it to the gas company office in time to have the gas turned on today.

But Mr. Coleman wasn't in any shape to leave alone.

"Does anybody come in to help you, Mr. Coleman?" I asked.

He frowned. "Help me?"

"Yeah. You know, like fixing you dinner or cleaning the house or helping you take your meds?"

His eyes teared up. "Rosa is supposed to come in for a few hours every afternoon. But I haven't seen her here since the day Mildred died. She said she came in and found Mildred at the bottom of the cellar stairs. She called for the ambulance. But she didn't wait for it to get here."

That seemed kind of strange. And then she hadn't shown up for work since? Could she have had something to do with the fall down the stairs? Should I call Detective Montgomery and make sure he knew about Rosa?

Rosa and the Rose Aaron mentioned were probably the same person. If Aaron were a police informant, Montgomery would be privy to everything Aaron knew. Montgomery would likely ask me how I found out that she'd been in the house. I wouldn't have a good way to answer that.

If I couldn't find somebody to come over, I'd have to call 9-1-1 or something and take whatever grief that came with it. And they'd probably take Mr. Coleman to the hospital. "Is there anyone else?"

"Mrs. Williams," he said. "She was Mildred's friend. And she's a nurse. She stops in sometimes."

"Has she been here lately?" I asked.

"I don't know," he said. "Last time I remember her coming, I was just heading out for my walk. So she walked with me. But that was a while ago."

"Like today?"

"I don't think it was today."

"Or maybe yesterday?"

"I don't know."

"Does she work for an agency or something?"

"She used to work in the hospital. Now she's retired. But she belongs to the same church as us."

"What church do you go to?" I asked. When I was a kid, they'd gone to the Church of The Savior, a fundamentalist Christian church.

"Church of The Savior," he said.

I remembered all the ladies standing around him at Mrs. Coleman's viewing. They'd looked like church ladies. At least at that church, the church ladies could be depended upon in an emergency for one of their congregation.

Taking the phone book, I looked up the church number and dialed. I got an answering machine. I wasn't sure it would do any good before tomorrow morning, but I left a brief message anyhow.

"Any other way to get in touch with Mrs. Williams? Or anybody else from the church?"

He gestured across the room. "Her phone number's on the refrigerator."

"Where does she live?"

"The next street over."

"I'm going to call her."

Mrs. Williams answered on the second ring. Without giving my name, I explained I was a former foster child who had stopped by and how I'd found Mr. Coleman. She said she'd be right over.

Mr. Coleman was sitting up straighter, and his eyes were brighter. Maybe because he'd gotten something to eat. I wasn't quite so worried about him now and wondered if I could just leave. Mrs. Williams would be over soon.

Before I could act on that thought, the back door opened and a sturdy middle-aged woman bustled in.

"Mrs. Williams?"

She adjusted her glasses. "Yes. What seems to be going on here?"

I shrugged. "I just came by to see how Mr. Coleman was doing. He was outside without a coat or anything. And he fell."

She raised her eyebrows and looked me over. "And just how did he fall?"

My gut froze. Mrs. Coleman had died from a fall. "Looked like he'd dropped his cane and kind of tumbled over when he tried to pick it up."

"And exactly who are you?"

"I was one of the foster children they took in. Years ago."

"What's your name?"

I didn't want to give my real name, but I knew Montgomery would probably be talking to her. If he found out I'd lied, he'd be even more suspicious than ever. "Jerry," I mumbled, hoping she wouldn't ask for a last name. They must have had a Jerry or two sometime over the years, and it sounded enough like Jesse that I could claim she'd misheard if it ever came to that.

She smoothed the afghan over Mr. Coleman's lap again. "It's cold in here," she said.

"Yes, ma'am. The gas is off. I called the gas company and they said if I got a check in by three this afternoon, they'd get it turned on by five."

"Where're you going to get a check?"

"Mr. Coleman gave me one." I pulled it out of my pocket and held it up.

"Let me see that," she demanded.

I handed it over to her. She looked at it suspiciously, turning it over in her hands before she gave it back to me. "I'm going to be calling the gas company to make sure this gets to them," she warned me.

"Yes, ma'am."

"Has he had any lunch?" she asked.

"I fixed some canned soup. And a cup of tea."

Mr. Coleman stirred and peered up at me. "How long have you been here?"

"Just a little while. You fell out in the yard, remember? I helped you back inside."

"I don't like you young men coming around. You're never up to any good."

I was thirty-six, not exactly a young man. But maybe I looked that way to Mr. Coleman. "Have there been other young men around a lot, Mr. Coleman?" I asked, remembering Montgomery's claim that I'd been seen in the neighborhood.

His lips formed a thin stubborn line. "I told Mildred not to have anything to do with any of you. We're old. We get confused. We can't take care of ourselves."

It wasn't the first time he seemed to be forgetting that Mrs. Coleman was dead. I wasn't going to be the one who reminded him.

His eyes softened. Tears gathered. "But it didn't help, did it? I told her not to give you any money. You'd just be back again."

"Mr. Coleman, I haven't been here in years."

"But you're here now. And rummaging around in the house."

I guess he was right about me rummaging around, at least in the office.

Mrs. Williams took his thin wrist in her hand. Was she taking his pulse? "Why were you outside, Mr. Coleman?" she asked. "And without your coat."

"I don't know," he said.

"You should stay in the house until someone else is here to help you."

"I thought I heard someone out there. I went to check."

"Have you been taking your meds?" she asked.

"Yes. Some of them. Sometimes."

"When did you take them last, Mr. Coleman?" she asked.

His gaze shifted to the wall. "I don't remember. They're gone," he said flatly.

"What do you mean, they're gone?"

"The medicine cabinet's empty," he said. "I don't remember moving everything. But I must have."

Mrs. Williams persisted. "Did you call the doctor and tell him you couldn't find them?"

He nodded. "The person who answered the phone said to look for them. She said they couldn't give me any more until those were supposed to be gone. She said they have to be somewhere. I looked."

"What meds did you have?" she asked.

"Blood pressure medicine. Cholesterol medicine. Thyroid medicine. Arthritis medicine. Pain medication."

Mrs. Williams looked at the row of pill bottles on the counter. "Could you bring those over here?" she asked me.

I gathered them up and moved them to the table.

"Are these them, Mr. Coleman?" she asked.

He rubbed his eyes. "Why, I do believe they are. Where did you find them?"

"On the counter." Mrs. Williams starting reading the labels and taking pills out of the containers. "You haven't taken any at all today?"

He poked at one of the pills. "No. I couldn't find them. I thought he took them." He nodded toward me.

"Why would the young man have taken your pills?" she asked.

Mr. Coleman shrugged. "Mildred said he wanted some of her pills. When she told him it wasn't good for you to take someone else's medicine, he said he didn't care."

"Did she have pain medication?" I asked.

"Yes. Some of those oxycodone things. I have some too. But I don't like to take them."

"Why is that?" Mrs. Williams asked.

"They make me feel dizzy. Sometimes, if my back hurts, I take one before I go to bed." Mr. Coleman picked up a pill bottle. "But the bottle seems to be empty now."

Mrs. Williams was busy sorting out the pills. "Can you get him a big glass of water?" she asked me.

I let the water run for a minute until it got cold, then filled the glass and brought it over to the table.

Mr. Coleman looked up at me. His eyes darkened.

"Where are your friends?" he asked.

I started to say I had no friends, but that sounded pretty pathetic, even to me. Even if it was pretty much true. "I came by myself," I said.

He started to get up. "I bet your friends are outside."

Mrs. Williams looked at me suspiciously. She glanced at the empty oxycodone bottle. "What did you say your name was?"

This conversation was headed nowhere good. "I'd better get going if I'm going to get to the gas company office in time."

As I closed the door, I looked back through the window at them. He was fingering the checkbook where I had ripped out the checks. Mrs. Williams was fussing by the stove.

The walk to the gas company office took close to forty-five minutes, but I made it with time to spare. I handed in the check and made sure they would send someone out to turn the gas on that afternoon. I pocketed the receipt. It should go back to Mr. Coleman, but it didn't seem like a good idea for me to go back there again. Maybe I could mail it to him. Without a return address.

CHAPTER 9

Sunday morning was cold but sunny. Light even made its way through the ground level window off the alley into my basement apartment. I fixed myself some instant coffee, fed the cat, and headed out. The center of town boasted a cluster of churches, and as I walked by, I would be able to hear some of the choirs singing. And the church bells.

There was a good chance I would be back on home detention by next Sunday morning, so I decided to take advantage of my freedom while I had it.

In the early afternoon, after the church crowds had scattered, I returned to my apartment.

Montgomery's commanding and cultured voice reached me. "Stop, Jesse. Now."

The hair on the back of my neck tingled. I halted, pulling my hands out of my jacket pockets and letting them hang loose by my sides.

He and Belkins got out of a parked car and stood in front of me.

"Why don't we step into the alley, Jesse?" Montgomery said. "Make less of a spectacle for the neighbors that way."

Not much I could do but walk down the alley until he told me to stop.

Belkins coughed and spit on the ground. "Assume the position, Damon." His voice was hoarse and nasal.

I turned to the wall and leaned onto it, bracing my weight on my hands.

"Spread your feet," Montgomery said.

Belkins kicked the toe of my boot, knocking my unresisting foot back. He grunted.

I tried to keep a smile off my face. My boots were steel-toed work boots. Belkins was wearing worn loafers. I bet he'd hurt his foot.

Expert hands skimmed under my jacket, between my legs and over my pockets. I felt my wallet and keychain being whisked out of my pocket.

One of my hands was pulled back behind me, followed by the other. Cold steel cuffs snapped in place. I struggled not to fall.

"Turn around."

I brought my feet closer together, which let me regain my balance, and turned to face them. I took a step back so the rough brick wall was at my back.

Montgomery leaned back, his guarded dark eyes glittering in his dark face. He slipped his manicured hands into the pockets of his immaculate overcoat.

Belkins bounced my wallet and keychain in his palm. I hoped he didn't drop them into the dirty slush. Or that he would pick them up if he did. Finally he put them in the pocket of his wrinkled trench coat. He spit on the sidewalk again.

Leaning on his hand against brick wall, he put his face close to mine and grinned. We were much the same height, although he outweighed me by maybe a hundred pounds. His boozy breath was hot on my face.

"So," he said. "Wanna tell us about your visit to Dennis Coleman?"

They'd found out about that. No real surprise. I knew I was taking a chance when I went there.

"I just went to check on him," I said lamely.

Montgomery raised his finely chiseled eyebrows. "I thought I made it clear you should stay away from Mr. Coleman."

He had. I kept my mouth shut.

"The poor man has had enough to deal with without having you show up and harass him," Montgomery said.

"I hadn't planned on actually talking to him. I was just going to see how he was and leave."

"So why did you change your mind?"

I shifted uneasily on my feet. "He was outside in the cold without a coat. His cane was on the ground. And he fell when he tried to pick it up. I couldn't leave him there."

"So you went to the house, planning on not talking to him, but ended up going inside? And messing with his checkbook? Makes no sense to me." Montgomery pulled his cashmere scarf a bit tighter around his neck.

"No. He'd fallen outside. I helped him get inside."

"Where outside had he fallen?"

"On the back path that goes to the garage."

"What were you doing around back? That's trespassing. In this case, criminal trespassing."

Montgomery was undoubtedly right. I didn't answer.

Belkins leaned closer, his head tilted back and his eyes narrowed. I could see wiry hairs in his nose. "And if you were so concerned about his welfare, how did you find him?"

"Not well."

"So what did you do?"

"After we got into the kitchen, I fixed him some tea and some soup."

"Then what?"

"Then I called a neighbor to check up on him. She came. So I left."

"You just left?"

"Yeah. He seemed better."

"And you didn't mess with his meds?"

"No."

"So if I told you we'd found your fingerprints on the bottles, you'd say it had to be a mistake?"

"I guess not really. They were on the kitchen counter. The neighbor lady asked me to bring them over to her. Then she took care of them. I think she's a nurse."

"How many of his meds did you take for yourself? Especially the pain medication?"

Of course they'd think I took some oxys if I could get hold of them. "None." I didn't expect them to believe me. I was right.

"You seriously expect me to believe that? He was supposed to have pain meds. They were gone. What did you do with them?"

"I didn't take them. You can run a piss test if you want." As long as I didn't have to pay for it. Which I would have to do if they asked Mr. Ramirez to get the sample.

"We may." Belkins narrowed his eyes. "But maybe you sold them. To your buddy Aaron. Then it wouldn't show up, would it?"

Montgomery stepped forward. Now his face too was inches from mine. His breath smelled of minty mouthwash. He inhaled deeply. Then his gaze jerked to the side, focusing on Belkins, not me. He sniffed. He must have caught the sour scent of whiskey on Belkins' breath.

He turned his attention back to me. "Tell us about the checkbook."

My heart sank. Of course they knew about the checkbook. "The gas was turned off. Mr. Coleman wrote a check to the gas company. I took it to the office to pay the bill and get the service turned back on. He has gas heat."

"How much was it?"

"Over a thousand dollars," I said.

"That's a hell of a gas bill," Montgomery said.

"True, that." I would have retreated a step if I could have, but I was as far back against the wall as I could get. My hands were pressed into the wall and were beginning to ache. The cuffs were cutting off circulation and my hands tingled. "That's why service was shut off."

"We can check that, you know."

Of course they could.

"What happened to the other checks?" Montgomery asked.

"The other checks?" I was puzzled.

Belkins' face came even closer. "Yeah. There are a few checks missing. We figure you got them somewhere."

I thought back. "They should be in the wastebasket in the kitchen," I said. "Mr. Coleman was pretty out of it. He messed up a few checks."

"So you admit he was 'out of it' when you made him write the checks," Montgomery said. "Big man, making a grieving, feeble old man write checks to you."

"I didn't do that," I protested.

"But before she died, you did make Mrs. Coleman write you checks. And give you money."

"No."

Montgomery stepped back and stood up straight again. "That's pretty low, Jesse. Even for you."

"I didn't do that. I wouldn't do anything to hurt Mrs. Coleman."

"What I'd like to know," Montgomery said, "is who was the woman who called 9-1-1? I thought it might be your girlfriend."

I didn't want Kelly mixed up in this. "It was Rosa."

"Rosa?"

"Yeah. She was kind of a housekeeper or something."

"And how," Montgomery asked, drawing himself up to his full height, "do you know about the Colemans' housekeeper?"

I should have kept my mouth shut. "Mr. Coleman mentioned her."

"What else do you know about this Rosa? We can't seem to find her."

I was pretty sure that the Rose Aaron said Zee was screwing was the same person as Rosa the housekeeper. "She might be an illegal alien," I said.

"The caller did have a Hispanic accent," Montgomery said to Belkins.

Belkins wasn't interested. "You say you wouldn't do anything to hurt that poor old lady. But you just might shove her. Down the stairs." He raised his hand and brought it down hard against my cheek. I tasted blood.

Montgomery stepped forward and grabbed his hand. "Stop. That's going to leave a bruise."

Belkins glared at me. "So?"

"So now if we take him in, he'll have bruises. Not good."

"He's not going to complain. Not unless he wants to be arrested and booked. For murder." Belkins took a fresh cigar from his pocket and unwrapped it. "Are you, Damon?"

If that happened, I was totally screwed. Even if by some miracle a magistrate did set bail, who would post it? "No, sir," I said.

Montgomery was shaking his head. "It taints the testimony," he said. "We need a clean case. I don't want any grounds for appeal."

"Damon knows better than that," Belkins said, chomping on the cigar. "He wouldn't push an appeal."

Montgomery's handsome face drew into a frown. "At that point, why not? If he's facing another murder charge, what's he got to lose? This might be a capital trial. He could get the death penalty. You know what kind of scrutiny those cases get from the courts? Not to mention the press?"

Belkins turned away from me in disgust. "He's not worth it."

"He may not be," Montgomery agreed. "But that won't stop it from happening. This would be the first capital case investigation I worked on. I don't want it blowing up in my face for something inane."

"You worry too much," Belkins said.

"That may be, but I'm not going to lose this on appeal if there's any way I can help it. Either we have a clean case, with testimony that can't be successfully challenged, or we don't bring it."

Belkins shook his head in disgust. "So what do you want to do now?"

"Not bring him in for questioning, that's for sure. Or lock him up. Not until that bruise is gone."

Belkins gave me a mean grin. "Next time, I'll make sure the bruises don't show."

"That'd be a little better," Montgomery said. "But still dangerous. If we had him locked up, the nurse would see the bruises when he was processed. And they might be photographed."

"He could have gotten them anywhere," Belkins argued.

"Why take the chance at all? He's not going anywhere."

"How can you be so sure?"

"Well, if he does take off, he'll be violating parole. Ramirez will have him picked up. He won't get far."

They both stared at me. The wind was picking up, and a chill was beginning to set in. I wondered if the cat would miss me. Probably not me, but she'd want to be fed.

"Turn around, Jesse," Montgomery said, taking a cuff key out of his pocket.

Belkins was still standing so close I brushed him as I turned around. I felt the cuffs loosen. I stood facing the wall, waiting for them to either leave or tell me I could turn around.

"Give him back his stuff," Montgomery said.

Taking my wallet and keychain out of his pocket, Belkins tossed them into a slushy puddle. Anything I bought in the next few days would be paid for with damp money.

"Come on." Montgomery turned and walked to the entrance of the alley.

I bent down to retrieve my things.

Belkins shoved the heel of his hand into the back of my head, slamming me face first into the asphalt. My forehead hit hard, and I felt blood gush from my nose.

I hadn't expected that. I tried to get up and stumbled as I reached my feet.

He brought his knee sharply into my groin. I covered my crotch with my hands as I fell. My head hit the wall behind me. He drew back his foot and kicked me in the leg.

Montgomery came back and grabbed him. "Come on. Let him be."

Belkins stood, watching as I lay in the slush on the sidewalk. "Might as well give him a few more bruises to heal, if we have to wait for that," he said, drawing back his foot again.

I didn't try to move. I closed my eyes and waited for the next kick.

"What kind of idiot are you?" Montgomery hissed. "You promised me you wouldn't drink before we went out on this investigation."

"Yeah, well, the road to hell and all that," Belkins said.

I forced my eyes open. Montgomery had Belkins by the arm and was dragging him out of the alley.

CHAPTER 10

My groin throbbed. I could feel a sticky trickle of blood on my face. I was soaked and dirty from lying in the filthy, half-frozen puddle. And cold. My head throbbed.

I closed my eyes again. I was so tired. The thought that maybe I could take a short nap here flashed through my mind. Then maybe I could get up and struggle to my apartment. I was shivering in the cold. But if I got just a little sleep, I'd feel so much better.

"Hey, mister, what's the matter?" a voice said near at hand.

I hadn't heard anyone approach. A dangerous lapse. I opened my eyes and tried to sit up. My head spun when I looked up.

A thin, bearded figure stood in front of me. Saffron robes flapped around his bare legs. One of the young men from the temple. I tried to look up again at his face, but my neck didn't seem to be working, and all I could see were those hairy legs and his bony feet in sandals.

"Must have slipped on some ice," I said, trying to gather my legs underneath me. My voice sounded thick and slurred.

"Two men just came out of this alley. A short white one and a tall black one. I saw them. Did they mug you? Shall I call the police?"

Despite how I felt, the thought of someone reporting Belkins and Montgomery to the police for mugging me made me smile. I had a pretty good idea how that would play out.

"No. Don't call the police." My breath was beginning to come back.

"At least they didn't get your wallet," he said, picking it up along with my keychain and handing it to me. "I didn't check to see if they took the money."

"Wasn't much in there anyhow," I said, reaching out for it and almost dropping it again. My hand didn't seem to be working well, either. "Thanks."

He reached a bronzed arm, wiry but strong, out of the folds of saffron fabric and extended a hand for me to grab. Gratefully, I did so and lurched to my feet. I had to concentrate on keeping from falling again.

"You probably ought to go to the emergency room," he said. "It looks like you hit your head pretty good. And your face is all bloody."

"Nah. I'll be okay. Thanks for the help, though. I don't know how much longer I would have been lying there if you hadn't come along."

"I'm a member of the Tabernacle," he said, nodding toward the building. As if his robes and unkempt beard left any question. "We're supposed to help anyone we see who needs it."

"Thanks," I said again.

"My name's Isaac. Not my birth name, of course. But the one I was baptized into the Tabernacle with. I've seen you around."

I winced as I took a step. "Yeah. I live in the basement apartment. My name's Jesse."

He nodded. "The murderer."

In spite of the pain, I grinned. "Yeah. The murderer."

"It's cold out here. Do you want me to help you into your apartment?"

Trying to stand up straight, I said "I should be all right, thanks." I took another step. My leg buckled under me.

Isaac grabbed my elbow. "Let me help you."

With his support, I made it to the stairs and reached for the railing. I stood at the top, dumbly staring down. When had the steps gotten so steep? I felt myself sway.

Once again, Isaac caught me. He put one arm around my back and slipped the other under my arm. "Lean against me," he commanded. "We can make it down there."

The progress was slow, but he was right; we made it. The key dangled uselessly in my hand. He took it and opened the door.

As always, the room was dark and gloomy. But warm. Isaac flipped on the overhead light and eased me over to one of the two rickety chairs by the equally rickety table. He laid the key on the table.

Wincing, I sank into the chair. "Thanks," I mumbled.

He nodded at the phone on the wall. "You want me to call 9-1-1? You don't look all that good."

"Nah." What would I tell them? And my health insurance from work hadn't kicked in yet. How would I pay for an emergency room visit?

Frowning, he said, "You might have a concussion."

"Yeah, well, if I do, I'll deal with it. Maybe knock some sense into me."

He didn't give any indication that he appreciated my weak attempt at humor. "Well, at least you're out of the weather here. You want me to fix you a cup of coffee or something?"

I glanced up at him gratefully. "That sounds good. I got instant. Fix yourself one, too, if you want."

"We're really not supposed to use caffeine. It's a drug, you know."

"Yeah. At least it's a legal one. But suit yourself."

He filled the kettle with water and put it on the burner. Then he took both mugs from the drainer next to the sink and dumped a spoonful of the dark crystals in each one.

Standing next to the stove, Isaac glanced over at me. "Are you really a murderer?"

I shifted uncomfortably in my seat. I hated it when people asked things like that. Usually I just let the conviction speak for itself. But Isaac was looking at me thoughtfully, and he had just helped me out. I said, "I was convicted of murder and sent to prison."

"How long were you in prison?"

"Almost twenty years."

He looked surprised. "You don't look that old. How old were you then?"

"Sixteen."

"Sixteen? I thought you had to be eighteen to go to prison. A sixteen-year-old goes to juvenile court."

"Not for murder or rape. That goes right to adult court."

"Did you do it?"

"Do what?"

"Kill someone."

"Not directly."

"What do you mean, not directly?"

I sighed. "I was involved in a felony that resulted in a death. That fits the definition of murder in this state. So technically, I'm guilty."

He took the kettle with the now-boiling water off the burner and filled the mugs. "What kind of a felony?" He stirred the coffee.

I took the mug he handed me. The warmth felt good on my hands. "I was with my two older brothers, standing lookout. I thought they had gone to a crack house to make a buy. They'd gone to rip off the dealer."

"So how'd that result in a death?"

"I guess one of them shot him. I wasn't inside to see, so I don't know for sure. But he got shot. And died."

Isaac cupped his own mug and inhaled the coffee-scented steam. "I wouldn't have thought they'd have charged you as an adult with murder. If you weren't even there."

"Yeah, well..." I took a sip of my coffee. "We'd agreed I'd be the mule, take the heat if anybody had to. They were both adults with pretty impressive rap sheets already. They ran out of the building and shoved a few bags at me. I didn't know anybody'd been killed, and I didn't know the gun was in one of the bags. So when the cops stopped me, I just kept my mouth shut. I look a lot like my brothers. They thought I'd been the triggerman. And I had the gun. Murder charges were a no brainer."

It was a long speech. I was surprised how good it felt to have someone actually listen to my side of the story.

Isaac took a big gulp of his coffee and coughed.

"Hey," I said. "I owe you for helping me out here. I'm lucky you happened by."

He set the mug down on the table. "I was looking for our goddess. She's missing. They said she left when I was supposed to be sitting watch with her." Tears pooled in his eyes. "I was on the schedule. But Xavier told me he would stay with her."

My thoughts were pretty foggy right now, but even so, that sounded strange. "Your goddess?"

"Yeah. At first Father Peter thought she'd gone on a retreat or something, but it's been days, and she hasn't come back. I was sure she'd be back for the services in her honor this morning, but she hasn't shown up."

What kind of goddess could they have? A woman? That they all had sex with or something? Of course she'd leave. First chance she got. And definitely not come back for "services in her honor."

But I didn't know anything about their goddess—I was just speculating. My mind was certainly in the gutter. And Isaac looked genuinely distressed.

"Jesus was gone for forty days in the desert," I pointed out. "He came back." I wondered if the Tabernacle had any connections to Christianity as I knew it. Probably not, if they had a goddess. The Christian god was notoriously jealous of other deities and barely tolerated women as worshipers, much less in an exalted goddess status.

Isaac brightened. "That's true," he said. "And his disciples weren't sorry they waited for him. Maybe our goddess had something she had to attend to."

"What does your goddess look like?" I asked. "I could keep an eye out for her and tell you if I saw anyone who looked like her." Although I knew I would offer the so-called goddess any help I could to escape if she wanted to before I said anything to Isaac or any other of the nutsos up there in the Tabernacle.

"Would you? I'd really appreciate that. But I suspect she can change her appearance anytime she wants to."

"If that's true, how do you know she didn't come to the morning worship service looking like someone else?"

Isaac's eyes blinked rapidly behind his wire-rimmed glasses. "I never thought of that," he said.

Maybe they weren't supposed to use any drugs most of the time, but I wondered if they had any ceremonies that included peyote or something like that.

"I'd appreciate it if you could keep an eye out anyhow," Isaac said. "Her box on the altar is so empty. And she hasn't eaten any of the sacrifices."

Eating sacrifices was strange enough, but the idea of a box on the altar kind of freaked me out. "You keep her in a box on the altar?"

"Well, keep isn't really the right word. It's her bed. So she spends a lot of time in it. Or did before she left."

A bed in a box on the altar? The images I was coming up with weren't good. They sounded sick. Did they keep her chained up? "Could she just leave any time she wanted to?" I asked cautiously.

"Of course she could. We would never have kept her in the Tabernacle against her will. All she'd have to do was get someone to open the door for her."

"The door to the box?"

"Oh, no. You couldn't lock her in the box. It doesn't have a top. She can climb out of it. She does all the time. I mean the door to the outside."

It did make sense to keep the exterior doors locked in this neighborhood. Although why wouldn't she have access to a key herself?

"What was she wearing when you last saw her?" I asked.

"Sparkly stuff. Lots of jewels." Isaac closed his eyes. "A collar. Father Peter got it for her. He said it was a sign of her status, kind of like crown jewels. And he says it helps concentrate her powers."

"Was she wearing anything else but sparkly jewels and a collar?" I asked. Between the bed on the altar and the collar, my imagination was running wild.

"I don't think so."

"Didn't she get cold?"

Isaac blinked rapidly again. "I don't think so. Fur's pretty warm."

"She had a fur coat?"

"Well, yes."

Either Isaac wasn't making much sense or slamming my head against the bricks had rattled my thinking more than I realized. "She was wearing sparkly jewels, a collar, and a fur coat?"

"Well, I guess you could say that."

I swallowed my exasperation. Without Isaac's intervention, I might have fallen asleep outside on the pavement and stayed there all night. Maybe even have never woken up. The least I could do was be patient with him. "How would you say it?"

"Well, the last time the goddess lived among humans was back in ancient Egypt. So she's taken the form of a cat again. A cat with fur in all different colors."

Now I had a pretty good idea where their goddess had gotten to.

Leaning back in the rickety chair, I stared at Isaac.

The cat was with her kittens in the laundry basket under the bed. I could hear the low sound of her contented purr. If Isaac heard anything, he didn't mention it.

"Take a peek under the bed," I told him.

"What?"

"Just look under the bed. In the laundry basket. But move it gently. You don't want to scare her."

Isaac gave me a look of disbelief, then dropped to his knees, pulling the laundry basket out and peering at the little family. "My lady!" he breathed.

A look of reverence came over his face. "The goddess has given birth," he said. "The kittens must be young gods themselves. And they don't have a father. The Immaculate Conception."

"I wouldn't know about that," I said. Was it supposed to be "The Tabernacle of Immaculate Conception," not "The Tabernacle of Inaccurate Conception?" Made a certain amount of distorted sense, either way. How well could Father Peter and the rest of the cult members read, anyhow?

And from what I knew about cats, there would have been nothing "immaculate" about conceiving the kittens.

He turned agonized eyes on me. "She's chosen to stay with you. Did you witness the birth?"

"Nah. I found her in the stairwell in the sleet one night last week. I couldn't just leave her outside. She had the kittens while I was at work."

He looked around. "If she wants to stay here to raise the young gods, she must have a reason. I'll have to talk to Father Peter, but maybe we ought to leave her here. Would you mind if we sent an apostle down to worship her and meditate? Only one at a time. We usually switch off every six hours."

One of those crazies in my apartment 24/7? Over my dead body. I looked into Isaac's sincere eyes. I did owe him. "Look," I said. "I think she probably just wanted some privacy for the birth process. It is kind of messy and all, probably even for a goddess. And you're all male, aren't you?"

Isaac nodded solemnly.

"So she wanted to be alone for the birth. But now she probably wouldn't mind moving back to her altar."

Isaac brightened. "You think?" he said. "I could bring her and the little gods upstairs. Everyone will be so surprised when they show up for the worship service tonight!"

"And you'll be the savior," I said. My entire body ached, but I felt a lot stronger and I wasn't so dizzy any more. I wanted him gone. Even if he took the cats with him. "I'll help you carry them upstairs."

The mother cat jumped out as soon as Isaac lifted the laundry basket, so I picked her up and tucked her under my jacket. She snuggled up against my chest and purred.

Silly, but I would miss her.

We went up to the sidewalk outside my apartment, around to the front stairs and up into the Tabernacle. Glittering jeweled sunlight streamed through the colorful windows. I looked at them in awe. Stained glass was expensive. If they could afford that, what were they doing renting an old storefront in this section of town? Unless it was because people around here were pretty tolerant of other people's peculiarities and minded their own business.

"Are those real stained glass?" I asked Isaac, staring at a side window of an Egyptian scene, with pyramids and camels.

"What? The windows? No, man." Isaac put the laundry basket down on the altar and looked in awe at the tiny kittens, which were beginning to squirm. "We made them with colored tissue paper, glued on. Pretty good, huh?"

"Very good."

One of the kittens mewed.

The cat stopped purring and stuck her head out from under my jacket.

I unzipped the jacket and took her out. When I put her down on the surface of the altar, she climbed into the basket and started licking the kittens. The altar looked more like a worn kitchen table on which some demented child had scribbled abstract designs than any altar I'd ever seen. Of course, my experience in such matters was limited.

"Do you think we should put them in her bed?" Isaac asked.

I poked the luxurious cushion in the fancy bed-box on the altar. My finger sank deep into its soft, plush top. "I think it's probably too deep and soft for the kittens," I said. "They'd probably roll into the crevices and couldn't get out. Maybe have trouble breathing. And the sides aren't very high. She seems to like higher sides. Makes her feel more comfortable."

Isaac looked uncertain. "Someone will be with her all the time," he said. "They'd help if the kittens got stuck."

I thought about that. "And someone was with her when she left?" I asked.

"Yeah. Like I said, I was on the schedule. But Xavier said he'd stay with her and I should go. He said he had to meet someone and I'd just be in the way, so he told me to go."

"What did Xavier say had happened to her?"

"That she just kind of faded away. There one minute, gone the next. She *is* primarily a spirit creature, you know."

She seemed pretty substantial and generally cat-like to me, but what do I know? She certainly didn't ever fade away on me.

In the end, the cat made the decision on where to keep the kittens by lying down in the laundry basket with them. The kittens snuggled up next to her and began nursing. When Isaac reached in, she swatted his hand and growled. He jerked his hand back. "Yes, your holiness," he said. "Whatever you want."

By now my teeth were chattering, and my head was throbbing in time to it. They could have the laundry basket. Leaving Isaac staring in awe at the feline family, I made my way back to my apartment, took a shower ,and collapsed into my bed. It had been an interesting day, to say the least. I had a lot I would have to try to sort out. But now, I needed to get warm and get some sleep.

CHAPTER 11

My head ached and I was stiff, but at least I wasn't dizzy any more. I wasn't about to skip a night's work if I could possibly make it. It wouldn't look good on my parole record, and I needed all the money I could get. So I got up and got ready for work.

I went to put out cat food before I remembered that the "goddess" was back on her altar with her kittens. It seemed kind of lonely without her, but I had to admit that me having a pet didn't make much sense. I was having enough trouble taking care of myself.

When I got to work and punched in, John and the second shift foreman were huddled over their clipboards, frowning.

"Jesse," John called. "Come over here."

Adjusting my hardhat, I went over. "Yeah?"

He stopped short. "What happened to your face?"

I almost fell back on the standard prison inmate's explanation that I'd walked into a cell door but stopped myself in time. "Slipped on some ice."

"You must have landed face first."

"Kind of. I landed against a wall. Slammed my face into it."

"Are you okay to work?"

"Yeah."

"That's good. We got our work cut out for us," he said, tapping the stub of a pencil he was using on his paperwork. "Most of the shipments for tonight haven't been assembled yet."

The second shift foreman straightened up and ran his hand over his beard. "It's that damn new system. It didn't print out the stuff until after eight tonight. So dayshift didn't get any of it done, and my guys only had a little over three hours to work on it."

Ignoring him, John flipped through the paperwork.

"You want me to tell Ramon to stay over a few hours to help out?" the second shift foreman asked.

"Don't look like he managed to get too much done on his own shift," John said, holding the clipboard up. "And where is he, anyhow? I was out in shipping and back in the warehouse. I didn't see him either place. Or his lift."

The other foreman shrugged.

John turned to me. "Don't matter how it happened. We just got to deal with it. Jesse, you're on the clock as of when you punched in. Go get a lift and report to the dispatch office for the shipping lists. And start picking that stock."

"Okay. Am I looking for those printouts or what?"

"Nope. They called in a dispatcher to try to straighten everything out. There should be a real live person there who can give you the packing lists. And you can ask questions if you need to. Let him—or her—set the priorities. I'll take care of what I can in the shop with a hand lift."

I nodded and hurried off to pick up a forklift.

As I stepped into the charging bay, I stopped short. Nobody but the lift drivers, and maybe a foreman, should be there at this time of the night. But three men stood there in front of the big exhaust fan. One handed a fat blunt to another.

Clay, who ran a plater on my shift, looked me up and down. "What's the matter, snitch, all yer orange jumpsuits in the wash?"

Damn Aaron. He'd told Clay I was a snitch, maybe to divert suspicion away from himself. It seemed like Clay believed him. And probably spread the false rumor to half the shift.

The spot where the men huddled, between the charging forklifts and the wall, was poorly lit and just out of range of a security camera. I caught a whiff of the mixed tobacco and marijuana.

Clay stepped out into the edge of the light cast by the overhead fixtures, slipping his hands into the heavy work gloves plater operators wore. He planted his boots on the floor and slammed his right fist into his left hand. The thick fabric muffled the slapping sound.

I was just trying to do my job. I didn't want any trouble. Geez, I couldn't afford any trouble. In less than a week, I'd be through the probationary employment period and in the union. Until then, any problem and I could be fired, no questions asked. If Clay and his buddies would just let me alone, I'd be more than willing to take a lift and get out of there.

Didn't look like they were going to make it that easy. One of them snuffed out the blunt they'd been smoking and shoved it into his shirt pocket. They stepped out from behind the lifts, standing behind Clay, their faces tense and their fists clenched by their sides.

"You got something to say, jailbird?" Clay asked.

Ignoring them was not going to work. I backed up a few steps, into the middle of the bright light and closer to the security camera. I narrowed my eyes and set my face into the prison yard stare that had served me well for years.

One of the guys, a big, lardy fellow named Ramon who drove a lift four to midnight, shifted his feet, a worried frown on his face.

Clay tensed and brought his fists to mid-chest level. "You think you can take all three of us?" he asked. "Just try."

I continued to stare, my hands by my sides. "I'm sure not gonna violate parole for wusses like you." Any type of fight, no matter who started it, could be grounds for a parole violation. And I'd be on my way back to prison.

Veins on Clay's neck stood out and his face turned red. "I'll show you who's a wuss." He took a step forward.

Never back down. If I had to fight, at least I'd make a good showing. I nodded my head and raised my fists. "Bring it." I glanced away from them for a second, up at the security camera, then resumed my stance. I hoped the camera was recording—it might help if Mr. Ramirez could see a video that showed I wasn't the aggressor. Slim hope, but better than nothing.

Ramon followed my glance and lowered his hands. "Come on, Clay. We don't need to start no trouble here at work. Besides, he looks like he already been in a fight."

Clay didn't want to drop it. "He just called us wusses."

"So? I don't want to get fired over something stupid like that." Ramon tugged at Clay's elbow.

"We can settle this outside work," the other guy, Marcus, said, dropping his fists.

"You gonna meet us at Mickey's after work?" Clay demanded, naming a bar a few blocks down the street from the plant.

I laughed. "Yeah, right. So you can call my PO and report it? And have the cops standing by? You really think I'd go into a bar? If I was gonna violate, I'd get the satisfaction of wiping up the floor with your sorry asses. Gotta be some PCP or something in them blunts you been smoking there."

"Come on, Clay." Ramon pulled him a few steps toward the entrance to the warehouse. "We got enough to worry about. If he reports us, he reports us. We can deny it. Who're they gonna believe?"

Marcus glanced up at the camera. "Yeah. Let's not make it worse. Especially when it might be recorded."

Shaking my head, I laughed again. "You don't got to worry about *me* reporting nothing. I ain't no snitch." Stepping around them to reach the forklifts, I steeled myself to turn my back to them like I knew none of them would throw a sucker punch at my head. I knew no such thing. The muscles in the small of my back tensed, expecting a punch to land any second.

While I unplugged the lift and started to run it through check-off sequence, I strained to hear if the boot-steps were retreating. To my relief, they were.

They stopped as they reached the door. I tensed again but continued checking the gauges on the dashboard.

"You just wait. We'll make sure you're sorry," Marcus shouted from the relative safety of the doorway.

I wanted to say, "Sorry for what?" but I ignored them.

Swinging my stiff body up into the seat, I switched on the ignition. The forklift's silent electric engine vibrated to life. I shifted into reverse and eased it out from between two others.

"You just do that," I couldn't resist hollering to Marcus as I swung around and drove a bit faster than necessary toward them.

They ducked down an aisle. I continued out the door and down the passageway toward shipping where we needed to get the loads organized.

Kelly was already there, standing next to her bigger forklift, which was used primarily for loading and unloading over-the-road tractor trailers. Her brow was furrowed as she looked at the papers in her hand.

Seeing Kelly always stirred something in my gut and left me short of breath. Her long dark hair was pulled back in a ponytail that flowed from beneath her hardhat and brushed her ample rear. Her sweatshirt didn't hide the expanse of her breasts. I knew the feel of the iron muscles that hid under her soft-appearing skin.

I approached her cautiously. Sometimes Kelly treated me like I was the boyfriend I wished I was. Other times she was curt and distant with me. And we hadn't exactly parted on the best of terms when I'd left her place on Friday.

I eased the lift up next to her and climbed down. "What have we got?" I asked, hoping she'd be in a good mood.

Her dark eyes blazed as she looked at me. "What the hell do they think they're doing?" She waved the papers at me.

"You got me there." At least her anger didn't seem aimed at me. I wondered if I could ask her about the weekend.

"They're supposed to get all this crap together on first shift. Or second at the latest. We only got two drivers—you and me—and all the regular work's got to be done."

Not exactly the moment to go into a "What are you doing Saturday night?" conversation.

I held out my hand, and she gave me the shipping lists. They weren't exactly like the old kind, but they weren't the confusing multi-page ones the computer printed out, either. We should be able to handle this.

"Why don't I take these and pull the stock from the warehouse," I said. "I'll line them up by the truck bays in groups, and as soon as I get one done, I'll tape the paperwork on the last pallet. Then you and the truck driver can check over them before you load them."

"And just who's going to take care of supplying the machine operators while you're assembling shipments?" she demanded.

"John told me to concentrate on getting these out," I said. "He'll keep an eye on who needs what, and if he can't get it moved with a handlift, he'll find me."

Kelly flexed her fingers in her gloves. "This is gonna take a while."

I shrugged. "Yeah. But we got all night, and the shift hasn't even started yet. It's mostly root baskets and tomato cages, so it isn't that bad." Root baskets and tomato cages mostly went to wholesale plant nurseries. They weren't heavy and couldn't be stacked, so we'd only need a single layer for each truck. And they weren't easily damaged, so we could work quickly.

"Root baskets and tomato cages?" A faint smile played on Kelly's luscious lips. "A rush order for root baskets and tomato cages?"

I grinned back. "It's not really rush orders, I don't think. Just stuff that the new system lost. Probably they didn't even realize they were due to ship tonight until a trucker called for instructions or something."

A genuine smile played on her face. "Probably," she agreed. "I was worried it was something I'd done. Missed instructions last night or something."

"Nah. Even if we tried, we couldn't mess up like this."

She laughed. "We don't have enough authority to manage that."

"True, that." I got back on my lift and tucked the edge of the paperwork under my butt so it wouldn't blow away. Maybe later in the shift, if we managed to get everything loaded and the trucks out before six, I could ask her about the weekend.

I headed out of shipping, past the plating line and skimmed the edge of the production floor, driving carefully. Shift change was getting close. The workers on my overnight shift milled around near the time clock, waiting for John to give them assignments. The second shift crew pushed to meet their quotas, the welding rigs throwing sparks and the presses thundering incessantly. The scent of hot steel and oil filled the air.

I passed Clay, heading out toward the plating room. He stepped well back from the center of the passageway, glaring at me. I wondered if he thought I might try to hit him. I was tempted to swerve toward him, but even I realized that would be pretty juvenile so I just ignored him. He gestured toward me, probably flipping me the bird, but I didn't check to see.

Ramon, the lift driver for the four to midnight, cut ahead of me and headed toward the charging stations. I eased my speed back even more. No point in taking any chances.

The whistle blew, signaling shift change.

Back in the warehouse, I had to move a lot of pallets to get to the root baskets and tomato cages. They were seasonal items, and if I was going to rotate the stock like I was supposed to, I'd have to get to the ones way at the back. Oily dust lay thick on everything. I doubted anyone had been so far down these aisles in the last six months.

I needed two pallets of the largest root baskets. They were huge, big enough to handle large trees for commercial projects like shopping centers where they wanted the landscaping to look mature from day one. Good to know some places were still building projects like that in this economy.

The beep of a backing forklift sounded in the next aisle. With Kelly out in shipping, there shouldn't be another lift around. Had John relented and asked Ramon to work a bit of overtime? I could do without that kind of help.

Picking up the front pallet of tomato cages to move so I could reach the older stock, I eased it down the aisle toward the back end of the row.

A stack of piled crates came crashing down into the space I had just vacated.

CHAPTER 12

By the time I got the aisle cleared enough to go look, the lift and whoever had been driving it were gone. I didn't know whether it had been someone carelessly backing into a stack of crates and afraid to stick around to accept responsibility for a potentially dangerous accident, or a deliberate attempt to hurt me. Since I wasn't hurt and I didn't see any real damage done, I decided not to report it to John. No point turning into a snitch now.

Kelly and I worked hard all shift, cutting our breaks and lunches short. By the time the eight a.m. whistle blew, all the trucks that were supposed to be loaded were checked out and on their way. The day shift foreman griped about the low supplies of parts by some of the work stations, but John dealt with that.

Exhausted and sore, I hurried home, took a shower, and fell into bed. Errands and shopping would have to wait.

I slept all day and woke up in the early evening. I was hungry and stiff, but otherwise felt pretty good. I fixed some ramen noodles and tried to sort out my thoughts.

My next appointment with the parole office was fast approaching. If Belkins had followed through with his threat to request I be put back on home detention—and I had no reason to think he would not—I would have very limited time outside my apartment in the coming weeks. A depressing thought. Not to mention that paying the monitoring fee would put a crimp in my already tight budget.

At least I should be prepared for the worst and take care of the errands that would eat up my limited free time. Like getting my laundry done.

The Laundromat was a few blocks down the street, at the end of a block-long building that also housed a few now-closed stores, Mickey's bar which was frequented by a lot of the workers from Quality Steel Fabrications, and a bunch of apartments on the second floor.

At nine o'clock on a weekday night, the Laundromat was a peaceful place, unlike Mickey's. In here, the music, shouts, and laughter were muted. Two washing machines whirred toward the final rinse cycle. One held my clothes and the other my bedding and towels. I knew all about separating whites from colored clothes, but since the only whites I had were my underwear, and I didn't care what color they came out, I just shoved all my clothes in together.

I stood by with my bottle of fabric softener, waiting for the final rinse.

Fabric softener was a wonderful invention. I'd never even heard of it before I'd been assigned to a job in the prison laundry, washing sheets, blankets, and clothes. The pay was a dollar a day, but it was something to do, and it sure beat being locked on the housing unit all day. Of course we had nothing but cheap powdered detergent. The only way to get the dank odor out of clothes was to get some bleach from the CO on duty. To do that, he had to go to a locked cabinet, get the bleach, take it to the washing machine, and dump it in himself since we weren't permitted to handle anything that caustic. And the bleach was in limited supply, so even if he was cooperative, there was no guarantee there'd be any actually in the cabinet.

One of the old heads, who'd worked in a commercial laundry before he was locked up, spoke longingly of fabric softener. Not only did the clothes come out softer, but also they smelled good. Very few things in the prison smelled good.

The first time I went to buy supplies to do my own laundry after I'd been released, I read the labels and got a bottle of fabric softener. The results it produced were even better than I'd expected. It was pure luxury to drift off to sleep under soft sheets that smelled of fabric softener. It was an artificial, chemical scent, but I didn't care. It was a luxury I could afford.

The front door to the street chimed as it opened. I turned to see who else was doing laundry this time of the evening.

Aaron strode in, followed by Clay, Ramon, and Marcus. They weren't carrying any laundry baskets or bottles of detergent.

This couldn't be good.

And why wasn't Ramon at work?

I glanced toward the surveillance camera, mounted next to the door right by the change machine, and wondered if anyone was monitoring it. Unlikely.

The washers reached their final rinse cycle. I poured the measured capful of the fragrant blue liquid into one machine, then the other, watching the four of them out of the corner of my eye.

Clay spit on the floor and rubbed the palm of his hand on his stubbly cheek.

"My supplier got busted," Marcus said. "But I guess you already knew that. Didn't you, snitch?"

We weren't at work—no foreman to fire anyone for fighting. We all knew that. If the cops came, they'd get a slap on the wrist. And I'd get sent back to prison.

Turning to face them, I narrowed my eyes into a stare and said, "I *know* you ain't talking to me."

The arrogant smirk faded from Aaron's face, and he backed up uneasily. The others were looking at each other and laughing.

"Get his wallet," Aaron said. "I bet he's got some oxys or something in there. And a lot of money."

Marcus stepped around the folding table in one direction, and Clay went around the other end.

They outweighed me by at least fifty pounds each.

I set the bottle on the table and backed up against the dryer.

Marcus slammed a beefy fist into my gut, but not before I managed to tighten my stomach muscles to minimize the effects of the blow. Although it knocked the breath out of me and I hunched forward, I kept my feet under me.

Clay grabbed me from behind, hooking his hands in my elbows and pulling my arms back. He jerked me around to face Marcus.

Grinning evilly, Marcus raised a clenched fist and held it next to his face. As he moved closer to me, the smell of stale beer and cigarettes washed over me. "Thought we'd just let it go, did you, snitch?"

I forced myself to relax, and Clay loosened his grip. If he knew what he was doing, he would be keeping a tight hold and forcing my arms up at a painful angle behind my back. Then I'd be pretty much helpless. Obviously he'd never had any training in physical restraint, and over the years I'd been restrained by the best.

Marcus leaned close and pulled his fist back.

Moving suddenly, I leaned back, shoving Clay against the washing machine. His hands closed clumsily on my arms. Supporting myself on his bulky chest and arms, I lifted my right foot in its steel-toed boot and drove up between Marcus's legs, connecting solidly.

Despite his entire body folding into an agonized curl, Marcus got the punch off, hard. It caught me in the throat. I couldn't breathe for a few seconds.

Clay regained his footing and leaned forward on my back, slamming my face into the flimsy table in front of me. The table collapsed, taking me down with it. As I fell, I tucked my head under and heaved upward with my butt. If Clay hadn't been so heavy, he would have gone somersaulting over my shoulders. As it was, he tumbled off to one side, losing his grip on my arms.

Pain shot through me as I came down on my left knee and the side of my right foot, but I ignored it, scrambling to my feet. My breath came in jagged gasps.

Ramon froze as his eyes opened wide in shock.

Aaron cowered back. He looked at me, rubbing his nose with the side of his hand. "Man, somebody's gonna get hurt," he whined.

As if nobody'd already been hurt.

He wiped his hand on the leg of his jeans. "You better watch it. You're gonna get in trouble."

I leveled my gaze at him and grinned. After the blow to my throat, I wasn't sure I could actually form words, but I tried, and it worked. "I'm looking at a new homicide charge, and I already got one murder conviction. You think I'm worried about adding another one? Or four?"

Aaron blinked rapidly. "We was just trying…"

I kicked him in the balls, but only got in a glancing blow. "I don't care what you was trying to do. It didn't work."

He turned his face away from me as he slid to the floor and moaned, his hands clutching at his crotch.

Ramon roused himself and stepped toward me.

Taking my eyes off Clay had been a mistake. Rolling onto his side, he reached out and grabbed my foot, yanking hard. I fell into Ramon, who landed on another folding table, collapsing to the floor along with it.

Clay struggled to get to his feet. He glared at Aaron. "Come on, you wimp. Kick him in the head or something."

Out of the corner of my eye, I saw Aaron approach. He was still holding his crotch with one hand, but he was balling his other hand into a fist, trying to look menacing.

The bottle of fabric softener lay next to me, its contents dribbling out on the floor. I snatched it up and, as Aaron bent down to deliver what would have been at best a feeble punch, I jerked it toward his face. Enough of the thick blue liquid was left to splash into his eyes.

He issued a startled cry and backed off, wiping his eyes.

Clay, now on his feet, gave him a disgusted glance and raised his boot over my hand. I dropped the bottle, rolled onto my back and reached for his foot. Seizing it, I twisted sideways. He tumbled over, his head catching a corner of the end dryer as he fell to the floor. Blood gushed out of a gash on his forehead, and he lay still.

Sharp pains cut through my ankle as I clambered back to my feet. Aaron, still crying and wiping his eyes with one hand, threw his shoulders back and drew his other fist back.

I grabbed him by the shirt and lifted him off his feet. Although he was taller than me, he felt almost weightless. Not surprising, I guess, in a meth freak. And I had plenty of adrenalin flowing. I tossed him toward the door. He landed on the change machine and his head hit the surveillance camera, knocking it to the floor. It bounced onto the floor, narrowly missing Clay's still form.

Something stirred behind me. I whirled around to see Marcus lumbering to a standing position, fury in his eyes. "You bastard," he hissed, lunging toward me with his arms outstretched to grab me.

Dumb. If these guys didn't know how to handle themselves in a scrap, they had no business going around picking fights.

Sidestepping him, I brought my fist up hard under his chin. His teeth met with a resounding crunch and blood spurted from his mouth. He tumbled back to the floor.

Without getting up, Aaron skittered across the floor and sat, leaning back against a dryer and whimpering.

Ramon was trying to untangle himself from the overturned table and the legs that had broken free from it. I grabbed one of the table legs and swung it at the side of his head. He let out a cry and held his hand to his ear. Blood trickled from between his fingers. He covered his face with his other hand.

Clay still hadn't moved.

Marcus sat up, fingering his chin. Blood dribbled onto his shirt. "You broke my jaw," he said. He was having as much trouble talking as I was. He lurched yet again to his feet and approached me.

This time I hit him in the gut. He doubled over and retched.

His wallet, attached by a chain to his belt, swung next to his leg.

They had been planning to take my wallet. Turnabout should be fair play, if I cared about fair. In my experience, fair play didn't usually enter into it.

I reached down and snatched it. A quick yank broke the chain. I stuffed the wallet in my pocket and took hold of him by the shirt collar and the seat of his pants.

He was too heavy for me to lift, so I dragged him across the floor to the door, shoved it open with my foot, and maneuvered him outside. My ankle protested, but I ignored it. He landed face down on the sidewalk and tried to get to his feet. All he managed was to get to his knees. He retched again and threw up on the pavement. And all over his shirt.

Ramon turned away from me when I stepped up to him. I pulled the bits of broken table off him and put my hands under his armpits. "Stand up," I ordered.

With my assistance, and at great expense to my ankle, he rose unsteadily to his feet. I reached into his pockets, transferring whatever I found there to my own, and then propelled him out the door. I shoved him up against the outside wall. He leaned against it and slid down to a sitting position. Still holding his head.

I went back inside and stood in front of where Aaron cowered against the dryer. His bleary eyes opened wide, and he tried to edge backwards, but he was already pressed up against the dryer.

"Hey, Jesse." His voice came out high pitched and squeaky. "Can't you take a joke, man?"

"Some joke." I stepped by him and stood over Clay. Was he still alive? I didn't really care. Although if he were dead, there would be a serious investigation. It would be hard to hide my part in this fight. And I'd hate to have to get rid of a body. I'd heard lots of tales of killers who would have gotten away with murder if they had figured out how to get rid of the body effectively. Bodies tripped people up all the time.

Bending down, I ran my hands over his pockets, pulling out keys, a few small items and some cigarettes. I took his wallet, also on a chain, from his back pocket. I yanked on it, but the chain didn't break. I reached down and unclipped it from his belt.

As I stood over Clay, he stirred. So he wasn't dead. But he was a dead weight. I grabbed his legs and pulled him toward the door. His arms sprawled out behind him, and his head banged against table legs. And he left a trail of blood behind him.

Headlights moved out on the street. I stopped at the doorway, looking out. The headlights picked up Marcus, who was on his knees by the curb, clutching a fire hydrant. He was leaning over, puking his guts out.

The car pulled in and parked. Its lights winked out.

I stood still, the door half open. I could do without any additional witnesses. The bright lights from the Laundromat were at my back, so my face was in shadow and my body blocked any view of the interior, which was pretty banged up.

A woman got out of the car, keys in her hand, and looked at Marcus, wrinkling her nose. "Disgusting," she said. Then she caught a glimpse of Ramon, who had slid to a sitting position against the wall and was holding his head. She shook her head and headed to a poorly lit doorway a few yards down. She unlocked the door and slipped in.

I dragged Clay the rest of the way out and dumped him against the wall on the other side of the door from Ramon. Rain was beginning to fall. I hoped it would wash away the blood and vomit on the sidewalk.

Aaron was trying to get to his feet. Roughly, I helped him up.

He didn't protest as I ran my hands over his pockets, taking his wallet, keys, cigarettes, and a few things I didn't take the time to identify.

"You best be telling me what you been saying about me," I said.

"Nothing, really," he whined.

"What's 'nothing'?"

"Just that you took some crystal meth I was supposed to sell off me and when you got busted with them, you rolled over on the guy who was supplying Marcus."

"What was he dealing?"

"That's just it. Only weed. So I didn't think it'd cause too much trouble."

"Aren't doing too much thinking there, are you?"

"You just don't understand, Jesse." Aaron sniffed. "I got to do something, or I'm in real trouble."

"I think you're already in real trouble. When the cops find out what they want to know from you, you're going down for whatever they can pin on you."

"That's not what I mean. I promised some guys I'd get some oxys for them."

"Who?"

"Zee."

"The guy from the Tabernacle?" The one I wasn't sure existed.

"Yeah."

"You're not making any sense at all. Why would you get him oxys?"

"Cause he gave me some money to go get crystal meth, but I used it all myself."

"Stupid."

"Yeah."

"Where are you gonna get oxys?"

Aaron pressed his lips together and looked toward the door. He must have decided he couldn't make it past me. "At the old lady's house. In the garage."

I was pretty sure I knew, but I asked, "Which old lady?"

"The one who died."

"Why in the garage?"

"I dunno. Zee said he took all the oxys he could find and hid them in the garage. Hid them so even if they brought in a dog, they'd never find them."

"Why didn't he just take them with him?"

"If he got stopped leaving, he didn't want to have anything on him. And he didn't realize she was dead. Now he's afraid to go back himself. So he's gonna make me go."

"Where in the garage?"

"He didn't tell me that."

"Why don't you take your buddies and go on home." I eased my weight on the injured ankle and moved out of the way so he could leave.

Aaron looked out the door in dismay, from Clay's inert figure to Marcus, still on his knees and heaving. "They're hurt," he said.

"And you're not?" I balled up my fist and took a step closer to him. "I can fix that."

"No, no. I mean, they should go to the emergency room or something. Especially Clay."

"So take them."

He felt in his pockets. "I don't have no keys."

"Not my problem."

"But you took them," he whined.

I reached into my pocket and pulled out his keys. I tossed them out the door, onto the sidewalk.

"Like I said, not my problem." I didn't take my eyes off him.

"You gonna give me the rest of my stuff back?" he asked.

"Not now."

"Later?"

"Maybe. I'll think about it."

I watched as he limped out the door and down the street toward his truck. I closed the door and turned the lock. I hoped he'd be able to get his buddies into the truck and away from here so I wouldn't have to decide what to do with them.

Back inside the Laundromat I surveyed the damage. I put my stuff in dryers and fed quarters into the slots, wincing with every step.

The mess wasn't that bad. Except for one of the folding tables, which had shattered when it hit the floor. The other one was pretty much okay. One of its legs had come off and another one was bent.

And the camera.

I picked up the pieces of the broken table and carried them out the back door, heaving them into the dumpster. If I rearranged the tables a bit, it might not be immediately obvious that one was missing. Maybe the dumpster would even get emptied before anyone thought to investigate.

Turning my attention to the other table, I tried to straighten out the bent leg. I couldn't get it entirely, but I got it to the point where it would support the table. I had no way to reattach the one that had broken off but I propped it under the table. As long as I didn't knock against it, it didn't fall over.

The camera's casing was cracked and the wires were ripped out of the wall. I turned it over to examine it. It had a tape inside it, so it was probably the type that just recorded on site, not one hooked up to a remote. If anyone had been monitoring it, all they would have seen was the first little bit anyhow. I removed the tape and debated what to do with it.

If the cops viewed it, it would make it impossible for me to deny that I'd been involved in the fight. On the other hand, it would clearly show that it hadn't been me who started the whole thing. And that the odds had been four to one against me.

I put the tape in my laundry bag. I dumped the wallets and other stuff on top of it.

The door to the janitor's closet in the rear was locked, but it was the kind that snicks open with a stiff card. I had four wallets' worth of licenses and bank cards. I retrieved one and slipped it under the latch, opening it.

Dumping a little detergent, a fair amount of bleach, and some water into a bucket, I pulled it out and went back for a mop. I swished the sudsy concoction around the entire floor, making sure I got all the blood. I swiped the mop head over the dryers where Clay had hit his head and where Aaron had crouched.

I debated changing into some of my freshly laundered clothes. Then I could run the mop head and the clothes I was wearing through a wash. If I used a lot of bleach, it should destroy any traces of any DNA-carrying bits, including blood.

It would take me the best part of an hour to do that. And would cost a few dollars.

If Aaron and his buddies decided to go to the police, it wouldn't make any difference if the cops could find any blood or anything. If, as was more likely, they lied about what had happened, it also wouldn't make any difference.

Unless Clay—or somebody else—died.

So I thoroughly washed out the mop head, rinsed the bucket, and put everything back where I'd found it. The closet door locked itself when I shoved it closed.

I looked at my reflection in the window of one of the dryers, touching my face. The place where I'd slammed my head into the wall yesterday was swollen and turning an interesting shade of purple, and my nose looked a bit misshapen. But I couldn't see that the recent fracas had made it any worse than it was before. Of course, the bruises might take a while to show up. Not much I could do about it.

The dryers were finished. I folded my clothes and put them into the laundry bag on top of the camera and other things. My right ankle was throbbing. I laced my boot tighter, trying to give it a little more support. Not for the first time, I wished I had a pair of high top work boots, not the ankle length ones. For the first few months after my release, I'd been on house arrest and had to wear a box, a black plastic monitor strapped to my ankle so the parole office could keep track of my whereabouts. It wouldn't fit above a regular work boot.

At least I wouldn't need new boots if I got put back on a box. I wouldn't be happy about that—I loved being able to set my own schedule and go out whenever I wanted to, and the fee involved would make a real dent in my income. But I'd take it. It sure beat being locked up twenty-four-seven again.

I gathered up my things and set out on the several blocks walk back home. A steady drizzle was falling. I flipped up my hood.

As I approached my building, I heard running footsteps pounding behind me. I dropped the laundry bag and backed up to have the wall at my back.

It was someone I didn't recognize, but he didn't seem interested in me. He ran right by me and swung down the alley.

I peered after him. He wasn't dressed in the usual saffron robes of the Brethren, but he stopped at the alley door and pulled something out of his pocket. As I watched, he unlocked the door and slipped in, shutting the door quietly behind him.

Picking up the laundry bag, I hobbled the last few yards to the stairs down to my apartment. It was going to be interesting negotiating those stairs with my hands full and my ankle protesting against supporting my weight. I'd try to let it rest as long as I could and then find something to wrap tight around it when I had to leave for work. Skipping a shift wasn't an option.

Flashing red and blue lights glared on the wet asphalt. A car skidded to a stop behind me.

Had Aaron called the police? Or had he gone to the hospital emergency room and been stupid enough to report what had happened?

With a pang, I realized I had no real idea what I had taken off those guys and stuffed into my laundry bag. What I did know was that I had four wallets that didn't belong to me, complete with IDs and bank cards. That would be more than enough for a possession of stolen goods charge. And I knew those guys were into drugs. Did any of the wallets have a few rocks of crack or a little baggie of crystal meth tucked inside?

I didn't turn to look at the patrol car but I could see the glare of the spotlight as it flickered on, catching me in the middle of it. The car doors slammed shut behind me.

Maybe it wasn't Aaron who was the stupid one.

CHAPTER 13

The muscles in my back and neck tensed up. I held the laundry bag so that my hands were in full view.

"You there," one of the cops said. "Turn around and face me."

I took a deep breath and turned.

"What ya got there?" he asked.

"Laundry," I said.

"Clean or dirty?"

"Clean."

"You just come from the Laundromat?"

"Yes, sir."

"Can we take a look at it?"

If they'd recognized me, they wouldn't have bothered to ask. "Sure."

The other cop took the bag and undid the ties.

"You see anybody run down the street here?" the first one asked.

I wasn't about to get any more involved than I had to be. "No, sir."

He stepped over to the alley and shone his flashlight down it. "Where does this go?"

"Dead end."

"Anything open off it?"

"Just the backdoor to the church upstairs," I said.

He took a few steps down the alley and tried the door. "This always locked?"

"I guess. Never tried to open it."

Passing me, he shone the flashlight down the stairs to my apartment. "What's down here?"

"My place."

"Your apartment?"

"Yeah."

"Anybody else down there now?"

"Shouldn't be."

"You see anything at the Laundromat?"

I licked my lips. "What kind of thing?"

"We got a report that a couple of people were fighting on that block."

"Fighting?"

"Or carousing. Or something."

"There *was* some guy blowing lunch by the curb. I didn't pay it no mind."

"Where'd he come from?"

"I guess the bar down the block. He had a couple of buddies with him, though, so I figured they'd take care of him."

He shone the flashlight into my face. "What happened to you?"

"I fell."

"Just now?"

"Yesterday."

He turned to the other cop, who was rummaging around in the laundry bag. "Find anything?"

"Mostly folded clothes. They smell real clean."

"Anything else?"

"Something hard down here." He snaked his hand down the side.

I stopped breathing. My wrists itched where the cuffs would press into them.

If they locked me up, at least I'd get a chance to rest the ankle. Maybe even get an x-ray and make sure it wasn't broken.

"What is it?" the first cop asked.

"Laundry detergent."

"What, a bottle?"

"Yeah. But there's something else down there, too. Something smaller."

My gut muscles spasmed.

"A bottle of fabric softener."

He handed it to his partner, who unscrewed the top off and took a sniff. "Fabric softener? No wonder the laundry smells good."

Placing it back in the laundry bag on top of the laundry, he handed the bag back to me.

"Better get inside before all your stuff gets soaked through in this rain."

I took the bag and tried to start breathing again. "Yes, sir." I turned to the stairs and, making a real effort not to limp, made my way down them.

When the red and blue lights stopped flashing through my one window, I fished out all the stuff I'd swiped from Aaron and his buddies. Four wallets, each with driver's licenses and union cards. I'd be getting one of those union cards after this week. I hoped. Two of them had credit or debit cards. Or maybe they were ATM cards. I didn't know how to tell the difference. Three wallets had a little cash. But not Aaron's. A few pictures, a VFW card, an IOU for $6.26, dated over six months ago. I stuffed everything back in the wallets and looked at the assembly of keys

I'd also acquired. None of them were those fat car keys with batteries, but some looked like they were for older model vehicles. A few house keys and one padlock key.

Why had I taken them? I might be a convicted murderer, but I wasn't a thief. Just because I'd been angry that they planned to take my wallet. And I'd had some vague idea I could offer to return them if they'd keep their mouths shut. Did that amount to blackmail?

Probably.

But I couldn't keep them here. Although no one had shown up to search my place so far, it could happen any time. No warrant needed.

Taking a roll of duct tape, I gathered them up into two bundles and taped them together securely. Wincing as I put weight on my ankle, I struggled upstairs and out to the alley beside the building. It was deserted. I knelt beside the dumpster and taped them on the bottom, behind the supporting framework. Once a week a refuse truck pulled into the alley, lifted the dumpster over its cab, and emptied it. That had been today. The bundles should be safe for a week. If no one found them.

Work was going to be a whole lot of fun with my ankle as sore as it was. At least John knew I'd been hurt the day before, so I could just pass this off as from the same incident.

I ripped up a T-shirt and wrapped the ankle tightly. Maybe the pain would work itself out some.

To my relief, the shift passed uneventfully.

The next morning I walked carefully the mile or so from work to the parole office. I wondered if Mr. Ramirez would show up this time, and if the detectives had convinced him I should be back on house arrest.

I breathed deeply, reminding myself how much better it was to breathe the cold, clear air than the stuffy, disinfectant scented air in an overcrowded prison. That could be pretty cold, too, but the damp smell of urine and unwashed bodies was always hovering under the disinfectant. I'd take house arrest, with all its limitations, over prison any day.

The waiting room was empty. I was early, but I signed in on the clipboard on the ledge and took a seat in the corner. Nothing to do but wait.

The window above the ledge opened and a pale hand with manicured fingernails reached out to snag the clipboard, drawing it inside. The window slammed shut again.

Ten a.m. came and went. No one else came in. Thursday mornings were not a busy time at the parole office, but I wasn't usually the only one there. I shifted uneasily on the bench. Was there something going on I'd missed? Like that the entire building was in lockdown. Or the world was coming to an end.

The crooked clock with its cracked face said close to eleven a.m. before the door opened. A very large lady with a yellow sweater stretched tight against a bosom that would be right at home in a porn flick frowned down at the clipboard in her hand.

"Jesse Damon?" she said, looking around the room as if expecting a more suitable Jesse Damon to materialize before her eyes.

"Yes, ma'am," I said, getting to my feet.

"Mr. Ramirez will see you now."

I followed her through the door and down a hallway. The temperature had to be fifteen degrees cooler in here, and the air was drier. I suppose the union would get on the county's case if they tried to make people work in conditions like the ones in the waiting room. The only people who had to stay in the waiting room, of course, were parolees like me.

Mr. Ramirez was leaning back in his battered desk chair with his eyes closed, his head almost touching the file cabinet behind him in the cramped office. When I knocked on the open door, he swiveled in the chair and brought his feet down on the floor with a thud.

"Made it, did you, Jesse?" he asked.

"Yes, sir." I was tempted to say, "So did you, this time," but that was a much too chummy thing to say to a man who could send me back to prison with a stroke of his pen.

His hands were clasped on top of all the papers on his desk, his fingers entwined. Little tufts of dark hair sprouted on his fingers above the knuckles. "Did you walk?"

"Yes, sir. It's not far from work."

He nodded. "Think we should give you a drug test?"

I blanched. Had Aaron been complaining that I had access to drugs but wouldn't hook him up? If so, to whom? Why else would Mr. Ramirez want a test all of a sudden?

"Your call, sir." No reason why I shouldn't piss clean. I just hoped he wouldn't make me pay for it. The tests were expensive.

His dark eyes studied my face. "Sit down," he said, nodding toward a worn wooden chair in front of his desk.

I sat.

"You look like you been through a wind tunnel. Care to tell me why?"

Reaching up, I touched a swollen cheek. "I'd rather not, sir."

"Recent, those bruises?"

"Yes, sir." If Mr. Ramirez didn't know about the fight with Aaron and his buddies, I wasn't about to volunteer the information.

He leaned back in his chair again. "Anything to do with an encounter with a couple of detectives?"

Of course Belkins and Montgomery had told Mr. Ramirez that he wanted me back on home detention, but they wouldn't have mentioned roughing me up.

"Maybe," I agreed. I would be happy to let that assumption stand.

"I've been hearing interesting things about what you've been up to."

I didn't see what I could say that would help, so I didn't say anything.

"Detective Montgomery was in. He said he'd seen you at a funeral."

"At a viewing, sir. I didn't go to the funeral." I didn't add that I wouldn't have been welcome.

"While you were at the funeral home, did you talk to him?" Mr. Ramirez rubbed his pudgy hands together.

"Yes, sir. Him and Detective Belkins." He'd find that out easily enough if he asked.

"And why were you at this—viewing?"

I stared at a spot on the floor between my boots. "It was for my foster mother, sir. I wanted to pay my respects."

"Your foster mother, eh? How long did you live with her?"

"About five years, sir. She meant a lot to me."

"But I suppose she wasn't exactly thrilled with how you turned out." Mr. Ramirez shifted his considerable bulk in his chair.

"No, sir. I guess I should have thought of that. Before I went."

"Do you know how she died?" He leaned forward.

I could feel his gaze boring into me. "It was sudden, I think, sir."

He lowered his voice. "Murdered?"

"I don't know, sir." I did, really, but I didn't want to say so. "I suppose maybe."

"And did you have anything to do with that?"

I tried to take a deep breath, but my lungs wouldn't cooperate. "No, sir."

"Had you been in touch with Mrs. Coleman since you were released?"

"No, sir."

"If she meant so much to you, why not?"

"I didn't think she'd welcome the contact, sir."

"How about while you were in prison? Did she come to see you?" His chair squeaked in protest as he leaned forward.

"No, sir."

"Yet she was on your visiting list."

"Yes, sir. When I first got locked up, I hoped she'd come visit, so I put her on the list. But she never came."

"But you left her on the list."

I shrugged. "I just never bothered to take her name off the list. I didn't have anybody else to put on it."

"And she never came to visit you? I can check, you know."

"Then you'll find out I never had any visitors at all." Did I sound like a smartass? I'd better get a grip on myself.

"I find that hard to believe." Mr. Ramirez shuffled some of the papers on his desk. "Not in the whole twenty years?"

I didn't find it hard to believe. Depressing, maybe, but not hard to believe. Who would visit me? I had no idea what the visiting room at the prison even looked like. "No, sir."

"Did she write you?"

"No, sir. I wrote her once, but I got a letter back from Mr. Coleman saying she didn't want to hear from me. And not to write again. So I didn't."

"And yet you went to her funeral."

"Viewing, sir. It was stupid. I shouldn't have gone."

"And have you seen Mr. Coleman since?"

Belkins and Montgomery knew about the visit I'd made to the house, so there wasn't much point in not 'fessing up.

"Yes, sir. I went round the house to check up on him."

"For any particular reason?"

"Not really, sir. I was just concerned about him."

"You must realize I'm not happy you're involved in a murder investigation."

No surprise there. "Yes, sir." I wasn't too happy about it either.

The chair squeaked. "You must also have realized Mr. Coleman wouldn't be pleased to see you at his wife's funeral."

He was going to keep calling it a funeral. I was not going to keep trying to correct him. I stared miserably at my hands. "I was hoping I could kind of sneak in and get out without him noticing me."

"At a funeral home? During visitation for his recently murdered wife?" Mr. Ramirez sounded incredulous.

It did sound pretty stupid. "I never been to a funeral home before."

Mr. Ramirez shook his head. "Nobody you knew ever died before?"

"I only been out on the street for a few months," I reminded him. "And I was sixteen when I got locked up."

"So it'd be fair to say that you're not familiar with how a lot of things work?"

"I guess."

He shuffled a few of the papers around on his desk. "Are you aware that Detective Belkins, who is assigned to this case, is of the opinion that it was a mistake to grant you parole? He thinks the only reason you haven't killed anyone in the last twenty years is because you were locked up. And now, here we are, you've been recently released, and there's another dead body with connections to you."

I hadn't actually ever killed anyone. But I'd been convicted of murder. What really happened back then didn't matter much. Not to anyone but me anyhow.

I didn't answer. Mr. Ramirez sat silently. I kept staring at the floor between my boots. Worn wood, probably pine. Needed a good refinishing.

"Why did you go to the viewing?" he finally asked.

"I don't know. I shouldn't have gone."

"Sometimes murderers can't stay away from the funerals of their victims. Kind of like a lot of arsonists are the first on the scene to help put out the fire. You know that?"

"Yes, sir. I didn't know she'd been murdered."

"You expect me to believe that?"

I winced. As parole officers go, Mr. Ramirez had been pretty supportive. If he thought I was lying to him, that would change.

"And then you went to Mr. Coleman's house. Any good reason for that?"

"No, sir."

He got to his feet and drew himself up to his full five foot two inches. His expansive gut hung over his belt.

I knew better than to stand up. At just about six foot, I would tower over him.

"Have you heard about the grant the county has gotten for law enforcement?" he asked.

"No, sir." Why was he bringing this up? I'd seen something about it in the newspaper, and of course I was interested, but the article hadn't gone into details.

"Money from seized assets from convicted drug dealers. The county law enforcement can use it any way they want, but they've mostly used it for electronic communication and surveillance equipment," Mr. Ramirez said. He held up a black plastic box with a screen. "Hand-held computers for patrolling police. Pocket cops, they call them. Upgraded bugging devices. GPS monitors for parolees and people out on bail. You know what they are?"

"Yes, sir." I wondered if one of the upgraded bugging devices had made its way to Aaron.

"High tech replacements for the ankle boxes we've been using, the ones that are read with a phone land line."

I knew all about the ankle boxes. I'd worn one for three months. It had cost me forty dollars a week in monitoring fees. I'd had to have a phone installed in my apartment. A phone that was never used now that I wasn't on the box. I'd decided to leave it until I was pretty sure I wouldn't need it again. It had been expensive to get hooked up.

Mr. Ramirez reached over and removed some pamphlets from the top of his file cabinet. "Some of us have our doubts as to how effective the GPS systems will be here in the hills. Lots of places we can't get cell phone signals. Still, the GPS uses satellite signals. You wear the box and carry a transmitter. Might work."

I didn't like where this was leading.

"We need a few people to run a trial."

Definitely not heading in a good direction.

"I'd like to fit you with one," Mr. Ramirez said, handing me a pamphlet. "We can't use something experimental on anyone released on bail, since the court controls the terms of the monitoring. And we're not going to replace the box on people presently on home detention. Are you willing to be part of the trial?"

"Do I have a choice?" I asked, trying to keep the agony out of my voice.

Mr. Ramirez chuckled. "I guess not really. Unless you'd rather go back on the old box."

"How much will it cost?" I'd only recently gotten to the point where I had anything left over after I paid for essentials. I wanted to take Kelly and the kids out a few times. If she'd let me. And I wanted to save up to buy a pickup truck. Unlikely, maybe, but I could dream.

"No charge to you. Not while you're part of the trial. And if it works like it's supposed to, it could actually be an advantage for you. Belkins can check to see where you've been. Ought to eliminate you as a suspect if anything else happens. Or—" he stared down straight into my face "—put you right where it happened."

The options were limited. And he was right—I might as well look at the bright side. Unless a crime happened right where I was, I would have an ironclad alibi. If the damn thing worked.

Mr. Ramirez was saving me the monitoring fee. That was something.

"You gonna fix me with it now?" I asked. I hoped my ankle wasn't too swollen. My socks and boots were pretty damp, but at least the socks had been clean when I put them on last night. They might smell of wet wool but shouldn't stink of sweaty feet.

"I have to put in a requisition for the unit," Mr. Ramirez said. "They don't have that many of them yet."

Just my luck to get one of the few.

"I'll probably get it in two or three weeks. Until then, shall we just continue with the present conditions? With the exception of your propensity to become a suspect in murder investigations, it seems to be working pretty well."

"Yes, sir."

CHAPTER 14

John met me as I approached the time clock. "Another shipping disaster," he said gloomily. "You're on the clock as soon as you can get punched in."

"Same deal as last time?"

"Pretty much. But they printed out a bunch of shipping lists rather than leave a dispatcher on duty tonight. You'll have to work from them."

He peered more closely at me. "What happened to your face this time?" he asked. "Now you've got a cut on your lip. And the bruises look worse."

"Fell again."

"And landed on your face again?"

"Slipped in some ice and hit one of them newspaper vending machines on the way down."

"Is that why you're limping?"

I guess I hadn't been doing as good a job as I'd thought of walking normally. "Yeah. Twisted my ankle."

"You okay to work?"

"After tonight, I'm done with the three months probationary employment. You bet I'm okay to work."

John grinned. "Good for you."

When I went to get a lift from the charging station, I was relieved that no one was hanging around smoking anything. None of the group had showed up for work last night, and I hoped they decided to take tonight off, too. That would give us the whole weekend before we had to face each other. I was still undecided what I would do with all the wallets and keys I'd collected, but they should be safe until next week.

Kelly was in the shipping room, frowning as she tried to sort the paperwork. Several sheets drifted to the floor. "This whole damn system's messed up," she complained.

"True, that." I picked up the papers from the floor.

She glared at the sheets. "Look at all these shipping lists! I can't make heads or tails out of this."

"Let me see." I laid them on top of a packing crate, sorting them first by order number, then by page number. "It's not so bad as it looks. Each one has a couple of pages. It'd help if they'd staple them together so they wouldn't get mixed up." When I got them in proper order, I took the first bunch and folded down one corner. Then I ripped a narrow strip down the dog eared corner, pressed it back behind the last page and gave it a twist. It wasn't foolproof, but it would keep the pages together.

"How'd you learn to do that?" Kelly asked, taking the papers and putting them on her clipboard.

"Can't have no paper clips in prison." I repeated the procedure with all the shipping lists. "What's first?"

"This order of root baskets. The truck's already here. The driver's gone to the head, then he said he's gonna work on his log. But he wants to get going ASAP."

"Root baskets again. Weird. What size and how many?"

Kelly peered at the paper. "Thirty six inch baskets," she said. "Forty eight stacks of them."

I swung up onto my lift and headed out to the warehouse.

It was still early to ship root baskets for the spring, and we'd pretty much cleared out the ones in the front of the warehouse. I'd have to move quite a few loads before I could pull the pallets with the root baskets on them.

Darius, a back-up driver on the afternoon shift, had gotten a fair amount moved, but the path he was clearing went to the place where the bigger root baskets, the forty-eight-inch ones, were stored. Not too many baskets were being run now, and they almost never got run on that shift. He probably didn't know where each size was stored. I started moving pallets back into the path he'd cleared to work my way to the thirty-six-inch ones.

When I finally got to them, I scooped up a pallet and drove it out to shipping. At this end of the shipping dock, the bay door was open with an idling truck backed into it.

Kelly was down at the other end of the dock, finishing loading one of the regular trucks.

I made a few more runs with more pallets of baskets. Kelly drove over and started loading them onto the truck.

We worked steadily for the best part of an hour, me carting the pallets out of the warehouse and Kelly loading them. When we were done, the driver came over for the paperwork. Kelly climbed off her lift and handed him the clipboard.

The driver checked the paperwork, then went into his trailer to check the load.

He came out and went back to Kelly, shaking his head. I couldn't hear what they were saying over the din of conveyors and the packing room.

Kelly's face turned red, and she folded her arms over her ample bosom. The driver continued to shake his head.

When I'd put my load down, I swung off my lift and went over to see if there was a problem.

Kelly turned on me. "You brought the wrong size!"

"Let me see that." I reached for the clipboard. "Size: forty eight inches," the bill of lading read. "Quantity: thirty six stacks, twelve per stack."

The old shipping lists had always put the quantity first and the size second. Although this one had the numbers in different places, it was clearly thirty six stacks of the forty eight inch baskets. We were doing it backwards. And Darius had been heading for the right ones after all.

I shook my head. "I thought you said thirty six inch baskets," I said to Kelly. "So that's what I brought out."

"Well, you thought wrong!" she fumed.

The driver stepped back. "Hey, I don't care whose fault it is. I need to get out of here as soon as I can. With the right load."

He had a point. Kelly glared at me, climbed on her lift and started to unload the truck. I picked up a pallet of the wrong size baskets and ran it back to the warehouse where I deposited it in a corner while I began to clear a path again to the larger size baskets.

Kelly would have to explain the mistake to John when he came to check on our progress. He wouldn't be happy, but right now that couldn't be helped. All we could do was fix it as soon as we could.

We worked right through our first break to get that truck loaded. Then we cut our lunches—already a scant eighteen minutes—short and skipped the six am break, trying to catch up with the rest of the night's work. At seven thirty, just as the foreman from the day shift was walking in the door, the last driver checked his load, pulled his trailer door shut, locked it, and climbed into his cab.

Kelly hit the switch to lower the door to that truck bay. She leaned back in her seat and sighed.

It hadn't been pretty, but we made it.

It was Friday morning. The weekend stretched before us. "You wanna go for breakfast?" I asked Kelly. "My treat."

She shook her head, not meeting my eyes. "I got stuff to do," she said, and headed off to plug in her lift to recharge.

I wondered if she was mad at me over the mistake in the root basket sizes. I was pretty sure she'd told me the wrong thing, but the trucker had been right; it didn't really matter whose fault it was. We'd been able to fix it, although it had thrown the whole night's work behind.

Not much point in worrying about it. I let her get a ways ahead of me, then swung my lift to follow hers.

A few minutes after eight, she beat me to the time clock and punched out. I tried to step up next to her and see if she'd talk to me, but she circled around the tables by the vending machines and left. I still had to go find John and get my paycheck. Most everyone else had direct deposit. I didn't even have a bank account.

Probably about time to face the fact that there was no future for us. She was pretty moody, and she drank. On top of everything else, that was not a good place to establish a solid relationship.

I could get sent back to prison at any time, either on a new conviction or just a violation. Not exactly the best basis for making plans. I didn't have a damn thing to offer a woman. Especially a woman with vulnerable kids. They'd already been through hell when their parents divorced, and she was still mad at me for what she saw as interfering with the way she took care of them. Much better that I bow out, at least for now.

Boy, would I miss the evenings in her comfortable old house, spending time with the kids. Not to mention the sex.

I walked to the bank to cash my check. Someday soon I'd open a bank account and start saving for that pickup truck. Of course, I'd have to get a driver's license before I could drive it. That in itself was a major hassle and expense.

Kelly's old station wagon was parked across the parking lot of the half-vacant strip mall where the bank was located. What store had she gone into? I paused to look around. Maybe I should be more tolerant of her moods, and maybe she'd settled down some. She did that. Maybe I could still ask if she wanted to go get breakfast.

She was coming out of a liquor store. With two heavy bags clutched in her arms.

She saw me and stopped. "What the hell are *you* looking at?"

That wasn't a good sign. "Nothing. You want some help with those bags?"

"These bags are none of your business. Are you following me around?"

Better not ask about breakfast. "No. I'm just going to the bank. You okay?"

"I'm just *fine*, thank you," she said, shifted the weight in her arms. I heard glass clink on glass. Bottles. Southern Comfort? Didn't seem to bring much comfort in the long run.

Out of the corner of my eye, I saw a black and white patrol car pull into the parking lot.

I considered turning around and walking in the opposite direction. No reason they should be looking for me, but cops made me nervous.

"You're judging me, aren't you?" Kelly's voice was beginning to rise. "You, of all people."

I said nothing. From where she was standing, I was pretty sure she couldn't see the patrol car. I wished she would just shut up, and we could both leave. I'd rather go together, but at this point I'd certainly be satisfied with apart. As long as I could get away from there.

But she was getting more upset. "Just leave me alone," she practically shouted.

The patrol car pulled into a parking space. The window rolled down. I winced. "See you around," I said, hoping to sound friendly and neutral. Poor choice of words.

"Not if I see you first," she retorted. She took a few steps toward to me. I smelled whiskey on her breath already. Did she have an open bottle in the car? I didn't want her to get in trouble, either.

"Okay." I kept my voice calm. "I'll just be going now."

"Oh, sure. You just get going. And stop stalking me. Or I'll call a cop."

That was a deliberate taunt. Kelly knew how much trouble she could get me into if she complained that I was stalking her. She probably didn't really mean it, but I didn't want to take a chance.

And if she didn't mean it, she'd picked a really bad time to say it. Two uniformed officers climbed out of the car.

"Is this man giving you a hard time, ma'am?" the tall one asked.

Kelly turned in surprise. "Nothing I can't handle," she said.

"What's he to you?" the cop asked.

"We work at the same place. On the same shift."

"That's all?"

Kelly shifted the bags nervously in her arms. "Well, we dated a little. Nothing serious."

"He ever threaten you? Or hit you?"

"No. No. I got to get going." Kelly turned and opened the car door. She dumped the bags in the backseat and climbed into the driver's seat.

The cops and I watched as she drove out of the parking lot.

Hadn't they noticed the alcohol on her breath? Evidently not. Not something they were looking for at nine in the morning, especially from someone in work clothes.

The two cops now turned to look at me.

Oh, great. They were both young. One was much taller than I was. The other only had me by a few inches, but he was solidly built. They were probably both rookies.

What happened to the idea of pairing an experienced cop up with a newbie? They'd probably just started their shift, and things were pretty quiet on a Friday morning in the late winter. They were bored. Did they recognize me? I had no doubt my picture hung somewhere in the briefing room at the police station.

"What's your name?" the taller cop asked.

For a fleeting minute, I thought about lying. They really had nothing on me, no reason to take me in.

But if they frisked me, they'd find my wallet. I didn't have a driver's license, but I did have my picture ID from Quality Steel Fabrications. I needed it to cash any of my check.

And I had my old prison ID. When I was first released, it was the only ID I had.

"Well?"

I licked my lips. "Jesse Damon."

No flash of recognition. I was relieved, but a little surprised. Maybe I was just paranoid about how much surveillance I was under. That would be nice.

He pulled something out. One of those pocket cops Mr. Ramirez had shown me. I watched as he punched my name in.

I could just imagine what he would come up with. I made sure my hands were in full sight, by my sides.

His eyes widened at what popped up on the screen. He backed up a step, his hand going to his holster. "Put your hands on your head," he ordered.

I sighed and followed his directions.

"What you got, Stan?" his partner asked.

"Look at this." He handed it over and reached for his handcuffs. "Turn around, Damon."

I did so. Then he ran his hands over my pockets, between my legs and under my jacket. He reached into my pocket and felt my wallet and keychain, but didn't remove them. He pulled one of my hands down and cuffed it, followed by the other. Then he pushed me over toward the brick wall next to big front window of the liquor store. I was still facing away from him.

"You know your parole could be violated for going into a liquor store?" he said.

"I didn't go in."

"You expect me to believe that?"

That could be checked easily enough. "Go in and ask the clerk." I could see her standing at her cash register, staring at us.

He looked a little less certain and turned to his partner. "Go ask the lady in there whether this guy's been inside."

"You sure you want me to leave you alone with him?" his partner asked, slamming his right fist into the palm of his right hand.

"He's cuffed. I can handle him."

That might not have been true if I had decided to do anything, but I wasn't going to.

The partner went in and out of the corner if my eye I could see them talking to the clerk. She was shaking her head.

He came out again. "She says no. She says thanks for stopping him. She says he was sizing up the place, and she thinks he was going to rob it."

"He don't have a weapon."

"Don't need nothing but your hand in your pocket. Or *say* you got a weapon."

I felt a rough hand on my arm. "Turn around and face us." He gave me a shove.

Turning, I faced them but kept my gaze on the sidewalk between them.

"I suppose you wouldn't tell us if you were planning to rob the liquor store."

I considered how much I could say without pissing them off enough to cause myself real trouble. "If I was gonna rob a store, I sure as hell wouldn't do it just after they opened. I'd wait until they had a register full of cash."

They looked at each other.

"Later on there'd be more people around. Be harder to get away with it," the tall cop said.

The other one scratched his head. "Looks like now's not a good time, either. And all anybody'd get would be the change the cashier starts out with in her drawer. And maybe some booze."

He changed tactics. "What was going on with the girlfriend?"

"Not really my girlfriend," I said. "We saw each other a few times, but I think she's not interested in me anymore."

"I wonder why. She find out about your record?"

"She knew about it all along," I said.

"Working is usually a condition of probation. How come you're not at work?"

"I work nights. Just got off and went to the bank with my check."

"Stalking the former girlfriend, were you?"

"No, sir. She just got off of work, too. She stopped by to do some shopping."

They stood shoulder to shoulder in front of me.

The shorter cop's hand strayed to his service revolver. The flap was unsnapped. He rested his hand on the weapon. "What should we do with him?"

The other one shrugged. "He got no warrants. The girlfriend didn't sound like she was going to press charges. He hasn't got a weapon. He *didn't* actually go into the liquor store, and there's no way we can prove he was planning to rob it."

"So we just *let him go*?"

They stood menacingly. The taller cop turned back to the pocket cop, frantically tapping on it. "Nothing but the record," he finally said. "But he *does* come up 'armed and dangerous.'"

A woman dressed in a fashionable coat and boots walked by, a small boy in a snowsuit struggling to keep up with her long stride.

"Mommy!" the child said, stopping to stare at me. "What did that man do? Did he *kill* somebody?"

"He's a bad man, honey," the woman told him. "The nice police officers will make sure he doesn't hurt you."

"Are the policemen going to take him to jail?"

"Yes."

CHAPTER 15

Fortunately for me, she was wrong.

The minute the cuffs came off and the cops told me I could go, I headed straight for home. The wind picked up trash and blew it in eddies around the stairs down to my apartment. A cold rain began to pelt down. I hitched up the collar of my jacket. At least this might melt the chunks of dirty ice that littered the streets and sidewalks.

I tried not to think about Kelly. Without much success.

Someone was huddled on the front steps of the old pizza parlor, now the Tabernacle of the Inaccurate Conception. It was one of the cult members, dressed in the saffron robes they wore, his sandaled feet drawn up against the stained concrete stairs. He didn't have a jacket or a hat and was leaning forward, burying his face in his crossed arms on his lap. Not surprisingly, he was shivering.

I glanced at him. None of my business if he wanted to freeze his ass off sitting on the steps.

As I came closer, I realized it was Isaac.

What made someone young like that, with his whole life ahead of him, throw himself away on a bunch of religious lunatics?

Walking up to him, I said, "You're gonna freeze if you sit there much longer. You okay?"

He looked up at me, his face white and drawn behind his straggling beard. "I'm fine, thank you."

"What're you waiting for?"

His teeth were chattering. "I overslept and was late for the morning service. I can't go in until Father Peter says it's okay. Then he'll tell me what my penance will be."

"I would think sitting there freezing your buns off would be penance enough."

He lowered his eyes. "I brought it on myself. I have a long way to go before I can be declared worthy."

He must really buy into that stuff. But he'd have to. Otherwise why would he be hanging out with these freaks?

"How come you overslept?" I asked.

"I was up late sitting with the goddess. I guess I was just so tired I didn't wake up."

"How long before Father Peter shows up?"

"I'm not sure. He said he'd be back before noon."

"It's only about nine now. That's a long wait."

"He might be a little earlier."

"Can't you wait inside?"

The kid shook his head. "I'm a novitiate. When I missed the service, I broke my contract with the Brethren. So I can't enter the holy sanctum until we come to a resolution on my sins."

I sighed. I was probably making a mistake, but I owed Isaac. "You wanna come wait in my place?"

He looked at me, his eyes wide behind the wire rim glasses. "Father Peter said we're not supposed to talk to you. He said spending time with criminals can corrupt us."

I laughed. Like I could corrupt him any worse than Father Peter and his cult were already corrupting him. "True, that. But you already been talking to me. You even been down in my apartment. You tell Father Peter about that?"

"No. I was afraid he'd be mad."

"Did you get corrupted that time?"

He considered. "That was different. You needed help. We're supposed to help those in need. Even if it puts us at personal risk."

"Did you feel 'at personal risk' then?"

"Well, not really. But you were hurt. And now you're not."

"So what do you think might happen?"

"Well, you *are* a convicted murderer, even if you say you didn't kill anyone yourself."

"Tell you what. I promise I won't murder anybody today, you or anybody else. And I know what it feels like to be really cold. So come on in and get warmed up."

"The goddess will provide my comfort," he said, gazing at the wet concrete between his sandaled feet. His feet were turning blue.

His goddess was a calico cat who was busy taking care of two kittens. Hard to see what comfort she could provide for anybody.

"Ever think maybe the comfort the goddess is trying to provide is me asking you in to warm up?" I asked. "After all, she came and stayed with me herself for a while."

His head jerked up. "I never thought of that."

"The Lord works in mysterious ways. Probably goddesses do, too."

He sat with his mouth open, thinking that through. Rain plastered his hair to his skull and dripped from his beard. Uncertainly, he rose to his feet. "Okay. But why would the goddess want me to come warm up in your apartment?"

"Maybe so you don't freeze to death," I said.

"Or maybe I have something to learn from you," he mused.

I rolled my eyes. "Or maybe you're supposed to teach me something."

"I doubt that. I'm still pretty new. I don't know much to teach." But he followed me down the stairs and into the apartment.

The heat had just come on, and the room was still chilly. But it was dry and a lot warmer than outside.

This time, it was me who put the kettle on to boil and took the two mugs from the drainer.

"How did you choose the name Isaac?" I asked him. "That's a pretty exalted name to choose, Isaac." And dangerous—Isaac was intended as a sacrifice.

"Oh, I didn't choose it," he assured me. "Father Peter assigns the names. He said it honors Abraham, who was a good father, and since I'm still really only a kid, I needed a good father. A spiritual one."

I spooned the instant coffee crystals into the mugs. "Other than that you shouldn't talk to me, what does Father Peter say about me?"

"Just that we should be careful around you. He said you've done hard time in prison and know how to take care of yourself, so we shouldn't bother you. He said the goddess had decided to put you in the basement apartment for a reason. At first he said it was so she could retreat to your apartment to give birth and the police would be taking you away soon. But you're still here, so there has to be another reason. We'll just have to wait and see."

I wished I had some whiskey to add to the coffee when it was cold like this. It would do Isaac some good. But any alcohol would be a violation of my parole. It would certainly be stupid to take a chance on having something like a bottle of whiskey around my place.

Isaac looked down at the tabletop. "He says you deal drugs and will try to drag us all into the evils of heroin and cocaine if we're not careful. It might be a trial."

Shaking my head, I felt a pang of guilt about my unspoken wish for whiskey. "Big difference between being convicted of murder and dealing drugs," I said. "I don't use. Never did."

"But you've been to prison. You know lots of people who could supply almost anything."

He sounded like Aaron, who had been hanging around a fair amount. I wondered if Aaron had been talking to him. Maybe Aaron was even considering joining the Tabernacle. If it helped him kick his meth/oxy habits, I guess it would be a good thing. Somehow I couldn't see it, though.

"Other than that I was locked up for a while, you got any reason to think that?" I asked. "Somebody else tell you I could hook you up?"

"Father Peter says you attract the wrong element, that drug dealers hang around here because of you. He's afraid some of us will succumb to the evils of addiction. I think he's especially worried about Xavier."

"Why's that?"

Isaac shook his head. "Xavier's been lax in his morals lately."

Interesting way to put it. "What does that mean?"

"I don't really know. He's been missing from some of the services. He says he's visiting his son, but I don't think he is all the time he says he is."

"His son? Is that the young kid that I've seen around here a few times?"

"Yes. Father Peter gave him money to hire a lawyer and go to court to try to get custody."

"Away from the kid's mother? It'd be hard to convince the court that raising a kid in an environment like the Tabernacle would be a good idea."

"I know. And I think Xavier's been spending the money on...*inappropriate things*, shall I say, rather than paying the lawyer."

"What are 'inappropriate things'?"

"Some kind of drugs." Isaac stared at his mug. "Who am I to talk? I'm drinking coffee. With caffeine."

"Caffeine's not expensive enough to make a difference in paying a lawyer. And it's not gonna get you in trouble."

Isaac glanced around and lowered his voice. "I heard him talking about buying a *gun*. That might be expensive."

"That *would* be expensive. What did he want a gun for?"

Isaac's mouth twitched. "He says he's got lots of enemies, so he has to protect himself. And he says if the court doesn't give him custody of his son, he just might take him anyhow."

"That would be a dumb thing to do. After that, he'd *never* get custody. And he might lose whatever visitation he has." But Kelly's ex had done a couple of stupid things, and he was fighting for custody of *his* kids. The hearing was Monday, I reminded myself. I hoped Kelly didn't drink all weekend and show up for court hungover. Or not show up at all. "And what does the kid's mother do that Xavier and Father Peter think is so terrible?"

"She's sending him to the public school. Father Peter says that's indoctrinating him against all the values of the Tabernacle."

I warmed my hands on my coffee mug. "That doesn't make sense. Didn't most of the members of the cult...*Tabernacle*...go to public school? Didn't *you*?"

"Yes. But that's one of the reasons why it's so hard for me to become worthy. I have so much I need to put behind me."

"So Xavier thinks he's going to use a gun to go get the kid away from his mother?"

"That's what he says. But Father Peter says they must be patient and let the goddess settle things. He says now that she's got her own children, she'll understand what Xavier's going through and arrange for his son to come to him."

I considered pointing out that the goddess was a mother cat who had no notion her kittens even had a father, much less think that he should take them away from her. Isaac looked so sad and confused, though, that I decided not to add to his mental overload.

"*Do* you sell drugs?" Isaac asked.

"Look," I said. "I'm on parole. I've got years of back up time. If they decide I've violated, I get locked back up to finish it up. I don't need a new conviction. You can be sure that, if they found any drugs on me—or in me—I'd be back in prison so fast it'd make your head spin."

"How would they find out?" he asked.

"When you're on parole, you don't get normal rights. They can search you anytime. Pull you in without a warrant. Search your place. Demand a piss test. No need for probable cause or anything else. Just cause they feel like it."

"That doesn't seem fair."

"Fair don't enter into it. You want parole, you agree to their conditions. Otherwise, you can stay locked up. Some people do—just mandatory out so they won't have to put up with all the bullshit of parole." Not me, though. Not when I would be looking at a minimum of twenty five more years.

Isaac looked around the room. "You like living here?"

"Sure as hell beats a prison cell. And I got the key in my own pocket."

He nodded and took a sip of his coffee.

"Can I ask you a question about the Tabernacle?" I asked.

Isaac brightened. "Oh, yes! We're supposed to encourage people to talk about the Tabernacle! Father Peter says you never know where your next convert is going to come from. Sometimes it's people you'd never expect. Rich people, who donate their money to the Tabernacle. And since the goddess has already shown that she likes you..."

"Whoa. Don't get your hopes up," I cautioned. "And I got no money to donate. I just wondered about the name—it's kind of an odd one. Why do they call it that?"

He put the mug on the rickety table. "Father Peter says it's because none of us have proper fathers. Except maybe Xavier. Some of us aren't even sure who our father is. So it's like our conception was some kind of mistake, almost like no human man was involved. So Father Peter is father to all of us."

I guess that made sense in some distorted fashion. "What about Xavier?" I asked.

"Father Peter is Xavier's real father. Father Peter said it's really hard for him to share his own father with all of us, but we're brothers. That's why we call ourselves the Brethren. And why Xavier gets special privileges."

That part didn't sound especially good. But who was I to disagree? "Did you have a place to meet before you moved the Tabernacle upstairs?"

"I'm not sure." Isaac frowned. "I didn't join until they established the Tabernacle here. Father Peter says the goddess wants us here, so he can seek his roots. He was born in this town. Besides, his grandson, Xavier's son, lives here, and they have a sacred obligation to the child."

"The kid Xavier wants to take by force."

"Father Peter says we could all raise him, here in the Tabernacle." Isaac was warming to his subject. "Switch off like we do with the goddess. We could all be the kind of fathers and uncles we've never had."

I finished my coffee. Isaac's was only half gone.

"Did you know your father?" he asked me.

"Yeah, I did." I would have been a lot better off if I hadn't, though.

"Did you live with him when you were a kid?"

"From when the old man got out of prison when I was thirteen until I got locked up," I said. "Maybe three years."

Isaac brushed the damp hair out of his face. "You got sent to adult prison for murder when you were sixteen? Don't they keep kids locked up separate when they're that young?" he asked.

"Well, by the time it got all the way through the courts and everything, I was almost seventeen. Until then, I was in the county lockup. Believe me, prison's a sight better than the county lockup."

"Did your mother live with you, too?"

"My mother died when I was a little kid. Mostly I lived in foster homes."

Isaac bowed his head. "My mother died, too. About a year ago. I was supposed to go to a group foster home and finish up high school, but I ran away."

And ended up joining the Tabernacle. I wondered what I would have done if I'd had the opportunity to run away and been smart enough to take it.

CHAPTER 16

Twenty years of being locked in a cell most of the time had left me with very little desire to go out on Saturday night. I knew it affected some people differently, but as long as I had the key to the door and knew I could leave whenever I wanted to, I was content to stay in my apartment and read a book. The only place I'd prefer was Kelly's house.

That didn't seem like it was going to be a possibility any time soon.

My current read book was *Gods and Generals*. I was on a Civil War kick. We weren't far from the Sharpsburg Battlefield, and the whole area was steeped in Civil War lore. The local public library had a collection that would satisfy a far more intense appetite than mine for related reading material.

My two rickety wooden chairs weren't comfortable for long, so I lay on my bed. A cat cuddled up by my side might have been nice, but I knew the cat was far better off upstairs. The Brethren might be weirdos, but if Isaac were any indication, they would take good care of her and her kittens.

Tonight I was restless. I found myself wondering if the wallets I'd taped under the dumpster were still there. I'd planned to leave them alone until I'd figured out what to do with them, but they kept intruding on my thoughts, and I couldn't concentrate.

With a sigh, I tossed the book down. I could see if I had an easier read among the other library books I'd gotten out, but I really wanted to read this.

I glanced toward the single window that looked out on the alley. Soon it would be dark. Not much chance anyone would be hanging around, and I could slip out the alley to check under the dumpster. Meanwhile, I'd fix some supper.

My food budget didn't give me a whole lot of choices. I put a pot of water on to boil for both coffee and ramen noodles, and I sliced two hot dogs into my frying pan.

Fried hot dogs mixed into ramen noodles and a mug of coffee wasn't exactly gourmet, but it tasted good and was filling.

By the time I was done, the only light that showed through the window was a dim glow from the streetlight. I cleaned up and went outside.

I walked past the entrance to the alley and glanced down it to make sure it was empty.

It wasn't.

Someone was standing next to the door that led to the Tabernacle. Someone in regular street clothes, not the saffron robes the members wore.

Passing the entrance as if I had never intended to turn down it, I stepped into the dark recessed entry to the deserted storefront just beyond the alley. It was out of the wind, and I could see if anyone left or entered the alley. It couldn't be too long before someone let the person into the Tabernacle or he—it looked like a he, but I couldn't be sure—left.

After what seemed like forever—but was probably only ten minutes or so—I went back onto the sidewalk and approached the end of the alley, keeping next to the wall and in the shadows as much as possible. I peered down the alley.

He was still there. He was doing something to the lock on the door.

As I stood there, he stepped back and pocketed whatever he had been using, presumably in an attempt to pick the lock. He pulled a screwdriver from his pocket and went to work on one of the hinges.

I watched, fascinated. Getting through locked exterior doors without making a lot of noise or attracting attention was not easy. Not that it couldn't be done, but the people I'd known who did it specialized and did it quickly. This guy seemed to be clueless. And he wasn't paying any attention to anything going on around him, or he would have noticed me.

Why would anyone want to break into the Tabernacle? Not my concern. But I did wish he'd get going, one way or another, so I could see if the wallets were still there and get back to my book.

Evidently frustrated with his unsuccessful efforts to remove the hinge pin, he stepped back from the door and ran his hand over the door-frame. Then he moved down the alley toward me, still scrutinizing the brick wall.

I was about to retreat to the recessed entryway again when he stopped at the window to my place and inserted the blade of the screwdriver between the sashes.

He was trying to break into *my* place. I had no idea what he was hoping to gain, but I wasn't standing by and letting that go unchallenged.

I slid up behind him. He concentrated on his task and didn't notice me. I slipped one hand into his collar. I brought the other hand up under his chin and jerked his head back toward me.

As he tumbled backward, I sidestepped and got out of his way. He landed on his back on the asphalt. I raised my fists and drew my foot back, ready to kick him if he grabbed for me.

He let out a cry and covered his face with his hands.

Aaron.

I kicked the screwdriver down the alley so he couldn't get hold of it and stood over him. "What the hell are you doing?" I demanded.

"Don't hurt me!" He rolled over onto his side and curled up in a ball.

Reaching down, I took hold of the front of his shirt and lifted him to his feet. Glancing behind me to make sure no one was in sight, I slammed him back up against the wall. "I asked you, what the hell are you doing?"

He looked at me and sobbed. "Jesse."

"Yeah. Jesse. You try to break into my place?"

His eyes opened wide. "Your place? I thought that led to the church basement."

"The door you couldn't get through does go to the Tabernacle. But my apartment's in the basement and the window goes to my apartment."

"I didn't know. I thought it went to the church."

"So you was trying to break into the Tabernacle?"

"Yeah. Most of the people are at some kind of feast at Father Peter's place. Zee told me it'd be a good time to break in."

"What for?"

"What d'ya mean, what for?"

"Even a moron like you would need a reason to try to break in someplace."

"Oh. Yeah. Well, Zee says they got some expensive jewelry in there."

"Jewelry?"

"Yeah. He says Father Peter used to work in a jewelry store. The owner was an old guy, and he couldn't really run the store any more. So they took some of the most valuable jewels."

"What makes this Zee think that Father Peter didn't just go pawn the jewelry?"

"I guess he did most of it. That's what he used to start up the Tabernacle. But he kept some unusual pieces. The kind that would be really noticeable if he tried to pawn it. Zee says they're hidden in the church somewhere."

"How could you go searching in there? I thought they always left somebody in there. Praying or meditating or whatever."

"Yeah. They left that dumb kid Isaac. Zee said he would probably be asleep. If he wasn't, I was supposed to hit him over the head."

I looked at him with contempt.

"Look." He rubbed his nose. "I'm sorry about the mistake with the window. I *really* didn't know it went to your place."

I just kept my silence and continued looking at him. Finally I said, "What else you got to tell me?"

"Okay." He licked his lips. "I was supposed to get a gun Zee says was hid in there, too."

"What did you need a gun for?"

"I dunno."

Cocking my head to the side, I lifted my right fist.

"Don't hit me, Jesse. You got me good the other night."

"Not good enough, it looks like."

"Look," Aaron said. "I got to ask you about the guys' wallets."

"What about them?"

Aaron sniffed. "They figure you took the cash. But they was hoping they could get the driver's licenses back. They're a pain to replace."

"What about the credit cards and stuff?"

He winced. "Didn't you fence them?"

"What makes you think I might of done that?"

"Well, I thought you might not want to take a chance using them yourself, but you might try to make some money off them. You wouldn't have any problem finding someone to take them off your hands."

"So did they do the smart thing and cancel the cards?"

Aaron looked confused. "What?"

"The smart thing to do is tell the credit card companies and the banks that your cards are missing any they should cancel them so can't nobody use them."

"Oh."

"How are they doing?"

"Who?"

Dealing with someone whose brains are scrambled by drugs can be frustrating. "Your buddies. Clay and Marcus and Ramon."

"Them." A quick grin crossed Aaron's face. "You sure showed them."

Like he hadn't been part of it. "Why'd they want to bother me anyhow?"

He shrugged. "Marcus gets his reefer from some guy at that bar. And the guy got busted. So he got mad. And the madder he got, the more he drank. And the drunker he got, the more he thought maybe you'd snitched them out. Then we're walking down the street from the bar and there you are in the Laundromat."

"What did he think I'd snitched him out for?"

"For when you caught them with that blunt at work that night."

"How would that get his dealer busted?"

"I dunno. He just thought that."

"And he came to that conclusion with no help from you?"

Aaron looked stricken. "Why would you think that?"

"Just a hunch."

Nervously, he licked his lips. "I got to be going."

"Not yet, you don't. You got some more stuff to tell me."

His hand went to his neck. "No."

"None of you guys showed up for work on Thursday or Friday. We was real short-handed. They gonna come next week?"

"Yeah. They're okay, mostly. We all went to the emergency room. Said we'd been in an accident."

"Did they believe you?"

"No. But what could they do. Where'd you learn to fight like that?"

Even Aaron couldn't be that dumb, could he? "You believe I got all kinds of connections from when I was locked up to get drugs or fence stolen goods, but you don't think I learned to fight?"

"I dunno."

"I was a sixteen-year-old kid when I got locked up in an adult prison. You think I would have survived if I hadn't learned to fight?"

He looked down at his feet. "I guess not."

"At the rate you're going, you're gonna get hurt."

Aaron backed up a step. "Is that a threat?"

I shook my head. "No. It's a prediction. Stop trying to play these games."

"What games?"

"Telling people I'm a snitch."

"I was mad at you when I said that. I didn't really mean it."

"But Clay and them guys didn't know that. Did you ever tell them you were lying?"

"No. They'd be mad at me."

"And they're not mad at you now?"

"Well, yeah, but they're mad at you more."

"I can't help that. What was you going to do with the gun?"

"The gun?"

"Yeah. The one Zee said was hidden somewhere in the Tabernacle."

"I dunno. Sell it, maybe."

I took a menacing step toward him.

"Okay, okay." Aaron raised his arm to shield his neck. "Zee wanted it 'cause he wanted to go to the old man's place and get some stuff he'd hid there."

"The same old man whose wife died?"

"The one who you went to the funeral? I think so."

"He's just an old man. Not very strong. What'd he need a gun for?"

"He said the old man'd bought a shotgun."

That didn't sound like Mr. Coleman. "Why'd he buy a shotgun?"

"Protection. Zee was over there a lot. He took me a few times. At first the old lady was happy to see him. She'd fix frozen pizzas for us. We did some chores for her. Zee told her he'd paint the garage."

I recalled the half-painted garage. "Then what?" I asked.

"What d'ya mean?"

"You said she was happy to see him *at first*. What happened?"

"Then she found out he was screwing the housekeeper. And he'd make the old lady give him money. And some meds. Both her and the old man had some kind of good painkiller. Oxys, I think."

"Why would she give him anything?"

"He said she owed him."

That was what Aaron had said before. "How old is Zee?"

"I dunno. A little older than me. Not much."

The only way I could make sense of the "owed me" idea was if Zee was the baby Mrs. Coleman had given up for adoption. Even then, it wouldn't really make sense. But unless Zee were considerably older than Aaron—in fact, considerably older than me—he couldn't possibly be that baby. "Did you know this housekeeper?"

"Not really. He went over a lot without me. Until Father Peter got suspicious and started keeping a closer eye on him."

"Why was the housekeeper letting him screw her?"

"She was working under the table. No green card. She was hoping Zee would marry her."

Sad what some people would do to try to get legal status. "So you was gonna go over with the gun and take some more of the meds? Supposed the old man needed them for himself?"

"Well, Zee said he'd hid a lot of the meds in the garage. I'm supposed to get them, then see if I can get the ones from the house."

"Why'd he hide any in the garage?"

"He did that when the old lady got pushed down the stairs. He thought the housekeeper was gonna call 9-1-1, and he didn't want to have anything on him if he got stopped."

I shook my head. "You're just making things worse for yourself, especially threatening an old man with a gun."

"Zee said the old man isn't in his right head. He said he'd fix it so he thought I was you. Then you'd get blamed."

"How was he gonna do that?"

A car passed. Aaron's eyes darted hopefully toward the alley entrance. The car kept going. Aaron licked his chapped lips. "I'm not sure of all of it. But he said I should tell the old man I was Jesse. Not too many people named Jesse."

"I ought to just kill you now. And dump your body."

Aaron's face twisted in misery. "You don't understand."

"Damn straight I don't understand. You got a drug problem. No real shame there. Lots of people got problems like that. But you got to get a grip on yourself and tackle it."

He shifted his weight from one foot to the other. "You gonna let me go?"

"You gonna leave the old man alone?"

"*I* will. But I can't speak for Zee."

I knew I couldn't believe that. If Zee put him up to it, Aaron would be out at Mr. Coleman's, flashing the gun around and demanding his meds. And if Mr. Coleman really had a shotgun, somebody was likely to get hurt. It wouldn't bother me much if it was Aaron or some of his buddies, but I didn't want to see Mr. Coleman in any worse shape than he already was.

"I promise I won't say nothing more about you being a snitch."

Like I could really believe that. "You can go," I said. "But don't let me catch you around here again. Or at the Coleman house."

"I'll stay away."

"Go on. Get out of here."

Aaron eased away from the wall and started toward the street. I followed him to make sure he left.

At the entrance to the alley, he paused and looked back at me. "What should I tell the guys about their driver's licenses and stuff?"

"I'll *think* about getting it back to them at work Monday."

"Okay." He looked beyond me and strode abruptly away.

I turned in the direction he was looking. A small group of the Brethren in their saffron robes were approaching the stairs that lead up to the Tabernacle. They had the little boy with them, although he was dressed in regular clothes and a warm jacket. Aaron walked rapidly toward the little knot of flowing robes. The group split as he approached, half going on either side of him. They barely slowed down.

Except for the last one in the group, a tall thin young man with an acne-covered face. He hesitated ever so slightly, and his hand hovered near Aaron's shoulder, but Aaron shook his head and stuffed his own hands more firmly into his pockets. Was he selling drugs to cult members?

Why would a cult member be into drugs? Or more suspiciously, why would a drug user be a member of that weird cult?

Aaron continued walking down the street.

Was that the infamous Zee? Had he really seen Rosa or whatever her name was shove Mrs. Coleman down the stairs? According to Mr. Coleman, she had been there when Mrs. Coleman died. And had not been back since.

But Mr. Coleman wasn't a much more reliable source of information than Aaron. If I could come up with something reasonable, I could pass the information on to Detective Montgomery. Maybe it would take some of the suspicion off me.

The Brethren swept past me heading to the stairs. One of them bowed his head slightly in my direction. Isaac.

CHAPTER 17

I waited for a little while after the street and the alley were empty and checked under the dumpster. The wallets were still there, taped securely.

Now I could go back inside and concentrate on the book.

Only what would I do with the wallets? I had to do *something* with them by the time the truck came to empty the dumpster. I didn't feel like I owed those guys much consideration after what they'd tried to do to me, but I wasn't a thief.

And could I believe what Aaron was saying about going over to Coleman's house with a gun? To get oxys Zee had hidden in the garage. Was this the same gun Isaac had talked about? Aaron's mind was badly messed up, and he was a far from reliable source of information, but I was at this point inclined to think that this Zee character really did exist outside of Aaron's imagination.

I considered calling Detective Montgomery and telling him what I'd pieced together so far. He'd investigate, for sure. But he'd want to find out how I knew this stuff and what my involvement was. I wasn't sure how much I could tell him without getting in trouble myself.

Maybe I should just remove the temptation. Go see if I could find the oxys myself and let Aaron know there was no reason for him or anyone else to go looking for them.

Finally I gave up trying to read and turned out the light. Tomorrow I'd go scout out Mr. Coleman's garage. Early, when there would be less of a chance of someone noticing me.

I was up before daybreak and put on the heavy sweater under my hoodie. It was cold, and I wished I could wear my jacket, but I wasn't taking any chances on someone seeing it and describing it to the cops.

The streets were quiet. I'd timed the trip well. The sun was just rising, and I had enough light to see. On a Sunday morning, very few people would be going to work, and it was too early for church. I stuck close to the hedges that bordered the yard as I slipped down the driveway to the garage. First I tried the side door, but it was locked. The window, though, was cracked open a bit.

Placing my hands under the lower sash, I tried to heave it upward enough for me to climb in. It wouldn't move.

This was stupid. Suppose someone saw me trying to break into the garage? There'd be no explaining it away.

But the mental image of a crazed Aaron over here with a gun was worse. I gave the window another shove. With a wrenching sound, it flew upward.

I darted backward, diving under the sticker bushes. Had it been loud enough to attract attention? It had seemed really loud to me, but I'd been right next to it.

No one came running. No one shouted. The feeble morning light grew a bit stronger.

After a bit, I got to my feet, dashed to the window and scrambled in. I had to wait for my eyes to adjust to the interior dimness. I wasn't about to turn on the overhead light, although I might use a flashlight if I found one.

Where would someone hide pills? Aaron had said the dogs wouldn't be able to sniff them out. It couldn't just be that they thought no one would search the garage.

I moved away from the window and looked around. The car was covered with a layer of dust. The sticker on the license plate was over a year old. I eased myself around the side of the garage and looked at the shelves. Tools and gardening supplies and other stuff people tended to keep in the garage, all covered with dust.

One shelf had several cans of exterior paint in the same color as the half-painted garage and some old paint brushes that no one had bothered to clean. Hadn't Aaron said that Zee had been painting the garage? They shouldn't leave the paint out here in the cold weather. A deep paint tray gave off a pungent odor. Turpentine. An empty turpentine can lay on its side, the cap off. Why would anyone empty the turpentine into a paint tray?

I looked closer. Something square sat in the turpentine. I reached in and pulled it out. A plastic storage box, like for a sandwich. I shook it to get as much turpentine off it as I could, then tried to remove the top. It wouldn't budge.

I took a screwdriver. It punctured the side of the container, but it did pry the lid off.

The interior of the box was dry. Sure enough, several prescription drug bottles lay in the bottom. I held one up to the light. The name on the label was "Dennis Coleman." The medication was "oxycodone."

Wrapping the bottles in a rag, I shoved them into the kangaroo pocket of my hoodie.

Now I just had to get away with them and convince Aaron he had no reason to come back over here. Easiest way to do that was probably just bring the bottles, pills and all, and give them to Aaron.

There were three bottles, each half full. If they were oxys, they would bring at least thirty dollars a pill if Aaron sold them to his buddies. Or, more likely, kill him if he took too many himself.

Even if I didn't feel responsible for what happened to Aaron, I didn't want to be the one who supplied a fatal overdose. Besides, that could deliver a murder charge on top of a distribution charge.

Maybe my best bet would be to empty the pills down a storm drain or something and just bring him the empty bottles.

When I reached the end of the driveway, I stopped to look for anyone on the street. No cars, but someone was walking slowly down the side-walk away from me.

I could go around the other way. Tightening the hood so it would shield my face, I turned to walk past Coleman's house.

The front door was open. It was much too cold to leave it like that. I took a closer look at the figure hobbling away in the opposite direction. A man leaning heavily on a cane. Mr. Coleman?

I sprinted after him. Sure enough, it was Mr. Coleman. Once again, he had no coat or hat, just a shirt and pants. And the pants were wet.

When I got up next to him, my nose told me he'd wet himself.

What happened to the ladies who were supposed to be coming in to take care of him? Probably too early in the morning. Although he seemed to be beyond having part time household help. He seemed like he needed to be in a nursing home or some kind of residence.

I took him by the arm and turned him around toward the house.

When we got inside and the door closed, I steered him to a wooden chair in the kitchen. No point in sitting him on the upholstered furniture with urine-soaked pants. This time at least I knew who to call.

Mrs. Williams said of course she was up and dressed. She'd be right over.

Mr. Coleman's bottles of medication were on the counter, but they weren't in a nice neat row. In fact, some of them were lying on their sides with their caps off, pills spilling onto the counter.

Next to them was a compartmented plastic pill container, organized into days of the week and times of the day. The tops on a few compart-ments were popped open, but they were mostly full.

I took the bottles out of my pocket and studied the labels. They were all oxys, but one of them said Mildred Coleman. I put the two with Den-nis's name toward the back of the little collection.

The back door opened as Mrs. Williams let herself in. I slipped the other bottle back into my pocket. When she saw me, she frowned. "Aren't you the young man who was over last week? And found Dennis outside then, too?"

"Yes, ma'am."

"Jerry or Jeffrey or something."

"Yes, ma'am." I didn't correct her.

"I don't know what's gotten into him. Last time I thought he hadn't taken his meds or eaten, and he was dehydrated and disoriented. Usually he's quite lucid." She surveyed the counter with its pills. "Did he take his meds this morning?"

"I don't know, ma'am."

Her nose wrinkled as she got close to Mr. Coleman. "He needs a shower."

"Yes, ma'am."

"Do you want to help him get one?"

What I *really* wanted was to leave. But I said, "I guess."

"I'll fix something for him to eat. For you, too."

"I thought the people from the church were going to come over and help him out," I said, maneuvering him toward the bathroom off the master bedroom.

"Oh, they stop by, for sure. But you know how these church ladies are. Once they realize he's not wealthy and probably not interested in marrying one of them, they just do the bare minimum for him."

Granted, I didn't have much experience with church ladies, but I would have thought they were less interested in their own well-being and more in charitable works than that. But what did I know?

While I wasn't thrilled with the idea of helping Mr. Coleman wash up, he really did need a shower and clean clothes. And it was more appropriate for me than for Mrs. Williams to help him.

In the cramped bathroom, Mr. Coleman followed my instructions to unbutton his shirt. He was wearing leather slippers with a furry lining, so getting his shoes off wasn't a problem. I unbuckled his belt and watched as he unzipped his trousers and took them off. I had to tug his undershirt over his head.

I bundled the smelly clothes up and put them in an otherwise empty laundry hamper by the bedroom door.

The water seemed to take forever to reach a reasonable temperature, and I started to worry that the water heater wasn't working. I used the time to rifle through the dresser drawers and closets, finding clean underwear, shirts, and a folded pair of pants.

The drawers in Mrs. Coleman's dresser were still filled with her things. I slipped the remaining pill bottle under a stack of undergarments so sturdy I doubted they qualified as "lingerie."

Aaron would just have to take my word for it that the oxys were gone.

Mr. Coleman didn't seem to understand he had to step into the shower, so when the water had warmed up, I took his elbow and guided him in.

Not that different from helping fellow inmates clean up after they'd been in a fight, I told myself. If someone was all bloodied up but didn't want to go to the infirmary, we'd try to help him shower and get to his bunk without the COs noticing. Often a guy was trying to keep his disciplinary record clean, and having a report of a fight was a sure way to mess that up. And on the occasional case when one of the COs had gotten a little too free with his fists, the inmate often didn't want it reported, either.

I soaped up a washcloth and put it in his hand. Awkwardly, he followed my directions to lather up his body, spending extra time on the crotch and underarms. I rubbed a little shampoo on his sparse white locks. Then he stood under the shower, turning as I told him to, and rinsed off.

Once again I took his elbow and guided him out. I handed him a towel and watched as he dried himself off. His once-firm flesh sagged, covered by pale freckled skin. I toweled down his back where he had trouble reaching, and had him sit on the edge of the bed to so I could dry his feet well.

He struggled into his clothes. We didn't bother with a belt. I buttoned up his shirt for him and found another pair of slippers, identical to the first but looking cleaner and smelling fresher. He thrust his feet into them.

The kitchen smelled of baking biscuits and frying ham. Mrs. Williams looked up at me and smiled as I brought Mr. Coleman into the kitchen and sat him in a chair. She poured out two mugs of freshly made coffee. "The church ladies did bring food," she said. "They just didn't fix it for him."

Gratefully, I took a mug.

Mrs. Williams had gathered the meds from the counter. She looked at them and frowned.

"Would you be a dear and go get the list of his meds from the bathroom cabinet?" she asked me. "I think there should be a list taped inside the medicine cabinet door. Mildred always kept two lists there, one for each of them. I want to check it against what's here and see what he should be taking."

Obediently, I went back to the bathroom and carefully removed the list with his name on it. I put it on the table for Mrs. Williams.

She served up two big plates of fried ham, canned beans, and fresh biscuits. "I'm afraid that there were no eggs," she said apologetically.

I ate enthusiastically. Mr. Coleman picked at his food.

"These biscuits are wonderful, ma'am," I said, stuffing another one in my mouth.

She smiled. "I love to see a man with a good appetite."

She studied the list and the little bottles. After a few minutes, she took two bottles and shook a few of the little yellow tablets out on the table. "You have young eyes," she said. "Are these the same thing?"

I picked up one of each. "No," I said. "One's just a little bigger than the other. And they have different names on them."

"What do they say?"

"This one says 'Synthroid.'"

"Yes, that's his thyroid medication."

"And this one says 'Seroquel.'"

She frowned, studying the list. "I don't see Seroquel listed."

"What does it do?" I asked.

"It can be used as an anti-depressant."

"Maybe he got it after Mrs. Coleman died. You know, to help him cope."

"Maybe." Mrs. Williams picked up the bottle. "But the bottle doesn't *say* 'Seroquel.' It says 'Synthroid.'"

"Do you think he could be getting them mixed up?"

Instead of answering, Mrs. Williams pulled the compartmented pill container over to her and peered at it.

The container had four rows of seven compartments each. Each compartment had a hinged top. It looked like an abridged three dimensional multiplication table. I moved a bit closer. The rows were labeled *AM*, *Noon*, *PM*, and *Bedtime*. The little lids also had the days of the week printed on them.

Mrs. Williams started opening the lids. Some of them were empty, but others had pills in them. "He's not been taking them regularly," she said. "Maybe that's why he's so confused." She emptied the contents on the table and began to sort them.

I saw a number of Synthroid tablets, but no Seroquel ones, although they were hard to tell apart. She started sorting them into piles, then pulled the bottles over, and put each little hill of pills in front of its bottle.

Following the list carefully, she filled each little compartment with the appropriate pills. There weren't enough of the Synthroid ones, but the Seroquel didn't seem to go anywhere.

"May I have another biscuit?" I asked her.

"Of course. Have all you want. Put some butter and jam on them if you want."

I poured myself another mug of coffee, found a jar of raspberry preserves in the refrigerator, and slathered it on the biscuit. I'd bought myself some grape jelly, since it was the cheapest kind, but it had been years since I'd had any other flavor, and I'd forgotten how good it could be.

Mrs. Williams frowned again and picked up the bottle with the Seroquel pills that was labeled Synthroid. It was almost full. "This doesn't seem right," she said. "Seroquel could cause confusion. I wonder…"

"Can you call the doctor and check on those yellow pills?" I asked. "And see if he's supposed to be taking the thyroid stuff? They're almost gone. And the other bottle has the other kind in it."

"That could be a problem," Mrs. Williams said. "The doctor won't be able to discuss Dennis's medications with me. Confidentiality laws, you know."

"But Mr. Coleman isn't in any shape to figure out all these meds." I looked at the assortment in dismay.

"A common problem. I would imagine he'll end up in a nursing home one of these days soon. The church ladies will ultimately have to call social services."

I felt a pang in my chest. Wasn't a nursing home kind of like a prison? Maybe the people there pretended to be nicer, but a resident would have even less control over his life than any convict.

"And you said you're one of the Colemans' foster children?" Mrs. Williams asked.

"Yes, ma'am."

"I guess Mildred couldn't have children of her own. So she took in the foster children."

"I think she had one son, didn't she? Before she was married to Mr. Coleman?"

Mrs. Williams stopped what she was doing and stared at me. "I never knew that."

I probably shouldn't have told Mrs. Coleman's secret. After all, if she'd wanted the world to know, she would have said something. "I just thought so," I said meekly. "Maybe I'm wrong."

"Back then, of course, if it was before she was married, the baby would have been placed for adoption."

"Yes, ma'am."

"I wonder if that's why she was so compulsive about taking in children without homes. She wanted so badly to be a mother."

"Mrs. Coleman was the closest I ever had to a mother," I said.

Mrs. Williams raised her eyebrows. "Did you live here for long?"

"About five years."

"I thought the Colemans mostly did emergency foster care. Short term."

"I was an emergency placement when I was eight," I said. "But I had no place else to go, and Colemans kept me until my father could take me back." All he'd really wanted were the social security payments from the mother who'd died when I was a toddler, the food stamps, and the eligibility for Section 8 housing, I thought bitterly.

Mrs. Williams' brow was creased as she tried to remember. "I can only recall one long-term boy," she said. "A boy who went back to his own family when he was maybe fourteen or so. Mildred thought the world of him. Said he would amount to something despite the background. But then he killed somebody or something and went to prison. Tore her up something fierce. I think his name was Jesse."

I looked at the table top. "Yes, ma'am."

Her eyes widened. "You're *that* Jesse."

"Yes, ma'am."

She clutched the edge of the table, her knuckles white.

I got up. "I'll be going, ma'am. Thank you for the meal. And I hope you can see Mr. Coleman gets the help he needs."

I went out the door and headed back into town. I should've grabbed another biscuit on my way out.

CHAPTER 18

Isaac was sitting on the dirty asphalt in the alley, his hairy, spindly legs sticking out from under his saffron robes, the ends of which lay in a dank puddle. A cardboard box covered with a towel sat next to him on the cold pavement. His face was buried in his hands, and his shoulders shook.

Hesitantly, I went up to him. "Isaac?" I said. "You need some help, buddy?"

He didn't look up. "No."

"Well, man, you can't just sit out here in the alley. It's cold. Besides, it's gonna get dark soon. Somebody'll run you over."

"I don't care. Go away."

I looked at him for a minute, trying to figure out if I should just do as he said.

This was the guy who'd gone out of his way to make sure I got out of this same alley when I was too hurt to help myself.

I reached down and grabbed his arm. "Come on," I said, dragging him to his feet.

He didn't resist. I pulled him upright. He was a sad sight. The wet robes hung limply. His cheek was bruised above his beard, and he had a cut on his forehead. His bleary eyes swept over me. "I see you got your jacket back," he mumbled.

"What?"

He shivered. "Nothing."

"What about my jacket?"

"I guess I'm just confused." He swayed slightly.

I took hold of his arm, which trembled under my hand.

"What's in the box?"

"None of your business."

I pulled aside the towel. The cat huddled on the bottom, the kittens next to her. They'd grown quite a bit since I'd last seen them. "Why've you got them out here?"

A single tear rolled down Isaac's cheek. "It's a long story."

"Well, they can't stay out here. Neither can you."

Holding his elbow with one hand and tucking the box under my other arm, I propelled him out of the alley and down the stairs to my apartment where I deposited him on one of the decrepit chairs next to the kitchen table. I stuck my hand inside the box to see if it was wet, but the dampness hadn't yet seeped through the folded newspapers and piece of blanket in the bottom.

Isaac's eyes opened wide. "How come you can put your hand in there?" he asked.

"What d'ya mean?"

"She growls at me if I try to touch her. She'll bite if I don't move my hand quickly."

I shrugged and put the box on the floor, partway under the bed.

Isaac collapsed miserably, resting his head on the table. A shuddering sob escaped from deep in his narrow chest.

"You hungry?" I asked. I didn't know what or how much the cult ate, but it was pretty evident from the bony feel of his upper arm that Isaac, at least, didn't overeat.

He looked up hopefully, then lay his head down again. "No."

I opened a can of chili, dumped it in a pan on the stove and got out two bowls. When it was hot, I gave him a bowlful and tore open a loaf of bread, placing it on the table. I stuck spoons in each bowl and sat in the other chair. I began to eat.

Isaac sniffed. He lifted his head up and looked at his bowl.

I gestured with my spoon. "Go on, man. Whatever you decide to do, you need to keep your strength up."

Isaac reached over and pulled the bowl closer to him. He slowly put a spoonful in his mouth, then shoveled the rest of it in faster. He stuffed a piece of bread in his mouth and eyed the rest of the loaf.

"Have another piece," I said, getting up to make two mugs of instant coffee.

He took another piece and sopped up the remaining bits of chili in his bowl.

I made the coffee and put the mugs on the table. I sat down again and said, "So what's going on?"

Tears filled Isaac's eyes. "I got kicked out of the Tabernacle."

I scratched my chin. "I didn't know they did that."

"Oh, yes. I know I'm not the best disciple. But I try. And I *did* recover our goddess. You'd think that'd count for something. But they kicked her out, too." His eyes filled with tears.

I took a sip of the too-hot coffee. "I noticed. Why'd they do that?"

"Father Peter said she was losing her powers."

"Really?"

"Yeah. See, she used to have this bracelet or something on, like a collar. Father Peter said it concentrated the powers of the universe into her body. But when I brought her back, she didn't have the collar."

I remembered the collar. I'd taken it off the cat because it was so heavy, and she didn't seem to like it. I didn't remember taking it to the Tabernacle when we brought the cat and her kittens up there. It was probably still around here somewhere. "So what happened then?" I asked.

Isaac gulped. "Father Peter was praying about the collar. I know I should have kept my mouth shut. I have a lot to learn about humility. But I told Father Peter that the goddess seemed perfectly happy without the collar, and wasn't having the goddess back more important than the collar? We could maybe get her another one."

Made sense to me. "What'd he say?"

"He didn't say anything at first. Just hauled off and smacked me. I was surprised. He always says fasting and meditation, not violence, bring us answers. That's why he's always telling me I need to fast and pray."

I blew on my coffee. "I can see where that *would* be a surprise."

Isaac picked up his mug and warmed his hands on the hot sides. "Then he explained about the jewels on the collar concentrating the powers. And said that without the collar, the goddess might just as well be a regular cat."

I was pretty sure she *was* just a regular cat. I nodded.

"Then he accused me of *stealing* the collar. I said I hadn't seen it, and he hit me again." Tears overflowed his eyes and dripped down his cheeks. "He asked, if I pawned it, and he said that was stupid—it's a one-of-a-kind piece, and I'd get in trouble if I pawned it. He said I'd better get it back right away. I shouldn't come back to the Tabernacle until I had the collar to give him. He told me to leave. And to take the goddess with me. If I come back with the collar, he'll decide what my penance should be."

"Why penance? You didn't do anything wrong. Wasn't it Xavier or somebody who was there when the cat got out? And that's when she lost the collar, isn't it?"

"She didn't 'get out.' She faded away out of sight and reappeared somewhere else. And I was supposed to be there, watching her." Isaac bowed his head. "It was my turn to worship her overnight. She might not have left if I'd been where I was supposed to be."

It seemed to me that if the cat *had* faded away and reappeared somewhere else, she wouldn't have chosen a freezing outdoor stairwell. "But didn't you say Xavier told you he'd take care of it?"

"Yes. We didn't tell Father Peter, though. He'd've been mad."

"I'd think he'd be madder at Xavier than he was with you."

"You'd think. But Xavier gets away with *anything*."

"Why is that?"

"Well, he's Father Peter's natural son. And Father Peter says it's hard enough he has to share with the rest of us, he *should* get some breaks. Parents owe something to the children and grandchildren born to them. It's their natural right. And Xavier just wants what's due him. He said he and Xavier have been shortchanged all their lives by their natural parents."

If I looked around I could probably find the collar and give it to Isaac to bring back. But I wasn't so sure that would be the best thing for Isaac to do. "If he treats you bad and don't trust you no more than that, you sure you want to be a disciple or whatever?" I asked him.

Isaac took a deep breath. "Maybe not. But what else can I do?"

"Oh, I dunno. Maybe get an honest job and support yourself?"

He stared toward the single window where the daylight was fading. "Maybe. But how do I do that?"

I looked at him. He was skinny and probably poorly nourished. His hair hung below his shoulders, and his beard was overgrown and tangled. He was dressed in filthy robes and sandals. If he was kicked out of the Tabernacle, he had no place to stay. I doubted he had any money or ID or social security card. "You got no family you can go stay with?" I asked him.

He looked down at the table and shook his head. "My Mom died," he whispered. "OD'd, actually. There was nobody else. And now I'm eighteen, so I couldn't go into a foster home at this point. Even if I wanted to."

A dilemma I could sympathize with. "Look," I said. "First you got to decide whether you want to go back to the Tabernacle or not."

"They won't take me back unless I can find the collar," he wailed.

"I get that. That's what *they* say. What do *you* say?"

"What do you mean?"

"Do you *want* to stay in the Tabernacle or not? Completely apart from finding the collar or whether they'd ever take you back. Do you really want to live like that?"

He blinked rapidly. "They really aren't very nice to me, are they?"

"*I* don't think so." I took a swallow of my coffee. "But this isn't about what I think. It's about what you think. And what you want to do."

"And they're not likely to get any better, are they?"

"I'd bet not."

"So I'd be foolish to try to get back in."

"Your choice."

He leaned his elbows on the table and rested his chin in them. "Not much of a life there, is it?"

"I don't see it, myself."

"And no future to speak of."

"Not so's I can see."

Silence surrounded us, broken only by raindrops beginning to hit the glass of the window.

"And maybe the goddess is just a cat?" he said in a small voice.

"Maybe."

"So how do I go about doing something else?" he asked. "I mean, I got nothing, nowhere to go."

I'd faced the same questions when I was up for parole. But at least then, I had a place to sleep, even if it was a bunk in a prison cell. And the food, unappealing as it might be, was going to show up regularly, three times a day.

Isaac couldn't count on any of that.

"You probably got to go to the Rescue Mission," I said. "They got a shelter for homeless men."

He wrinkled his nose. "You mean down on Main Street? Next to Goodwill?"

"Yeah. They got a place for you to get a shower and sleep. They'll feed you. If you work with them, they'll help you find a job. Day labor at first, but it's money at the end of every day you work. It's a start."

Isaac looked down at his dirty robes. "Can I go in these? They'll think I'm a weirdo."

I refrained from saying that was *exactly* what they would think. With a great deal of justification. I got up and opened the drawers of my battered dresser.

Isaac was about my height. He was a lot thinner, but that couldn't be helped. I tossed a pair of jeans I'd gotten at Goodwill that were worn thin in the seat, and a grey hoodie that was a little small for me. I didn't know what the Brethren did for underwear, but whatever it was, Isaac would just have to keep on wearing that. Or go without.

My supply of clothes was pretty meager, especially the jeans. I only had two other pairs. I'd have to do the laundry more often if I had to wear one pair of pants while I washed the other. But Isaac had less than I did. When I got paid again, I could go to the Goodwill store again and see if they had any in my size.

"Go take a hot shower," I said. "And put this stuff on. You'll have to wear the sandals, though. All I got is my work boots."

A half hour later, Isaac stood in front of me, dressed in the jeans and sweatshirt. He'd trimmed his bushy beard. I handed him a hair band,

and he pulled his flowing, but now clean, hair back behind his head. He looked hollow and gaunt, but he was clean, and he was dressed reasonably. He looked only a little demented, not totally crazy like he had before.

"You sure you want to do this?" I asked, giving him a chance to change his mind. We could always look for the collar if he wanted to go back. I had no doubt it was around here somewhere.

Isaac nodded. "I'm sure. I've thought about it. I don't think I'd *ever* really be a son of the Tabernacle. Not as long as Father Peter's in charge. He doesn't really like me. If someone else took over, as long as it wasn't Xavier…" His voice trailed off.

I didn't say that there probably wouldn't *be* any Tabernacle if it wasn't for Father Peter. Crazies like that don't come around often, and when they do, they usually have their own ideas.

He stood by the door, tugging on the sleeve of the hoodie and staring at the empty bowls on the table, then he turned to face me. "Thanks."

"I won't pretend it'll be easy, and it'll take you a good while, but you'll be all right, Isaac," I said, holding my hand out. "Good luck."

He took my hand. "My name," he said, "is Roger."

CHAPTER 19

Looked like I was back in the cat tending business. I fixed up the litter pan again and put some dry food in a bowl. Maybe I could spring for another half-gallon of milk tomorrow.

My midnight shift would come around soon enough, and I needed to be alert. I straightened up my room, set my clock and lay down to catch as much sleep as I could.

A shrill noise woke me up before the clock went off. I lay there for a minute, trying to place the unfamiliar sound. Some kind of alarm?

The phone. I'd had to get the phone when I was on home detention. Then it would ring every once in a while when whoever was monitoring the signals from the ankle box decided to check on me. The installation was really expensive, so I'd left it in, even though I had to pay a monthly bill, in case I was returned to home detention and needed it again.

But I'd never in my entire life gotten a personal phone call.

How crazy would a telemarketer have to be to call this time of night? Had to be a wrong number.

I struggled up anyhow and answered it. "Hello?"

"Jesse?" a female voice asked.

"Kelly?" I said cautiously.

"Yeah. Were you sleeping?" Her words were slurred.

"Yep. Have to be at work tonight. You should be, too."

"Are you mad that I called?"

"No. How'd you get the number, though?"

"You wrote it down for me once. Said to call whenever I wanted to."

"Oh."

"And now I wanted to."

"Okay."

"Can you come over, Jesse?" she asked.

That caught me off guard. "I thought you wanted me to stay away. You even told me that in front of a cop. Remember?"

"Yeah. Well, I been thinking." That slurring again.

"Thinking or drinking?"

"Both."

This wasn't good. "Kelly, we got to be at work—" I checked the clock "—in less than two hours. Why aren't you asleep?"

She didn't answer for a minute.

"Kelly?" I said.

"I'd get fired if I went to work like this," she said. "I've had too much to drink to drive a forklift."

"Well, at least you know that."

"Can you come over here?" she asked again.

"I don't think I could make it to your place and still get to work by midnight."

"You could skip work."

I couldn't see that would help either of us. "I can't, Kelly. Tonight it'll be three months since I got hired. First night I won't be a probationary employee. I don't know what'd happen if I didn't show up." Nothing good, I was sure.

She sobbed. "I'm so *lonely,* Jesse."

"That's the alcohol talking, Kelly. You'll be fine." My stomach tightened. If I went over now, we'd be in bed in an hour. Guaranteed. Was there *any* way I could skip work tonight?

"No, I won't. I'm gonna miss work again, and I can't afford that."

"Show up drunk, and you get fired. Stay home."

"I have a custody hearing tomorrow for the kids."

"Then get a good night's sleep. Where are they now?"

"In bed. I didn't *really* start drinking until they were asleep."

"That's good, at least." I wasn't sure it was entirely true.

"And that new system at work is messing me up bad."

"What? The new forms? I know they're a pain. But why are you getting all bent out of shape over something stupid like that?"

"That's what I wanted to talk to you about."

Talking wasn't what was on my mind. "I *got* to go to work tonight. You get some sleep. Get the kids up and on the bus. I'll come over as soon as I get off work, okay?" Would she still be feeling "lonely" then? I hoped so.

"I don't know if I can do it, Jesse."

"You can do it. You just got to stop drinking *now* and be ready in the morning."

Her voice broke. "It's no use."

I gripped the phone and tried to keep my breath and my voice steady. Was she suicidal? She was strong, and I couldn't see her as that type. But then, what *was* the suicidal type?

"Look, Kelly. The kids need their mother. That's you. And tomorrow morning, they need you to be clean and sober."

"You don't understand!"

"Maybe I don't. But I *do* understand that you need to get a grip and stop feeling sorry for yourself. For Brianna and Chris. And for you."

All I heard in response was a few heaving sobs. Maudlin drunk stage. Even if I went over, there wouldn't be much I could do to help. She'd probably be asleep by the time I got there, anyhow.

"I'll be there in the morning," I said again. "Then we can see what's up with work. And get you to the hearing on time." And see if we could squeeze in a quick romp in her bed.

She sobbed once again. "I guess."

Maybe in the morning she'd be more sober, and I could make some sense out of everything.

Or maybe she'd forget she told me to come over and call 9-1-1 when she saw me on her porch.

I wasn't going to get any more sleep, so I got dressed and made a couple of peanut butter sandwiches for lunch.

What was I going to do about the wallets? Checking to make sure no one was around, especially that mysterious box truck, I went into alley and pulled them free from beneath the dumpster.

Getting caught with them wouldn't be good. Even if they hadn't been reported stolen, I would never be able to come up with an acceptable reason for having four wallets that didn't belong to me. And four sets of ID.

I tucked them into the voluminous pockets of my jacket and set out for work early. They'd fit through the slot under the window in the time-keeper's office and they'd end up in the lost-and-found box. If any of them said anything, I'd tell them where to go look. If not, sooner or later somebody would look in them and figure out who they belonged to.

That didn't take as long as I thought it would. When John came out of the office, he had a plastic shopping bag in addition to his usual clipboard.

When Ramon, who worked four to midnight, drove by on his lift, John waved him over. He checked the ID in the wallet and handed it over to him. Ramon flipped it open and stared at the cash and cards still in place, disbelief on his face. John held up all the sets of keys, and Ramon took one.

Then when Marcus showed up, the bruises fading and the swelling on his face almost gone, John repeated the process.

I didn't wait to see Clay and Aaron come in.

Because Kelly was out, I had to handle the trucks at the loading docks in addition to whatever loads John couldn't move with a hand lift, so I didn't have much time to worry about anything else. I did ask Hank, the plating room lead, to stash my lunchbox in his locked office.

Midway through the shift, John found me and handed me a union card and a health insurance card. "Congratulations," he said. "You made it."

I thanked him and put them in my wallet.

When I picked up a full pallet of heavy cabinets from Clay's plater, he didn't stop work—that would be next to impossible while the plater ran—but he did look at me with a thoughtful frown. The noise level prevented either of us from making any comments, which was fine with me.

Aaron never did show up.

At the end of the shift, I got the lift plugged in and made myself go through the checkout carefully, but I did it as fast as I could. I needed to get over to Kelly's as soon as I could.

Still pulling my jacket on, I hurried out the factory door.

To see Clay and Marcus waiting for me.

I didn't need this.

They stepped forward.

Shrugging my jacket over my shoulders, I felt for my gloves. They wouldn't provide much protection for my hands, but they'd help a little. Maybe keep my knuckles from getting all skinned up.

I moved next to the building. With the wall beside me, they couldn't attack from that side, at least. Maybe I could slide past them.

Wasn't gonna happen.

I stopped, keeping the wall to my back. Were they really going to make an issue of things here? It was daylight. People walked past at the end of the block. A tractor trailer slowed as it rounded the corner, positioning itself to ease through the shipping yard and back into a loading bay. A damn *patrol car* cruised by. We'd all get in trouble. Were these guys crazy?

Marcus shifted nervously from one foot to the other, not meeting my gaze.

Clay looked over his shoulder, than back at me. "You gave us back our wallets."

"Yeah." Where was this going?

"With all the cards and everything. Even the cash."

"Yeah. What of it?"

"We thought you'd take whatever you could use or sell."

I glared back at them. "I may be on parole for a *murder* conviction, but I ain't no thief."

"And you never reported nothing. Not the fight. Not the blunt we was smoking at work."

"Well, I ain't gonna start nothing. But I ain't no snitch, neither."

They glanced at each other. "We was wrong about you. Sorry about that, man."

I shrugged and turned away.

Clay called after me, "And sorry about that little incident in the warehouse. At least nobody was hurt."

That made twice recently somebody'd apologized to me. A new record.

The streets were clear, but mounds of dirty snow were piled at the corners. Melted snow had puddled in depressions on the sidewalks and frozen overnight into slick patches. As I walked, I pictured taking Kelly, soft and warm from a shower and wrapped in her bathrobe, into my arms and burying my face in her soft fragrant hair. I'd need to grab a quick shower myself, of course, after working all night, but that would only heighten the anticipation.

No lights showed through the windows at Kelly's house. I went up to the front door and rang the bell.

Chris opened it. Not good. Forget any tumbles in bed, quick or otherwise.

"Did you miss the school bus?" I asked.

He shrugged. "Brianna won't get ready again."

"Where's your mom?"

"She didn't get up yet."

Keeping a few choice words to myself, I went in.

Brianna, still in her pajamas and her hair a mess, was sitting at the kitchen table, two Pop-Tarts and a glass of milk in front of her. "I don't *like* chocolate Pop-Tarts," she said. "I only like strawberry ones. With frosting and sprinkles."

Chris rolled his eyes. "We don't *have* any strawberry."

What did Kelly think she was doing? Frustrated, I took the stairs two at a time and threw open the half-closed door to her room.

She lay face down, the bedding tangled around her. The room smelled of spilled whiskey.

I shook her arm. "Kelly! What are you *doing*? You got a hearing this morning. And the kids aren't even in school."

She stirred but didn't raise her head. "Let me sleep."

"You lose custody, you can sleep in whenever you want."

She rolled over and squinted at me. "What?"

"You gonna get up and get your kids to school so you can make the custody hearing?"

"I feel sick. I'll call and tell them I can't make the hearing."

"You do that and they'll probably hold the hearing anyhow. You just won't be able to present your side."

She sat up and started crying. "I can't do this."

"You *have* to do this."

"I don't *have* to do anything."

"You do if you want to keep what you got."

Anger flared in her eyes. "And I suppose *you're* so successful you can tell me what I should be doing."

I took a deep breath. I could just leave. Or I could try to reason with her, unreasonable as she was right now. Meeting anger with anger would do no one any good. "I don't got kids. I don't got near as much to lose as you do," I said. Just my freedom.

"So what?"

I looked down at her in disgust. "You got two great kids. You got a decent job. You got a nice house and a car. You're working on losing all that. So you can drink. Your choice, but make sure you're ready to live with the choice you make."

"I'm gonna throw up."

"So get into the bathroom. And when you're done puking, take a shower."

She rushed past me and slammed the bathroom door. From behind the closed door, I heard retching sounds. I headed downstairs to get the kids ready. Definitely not the morning I'd hoped for.

The kids went to get dressed. I made two mugs of instant coffee, cleaned up the kitchen, and started packing two lunches for school.

When everyone, Kelly included, was assembled in the kitchen, I handed the kids their backpacks. "All set?"

No one looked particularly cheery.

Chris was carrying a long, awkward shape wrapped in a beach towel.

"The solar system project?" I asked.

"Yeah. I brought it home to finish over the weekend."

It was long and clumsy. Maybe just as well he wasn't trying to carry it on the bus.

I helped Brianna with the zipper on her jacket and fastened my own.

Kelly put her hand to her forehead. "I *really* can't drive, Jesse."

"Well, *I* can't drive. What time is your hearing?"

"I dunno. This morning."

"You got the papers?"

She reached into her bag and handed me the envelope. I pulled the summons out and scanned it. "Holy shit, Kelly. It's for nine thirty. That's in, like, ten minutes."

We bundled out the door and into the car. Kelly fumbled with her keys and backed out of the driveway.

"You'd better just drop us off at the school and take off for the court-house," I said. "I'll sign the kids in."

Kelly turned sad eyes toward me. "I blew this good, didn't I?"

"We got no time for that nonsense. We can talk it out later if you want to. Right now you got to show up in court. And be able to tell them the kids are in school, where they belong."

She looked at the road again. "And I got to do something about work."

"Like show up? You sure do."

"No, I mean about that new system."

I looked at her. "Why are you so bent out of shape about the damn new system? Things change. We learn the system. Shouldn't be any big deal."

A sob escaped from her. "It is to me."

"What d'ya mean?"

Angrily, she wiped her eyes. "I worked so damn hard to be able to do that damn job."

I didn't see it was *that* difficult, but I just said, "Yeah. So?"

"So just when I think I've just about got it down pat, they go and *change* everything."

"Just changed the paperwork. What's the big deal?"

She gripped the steering wheel. Her knuckles turned white. "Jesse. I can't read."

"You can't read?" I repeated stupidly.

"Yeah. So I got all the packing slips and bills of lading figured out, where the stock numbers are and where the quantities are. And then they *change* them. And put all this extra crap on the paper so I can't find what I need."

I remembered the root basket shipment we'd messed up. "Does John know that?" I asked.

"Hell, no. He thinks you *got* to be able to read to do most of those jobs. I'm not gonna tell him."

Closing my eyes, I tried to picture what the paperwork looked like. Lots of verbiage. Lots of numbers. Complicated.

"Look," I said. "We'll worry about that later. There isn't *that* much in writing on our shift. Maybe we can show up a few minutes earlier and go over them together."

"You'd do that for me?"

"Sure. But that's not the biggest problem now."

"Oh?"

"You getting to the hearing is."

We pulled into the school's parking lot. The last of the buses was leaving. A big white van pulled into a handicapped space, its engine idling.

"Should I wait for you?" Kelly asked.

"No. You get to the courthouse."

"Are you gonna come over later?"

"To your place?"

"Yeah."

"Okay." Maybe there was some hope to salvage some time in bed with Kelly yet today.

CHAPTER 20

Wind whipped across the school parking lot as Kelly drove off. Chris was struggling to hang onto his project, so I took it.

A swirling gust tore Brianna's hat from her head and sent it skittering across the pavement and under the van parked in the handicapped space.

Brianna clutched at her head. "My hat!"

"Let's get you and Chris up on the sidewalk. Then I'll see if I can't get your hat."

Chris headed for the sidewalk, but Brianna just stood there, staring at the spot where her hat had disappeared. I tugged on her hand. She didn't move.

Sighing, I scooped her up and hurried to catch up to Chris. "Hold her hand," I told him as I deposited her next to him.

I went down on my knees next to the van and peered underneath. I could see the hat, but I couldn't reach it. I went around to the other side. Putting Chris's project down and lying on the cold damp asphalt, I inched my head and shoulders under the van until I could just snag it.

As I grabbed the project and stood up, a movement around the side of the building caught my eye, but when I turned and looked, I couldn't see anything.

The kids were looking toward that side of the building as I came up to them.

I handed the hat to Brianna. "Hang onto it."

Chris looked at me and then back to the corner of the building. "Weren't you just over there?"

"No. I was getting Brianna's hat from under the van."

"I thought I saw you around there."

"Must have been somebody else."

"But he had on *your* jacket."

"I got my jacket right here, on me. Must have been a jacket like mine."

"I guess."

Brianna still didn't want to move, so I switched Chris's project to one hand and lifted her up.

"You're getting too big for people to carry, honey," I said.

The same ladies as last time were in the office, including Mrs. O'Neill. She looked us over and raised her eyebrows. "I suppose Mrs. Mathias is sick again?" she said.

"Yes, ma'am." I didn't have much else to say.

"We're not very late this time," Chris said.

"Almost a half hour." Mrs. O'Neill turned toward us. Her lips were pursed, and I noticed the hand that clenched her clipboard was white. She had a funny look on her face. "How fortunate that Mr. Damon is able to bring you to school."

I wondered if she'd looked up information on me since my last visit. My conviction was, of course, public record.

A phone rang in the back office, a kind of funny ring. The secretary got up and went to answer it. She hung up, looked hard at me, picked up the receiver again and without putting it to her ear she punched in a short number.

Was she calling 9-1-1? I didn't see why, unless she was of the opinion that I was on the sex offender registry. Then I would not be permitted within so many feet of a school, and here I was *in* a school. But I wasn't a sex offender, and I wasn't required to register.

"Can we go to class?" Chris asked.

"As soon as Ms. Rivers gets back and can get you signed in," Mrs. O'Neill said. Her voice quivered. "She needs to write a late pass for you."

Ms. Rivers showed no sign of returning to the counter.

Two men came down the hallway and into the office. One was dressed in a suit and tie, the other wore sweats and had a whistle on a lanyard around his neck. Probably the gym teacher. Both of them were big men, towering over me. They stood on either side of the door, watching us as Mrs. O'Neill fumbled with the clipboard. The gym teacher bounced gently on the balls of his feet. He held his hands at his sides, but both of them formed fists.

I shifted Brianna's weight in my arms uneasily. Hairs on the back of my neck prickled; I wanted to be out of there. But I didn't want to upset the kids.

Chris set his backpack on the floor and unzipped his jacket.

"You want this?" I asked him, holding out the wrapped solar system project.

Mrs. O'Neill screamed and fled into the back office.

Chris grabbed my leg. His face was white and drawn.

I eased Brianna down to the floor. "Stand up, honey," I said. "You and Chris go on to your classrooms."

"We need our late passes," Chris said in a small voice. His hand clutched the hem of my jacket.

"I don't think you need to wait for the passes," I said, trying to make eye contact with the man in the suit. "Somebody will bring them down later if they need them."

Just as the big man nodded, we heard a sharp retort and the sound of glass shattering from the front entrance.

The two men bolted out the office door into the hallway.

The public address system crackled to life. "Code red. This is a code red. This is not a drill."

Couldn't be good. I might be in real trouble. For what, I didn't know.

A hall monitor dashed into the office, eyes opening wide as she looked at me. She darted toward the back office.

From outside, I could hear a siren screaming, heading in this direction.

"Take the kids with you," I said, pushing Chris and Brianna toward the women beyond the door. Whatever was going on, I didn't want them to be part of it.

The door slammed before the kids could get there.

I heard a burst of what sounded like automatic gunfire. A lone figure ran down the hallway by the office, with what looked like an AK-47. He was dressed in black except for his jacket, which was a red and black buffalo plaid hunter's jacket.

Just like mine.

He kept running down the hall, past the office.

The siren whined to a halt out in front.

I looked around. The kids were clinging to me. I *had* to get them someplace safe.

A female uniformed police officer appeared in front of the office, followed by several men, not in uniform but looking very much ready to take charge of the situation. They skidded to a halt, their guns drawn, and looked straight at me.

"Put it down."

What? I looked at my hands. The solar system project. I tossed it to the floor, trying to get it away from us.

One of the men swiped at it with his boot and kicked it away from us.

No one said to, but I clasped my hands behind my head and spread my feet.

"Don't move," the woman said.

"Yes, ma'am," I said. "Let the kids move away, though."

She stood silently, her left hand steadying her right, which held the gun.

"Chris. Brianna. Get under the desk," I said.

Chris let go of my jacket and took a step toward the secretary's desk. Brianna held on tighter.

"Chris. Come get Brianna. She *has* to go with you."

Chris's frightened eyes looked up at mine. "Get her, Chris," I said. "Now. Go sit under the desk and pull the chair in behind you."

He grabbed Brianna by the arm and pulled her toward the desk. She whimpered.

"Go, Brianna," I said.

As soon as the kids were no longing clinging to me, one of the men tackled me, sending me flat on the floor. I fell hard, smashing my already battered face into the floor, but I didn't resist.

I felt a knee in the small of my back. My hands were jerked back, and I felt the cold familiar bite of handcuffs.

"How many of you are there?"

I tried to make sense of the question. "I don't know what you mean."

I felt something jam into my neck just below my ear. Something metal. The muzzle of a gun? Good bet. The knee was still in my back, and someone was now holding my legs down.

"How many of your buddies are running around this school?" he asked.

I swallowed hard. "I'm by myself. Except for the kids."

"I'm not afraid to use this," he warned, shoving the gun harder into my neck. "We're in an 'active shooter' alert; that means we go by military standards, not civilian police. Shoot first and ask questions later."

But he *was* asking questions. Questions I couldn't answer. I fought down an urge to try to scramble to my feet and make a run for it. That would probably be a fatal move. I closed my eyes and wondered how quickly I could figure out how to pray. Or if there was anyone out there willing to listen to me if I tried.

"We got your one buddy. The one doing the shooting. And we've got you. Are there any more of you?"

I didn't have an answer for him, so I didn't say anything.

"Let's get him away from the women and children," someone said.

The knee left the small of my back, but my legs were twisted up behind me. I felt something tighten around my ankles, just above my boots. It didn't feel like regular leg irons. Probably those plastic disposable ones the cops carried.

Time seemed to stop, although I bet it was only a few seconds until I heard more boot-steps come into the office. I opened my eyes without moving a muscle. I was surrounded in all directions by polished boots, inches from my body and face. If they smashed into me, they'd do a lot of damage.

"What've we got here?" The words came from over by the door.

"One of the invaders," the man with the gun said as he shoved it harder beneath my ear. I felt the gun waver as he turned. I hoped he had a steady hand.

"Was he armed?"

"Over here," someone else said. "Wrapped in this towel. We haven't looked to see what it is."

I wanted to say, "A science project of the solar system," but I didn't think anybody would listen to me anyhow.

"Let's get him up."

Rough hands hauled me to my feet. The effort wasn't well coordinated—the guy leaning on my legs didn't let go until I was halfway up.

I was suspended by two men holding my arms as my legs tried to catch up with the rest of me. I finally managed to get my feet under me and stood up. I left a small pool of blood behind on the floor. Blood dripped down my throat, and if my nose hadn't been broken from before, I was pretty sure it was now.

A man in a quasi-military uniform seemed to have taken charge. "Has he been searched?"

"Not yet."

"Get that jacket off him and take it outside. The other guy had something sewn into the lining."

"Explosives?"

"We don't know yet. But we're not taking any chances."

My hands were uncuffed. The jacket was unzipped and pulled roughly off. Someone brought a waist chain, and my hands were cuffed again, this time in front of me and locked to the waist chain.

Hands from behind reached into my pockets and pulled out my wallet and my key ring. They felt under my shirt, around my belt, and between my legs.

"No weapons, lieutenant," the searcher said.

"What's your name?" the lieutenant said.

I didn't realize he was talking to me until one of the men holding my arms gave me a shove. "Answer him."

"Jesse Damon," I said. My tongue was thick, and I tasted blood.

"That's the name the secretary gave us last week," someone said.

"Last week? He's been in the school before?"

"Yes, lieutenant. Maybe to scope things out."

"Damon," the lieutenant said.

"Yes, sir?" I answered.

"Look at me."

Reluctantly, I raised my eyes to his face. He was clean-shaven with a scar down his left cheek. His steely eyes didn't blink.

"What's your buddy's name?"

"I don't know, sir. I came in by myself."

"Right. You expect me to believe that?"

Not much to say to that. I tried to shrug, but the grip on my arms was too tight.

"What did you come here for?"

"Dropping off some kids who go here. My girlfriend's kids." Not the time to discuss whether Kelly was really my girlfriend.

"Oh, yeah? And where are these kids?"

"I told them to hide under the desk," I said. "I think they're still there."

He narrowed his eyes and peered at me, but he moved behind the secretary's desk and jerked the chair out.

No one said anything for a long minute.

Finally, the lieutenant said "You kids okay?"

"Yeah," Chris said in a timid voice.

"Can you come out?"

"Yeah." I heard the kids scramble out of their hiding place. They were behind me. So I couldn't see them. I wished they couldn't see me.

"Get someone in here to pick up two kids."

"Medics?"

"Don't need medics. Social worker or something, if you got one."

I risked a look over my shoulder.

The female officer had taken the kids by the hand and was steering them toward the back offices.

Brianna looked back at me. "Jesse," she said. "You're hurt."

"I'm okay, honey," I said. "You just go with the nice lady."

"But you're *bleeding*," she said, pulling her hand away and running over to grasp my leg.

"I'll be fine, Brianna. The lady will take good care of you. Just go on with her."

One of the other officers pried her fingers off my leg and lifted her up.

Chris stood staring, his expression unreadable. He looked at his solar system project and took a step toward it.

"Leave it, Chris," I said.

I was jerked backward. "Shut up," one of the guys holding me said.

Why did the kids have to see me like this?

Chris stopped.

"Your mom'll be proud of how brave you guys are being," I said. "You tell her I'll be in touch as soon as I can." Which would probably be a while. If ever.

If I sent her a letter from jail, would she get somebody—maybe Chris—to read it to her? Or would she just throw it away? And if she did get somebody to read it, would she get them to write me back for her? Why should she?

Looked like I'd pick up some pretty heavy new charges. Or at least get pulled in on a parole violation. We'd both be old by the time I had any chance of being released again.

The lieutenant watched as the kids were shepherded into the office and the door closed. Then he turned back to me. "You put your girl-friends' *kids* in the middle of this? You're one sick pup."

He wasn't going to listen to anything I said.

"Let's get him away from the women and kids." They shoved me toward the door to the office.

"Is the building cleared yet?" the lieutenant asked.

A uniformed officer by the door to the office said, "I don't know. We've been maintaining radio silence."

Mrs. O'Neill slipped out of the back office. It must have been getting crowded in there.

The lieutenant nodded toward me. "Let's get this guy out of here."

The officer opened the door, and the two men holding my arms shoved me forward. The leg restraints only let me take a small step, and I stumbled, falling forward through the door.

From down the hall, several shots rang out.

My forearm felt like it had been stung by a giant wasp. It hurt so much I hardly noticed the sudden burn on my leg.

"Hold your fire!"

I felt myself being jerked upright. My arm was numb, but the left calf throbbed. I tried to put most of my weight on my right foot.

Two men in camouflage suits dashed up, They were both holding rifles. "Lieutenant."

"Is the building secure?"

"I think so. Should I make a round? Or should I use the radio."

"No sign of any explosives planted anywhere?"

"Only the jackets. Looks like a small amount of those plastic explo-sives. We put them out beyond the parking lot until the bomb squad gets here."

"How many intruders were there?"

"Just the two guys."

"This one and the shooter?"

"Yep."

"ID the shooter yet?" the lieutenant asked.

"Yeah. One Xavier Bradley."

I wondered if that were *the* Xavier. I mean, how many people are named Xavier?

"Any motive?"

"He's got a son in this school. And he's in the middle of a custody battle with the boy's mother."

"Xavier Bradley?" Mrs. O'Neill said. "He came in trying to take his son out of school late last week. I told him he couldn't. We have a copy of a restraining order."

"Did he seem upset about it?" the lieutenant asked.

"He said we'd be sorry, that it was his son and we couldn't keep him from taking his son. He said he'd be back. We called the police."

"Is that why this school's security level has been so high?"

She nodded toward me. "That and Mr. Damon there coming in."

"Wise thing to do," the lieutenant said. "We were ready for something to happen here. If we hadn't been on high alert, it would have taken a lot longer for someone to get here."

"Was anybody hurt?" Mrs. O'Neill asked.

"Just the gunman. The medics are getting ready to transport him to the hospital now. Otherwise it's just property damage."

I felt hot, sticky blood making its way down my leg and pooling in my boot. My eyes were so swollen I could hardly see out of them, and I had no doubt my face was a mess. I couldn't feel my arm. I guess I didn't count.

"Thank God," she said. "It could have been so much worse."

"You got that right."

"What are we going to do with this one, lieutenant?" one of the men holding me asked.

All eyes turned toward me.

"Take him downtown," the lieutenant said. "Have them hold him while we get a few things figured out."

"Should we get a medic to take a look at him?"

"Nah. The detention center intake ought to be able to take care of that."

"We're booking him? What are the charges?"

"We don't need charges. Damon here is a paroled murderer. Don't need no other reason to hold him. Find out who his PO is and let him know we've got him."

"Come, on, you." The men holding me propelled me forward.

"Lieutenant."

"What now?"

"Everywhere he steps, he's leaving a bloody footprint. I think he's been shot."

The lieutenant sighed. "All right. Have the medics take him to the emergency room. But see if somebody doesn't have a real set of leg irons. I don't want him trying to escape. And I don't want anybody hurt."

"Post a guard?"

"Of course."

CHAPTER 21

Hospital emergency rooms aren't my favorite places in the best of circumstances, and this wasn't the best of circumstances.

The waiting room was pretty full, but we didn't have to wait. Maybe "gunshot wound," like "heart attack," were magic words that assured immediate attention.

I was hustled through the waiting room, hands secured to a waist chain, leg irons locked firmly in place. I've never understood why those escorting someone fully shackled down, whether prison guards or police, don't take into account the length of the chain on the leg irons. I stumbled several times, saved from falling only by the burly officers who had a firm—and painful—grip on my upper arms.

My nose dripped blood. So did the sleeve of my shirt. Everyone around me had wisely taken the time to don gloves. The wound on my arm burned, but my entire face ached. My leg was somewhere between burning and numb. Without being able to see much, I had trouble keeping my balance.

It did mean, though, I was spared seeing the undoubtedly shocked looks from the people in the waiting room.

Why did I care what people thought? I didn't know any of them. I'd probably never see any of them again.

Not as humiliating as Chris and Brianna seeing me restrained, but bad enough.

Since the prison was nearby, the hospital was accustomed to receiving high risk patients and had its procedures well established. I was hurried to a cubicle at the far end where I was shoved onto an examining table and the chains rearranged so I was lying on my back, well enough secured that I could hardly move.

The two police officers flanked either side by my head.

The intake clerk came back to start the paperwork. No one talked to me. One of the cops tossed my wallet over. At least my medical insurance had kicked in. I had no doubt the bill would be in the thousands, and if I hadn't had insurance, I'd probably end up paying it off for the rest of my life.

Of course, if I ended up going back to prison, would it really matter? Not for years, at least.

I knew I had absolutely no say over what happened, so I lay back as comfortably as I could and closed my eyes. Blood began seeping down my throat, and I could hardly breathe. I turned my face to the side. Blood filled my mouth and pooled next to my face, but it beat dripping down my throat and making me choke. It wasn't long before I heard the rattle of the rings as the curtain was pulled back.

The triage nurse showed up with a big male medical assistant. "What have we got here?" She wasn't asking me.

"Injury to the left forearm and lower left leg. Possible gunshot wounds."

"What happened to his face?"

"He landed on his face when he was tackled. Maybe a broken nose. It's certainly bleeding enough."

"Head injury?"

"I don't think so. Although I guess the face *is* part of the head."

The nurse probed my arm. "You guys use precautions around the blood?"

"Yep. High risk."

"HIV positive?" she asked.

No one said anything. Someone poked my shoulder. "Answer her."

She was talking to me? "No, ma'am."

"Can't trust him to tell the truth," one of the cops said.

She turned to the assistant. "We need to see the injuries. Cut off the shirt, the pants leg and the boot."

"Don't cut the boot!" I managed to say. The damn things were expensive steel-toed work boots. Bad enough to be losing the shirt and a pair of jeans. "They're short boots. It'll slide off."

The assistant sighed. "I can get the one off. But the other one is all covered with blood. How about I just cut the laces and see if I can work the boot itself off without damaging it."

A cop by my head snorted. "He's headed for an orange jumpsuit and shower shoes anyhow."

Of course I couldn't have the boots while I was locked up. But I'd really like to have them waiting for me if I ever did get out again. Which seemed increasingly unlikely.

I could feel him work the boot off. The sore spot on my calf didn't like the manipulation, but I didn't complain. And I didn't protest when he cut into the fabric of the jeans leg.

Someone else came in. How were they all fitting in here?

The burning area of my forearm was poked. "That's a dirty wound. Might be something still in it. I'm going to numb it and give him some antibiotics. Maybe a sedative, too. He'll be less likely to give us problems."

I got two injections in my other arm.

And a series of painful little pricks in a circle around the area that was beginning to throb in earnest.

None-too-gentle hands began scrubbing at my very tender face. Prodding fingers felt my nose. I bit my lip to keep from whimpering.

One of the officers unlocked the cuff from around my left wrist. Someone roughly pulled my arm straight. I knew better than to do anything but let them handle the arm. I didn't especially want to be strapped down completely immobile so they could work on the wound.

I felt the area being scrubbed with something that burned, but then it became numb.

"Don't see anything in it," was the muttered verdict. "I don't see that it needs any stitches or anything."

A bandage was applied, then the arm was wrapped. The wound was well above my wrist; my hand was pulled back up where the cuff could be re-attached.

Fingers probed my face again. "Still bleeding. I think we'll need to pack this."

Something was shoved up my nostrils; I coughed on the blood in my throat and practically choked. I felt my nose being manipulated. It felt like portions of bone were grinding together and hurt like hell. Something was taped to my forehead.

"We'll have to wait until the swelling goes down to see exactly what we have here," the doctor said. "It might need some follow-up treatment. Maybe plastic surgery."

"Don't matter much, where he's probably headed," one of the cops said.

"You're taking him to jail?" the doctor asked.

"I imagine so. We haven't gotten our instructions yet, but he's definitely in custody now."

"Then the nurse there will be able to remove the packing in a day or two," the doctor said. "What's his substance abuse status?"

"Who cares?" the cop said.

"I mean, does he use street drugs? I don't see any needle tracks. I'm wondering if I should prescribe additional painkillers."

"Don't they all have drug problems?" the cop said. "Whether they admit it or not."

"Acetaminophen, then. With no codeine."

I felt drowsy. It seemed like if I could just get some sleep, I'd be able to make sense of all this.

Probably not.

My eyes would only open to narrow slits anyhow, so I let them close. I heard paper being shuffled.

They moved on to my leg. "This bled a lot. It looks worse than it is. It's really very superficial. We can clean it and bandage it. We don't want it to get infected."

The voices faded to murmurs. I knew I was in pain, but it didn't seem that important right now. I also knew I was in a lot of trouble and should be trying to figure out what—if anything—I could do about it. But first I needed to rest.

The curtain rings rattled as people came in and out, but it didn't bother me, so I didn't pay much attention.

No one said anything to me, but why would they? An injured dog at the vet's had about as much say in what happened to him as I did. And probably got a lot more sympathy.

I was in no particular hurry to find out what would be happening to me next anyhow. It was unlikely to be anything but very uncomfortable and very depressing. I lay there, getting a certain grim satisfaction out of not caring. When they wanted to move me, they would. At least I wasn't locked in a jail cell. Yet.

The sound of boot-steps approached. One of the cops guarding me stepped outside the treatment cubicle. I expected him to return to and to be jerked to my feet and hustled out, but that didn't happen.

When he did come back in, he removed the leg irons. Odd. Then the handcuffs. Even more odd. I flexed my stiff shoulder muscles, but didn't move my hands. No point doing anything that invited the use of physical force. I heard the chains clink as they were rolled up and several people in boots walked off, but I remained unmoving. I tried to make sense of what was happening, but my mind wouldn't cooperate. My thoughts just kept drifting off. I dozed.

I have no idea how much longer I lay there.

Finally the overhead rings clattered as the curtain was swept open. I hadn't heard anyone approach, so it was probably a hospital worker in quiet-soled nursing shoes.

"Well, you can go," she said.

She would be talking to the cops. I didn't say anything.

She touched my knee. "I said, you can go now."

I opened my eyes as well as I could and looked around. We were alone in the cubicle.

"Where are the cops?" I asked.

She shrugged. "I just got on duty. They must be gone. You're discharged. Just stop at the desk for your paperwork."

I eased myself onto the floor and stood in my grey wool socks.

"I can just go?"

"Far as I know. They'll tell you at the desk about any follow-up treatment or if they need any more information about your insurance or anything."

CHAPTER 22

I hobbled stiffly down the corridor between the cubicles, most empty but several with curtains drawn. The desk was at the far end.

The clerk behind the desk shuffled papers. "Name?" she asked without looking up.

"Jesse Damon."

She confirmed my birth date.

"Here's your instructions," she said. "You're supposed to go to your own doctor in two days to have the packing removed from your nose. Take acetaminophen for pain. You can use ice on the swelling on your face. Have the doctor check the wound on your leg and your arm. And call your doctor or come back immediately if you get any redness or additional swelling, especially on the wounds. It could be a sign of infection. If you can't get to your own doctor, come back here for follow-up care. Everything's written down for you. Sign here." She slid some papers toward me.

I took the offered pen and squinted at the paper. I signed it where she indicated. Then I took the papers she gave me.

"Do you know where I can get my stuff?" I asked.

"What stuff?" she asked.

I looked past the mangled leg of my jeans to my feet. "My boots. My wallet." My shirt was probably in the trash. It had been cut up pretty well. Last I'd heard of my jacket, it had been awaiting the bomb squad. Might not be too much left of it.

She frowned. "Didn't anyone come in with you? They probably have all your stuff."

"I came in with the police." Like they'd bother to keep track of my stuff.

"Ambulance?"

I tried to remember. All that came to mind was flashing lights and rough hands. "I think so. Might have been a patrol car."

She shook her head. "You can check at the registration desk. Sometimes the paramedics leave things there. Do you have insurance? They may have looked in your wallet to see if you have an insurance card."

"Yeah. I got insurance."

She didn't seem much interested in my dilemma once she got her paperwork back signed.

Great. I could hardly see. I was in my sock feet. I had no wallet or apartment key. My shirt was gone. One leg of my blue jeans had been cut off at the knee.

If I'd still been in custody, at least I would be getting a ride *some-where*. As it was, where ever I went, I guessed I was walking. Very possibly without boots.

I made my way out through the swinging doors that led to the waiting room. I'd have to ask at the reception desk if they had any inkling of where my stuff had ended up.

"Looking a bit rough, are we, Jesse?" a cold, cultured voice said behind me. Despite the packing in my nose, I thought I caught a whiff of mint. Montgomery.

I stopped, but didn't turn to face him. I almost hoped he would take me into custody. Then I wouldn't have to figure out what to do next.

"Have you been discharged from the hospital?" he asked.

I held up the paperwork. "Yes, sir."

"So where are you headed now?"

"Home, I suppose. I don't seem to be under arrest anymore."

He laughed. "Yes. I understand the lieutenant told the sergeant to cut you loose."

"Nobody told me that."

"They just took off the restraints and walked out, did they?"

"I guess. I didn't realize they'd left. I can't see too good." I touched the swelling around my eyes. "And I feel kind of out of it here. Dizzy and all. I hope it's the meds and it wears off."

"I hope you didn't put a lot of effort into planning to escape."

"No, sir. No point in that."

"You're nobody's dummy, Jesse. I'll give you that. Where's the rest of your clothes?"

"The boots, I don't know. The paramedics cut the shirt off. It was bloody. I imagine it's been trashed. And the bomb squad was getting the jacket. Maybe they blew it up."

He laughed. "The bomb squad gave the jacket to your girlfriend."

I wished I could be as sure that she was my girlfriend. "What was she doing there?"

"She came to pick up her kids. Most of the parents did."

"Are the kids okay?"

"As far as I know. Where'd they take your boots off?"

"When they put me in the cubicle back there. Unshackled my legs and took off the boots, then chained me to something or other. The examining table, I imagine."

"You don't *know*?"

"Well, a lot was going on. I couldn't see real well. Still can't. And I kind of, you know, went to my inner space."

He rocked back on his well-heeled shoes and considered. "Is what you call it when you drift off in the middle of an interrogation or something?"

"That's different. I got to pay attention then. Otherwise you'll tell Mr. Ramirez I'm not cooperating. And it's hard not to get tripped up."

He snorted. "You could just try telling us some version of the truth. Then it wouldn't get so complicated."

"That's pretty much what got me convicted of murder in the first place."

"Wait here. I'll see if I can dredge up your boots. Then I want to talk to you."

"Could you see if anybody's got my wallet and key chain, too?"

He laughed again. "Pathetic. You know that, Jesse? That's *really* pathetic."

I tried to grin, but it hurt. "True, that."

Gingerly, I sat in a waiting room chair, not leaning my bare back on the cold plastic. I let my fingers gently explore my swollen face. The thing they'd taped to my forehead was some kind of tube or string that led from the packing in my nostrils. The top of my nose throbbed worse when I pressed on it. The area surrounding my eyes was puffy and felt tight, but it didn't really hurt.

I just wanted to lie down and go to sleep. I knew it wasn't a good idea, but I didn't really care. I leaned forward, resting my chin on my chest and closed my eyes. That was more comfortable than trying to peer through the swelling. I dozed.

A thump right next to my vulnerable unshod feet woke me up.

Montgomery stood next to me. "There's your boots. And here's your wallet and key. You're probably right about the shirt. Couldn't find it anywhere."

Gratefully, I accepted the wallet and keychain and stuffed them into the pocket of my jeans. Leaning forward to deal with the boots made me dizzier. I lifted one up onto my lap, unlaced it and pulled out the tongue. Then I dropped it on the floor and wiggled my foot into it, just tucking the laces inside. The other boot didn't need to be unlaced—all it had were bits of cut laces in the eyelets.

"Ready?" Montgomery asked.

"I guess." Unsteadily, I stood up.

He caught me by the arm. "Let's go."

He wasn't calling for transport. He wasn't pulling out the handcuffs. That in itself was worrisome. "Where are we going?" I asked.

"Where ever you want me to take you," he said. "To your apartment?"

"You're giving me a *ride* home?" I could hardly believe that.

"If home's where you want to go."

"In your own car? Not in a cage in a patrol car? No restraints?"

Again the laugh. "I *could* call for a prisoner transport, if you'd be more comfortable. And talk to you in an interrogation room."

"No, no. I'm just not used to this. And I'm pretty confused. My brain's really messed up right now."

Montgomery grasped me by the elbow, more to guide than to restrain. "And your mouth's messed up, too," he said. "I've never heard you talk so much. I might as well take advantage of it."

"Could we swing by Kelly's?" I shivered. "See if she's home. I could get my jacket."

"If you want."

As we went out the door, the chill, raw air hit my bare shoulders. Montgomery's car was pulled up in the driveway just beyond the ambulance bay. He opened the passenger door of the front seat and let me sit down. Then he went to the trunk and pulled something out.

Opening the door again, he said, "Lean forward." I did so and he draped a zip hoodie over my shivering shoulders. It was one of the expensive kind, with soft fake fur lining. He pulled it around so it covered my back and met in the front.

I was surprised. "Thanks." Knowing how fastidious he was about his clothes and his person and mindful of the possibility of getting blood on it, I said, "I'll be sure it's been washed when I get it back to you."

"Don't bother," he said. "I always keep sweat pants and shirt in the trunk in case I have to go grunging around on an investigation. And have time to change. You can keep it. No big deal."

Maybe not to him, but a warm hoodie would be a welcome addition to my meager wardrobe. "Thanks," I said again.

Then he got in the driver's side and removed the "Official Business" plaque from the windshield.

Montgomery's car was every bit as meticulously kept as his person. It occurred to me that he might have decided he'd rather give me the hoodie than to chance I'd get his upholstery contaminated, but I reminded myself that he didn't have to be giving me a ride at all. If he wanted to talk to me, he had plenty of other ways to go about it.

"Why did they just release me?" I asked as he eased the big gray sedan away from the curb.

"They looked at the surveillance videos," he said. "It was pretty obvious that you were a victim, if anything. And they needed the manpower elsewhere."

"Any other people hurt?" I asked.

"You're the only lucky one," he said. "You and the intruder. Good thing you got those kids out of the way."

I'd asked before, but I wanted some reassurance. "They're okay?"

"A bit traumatized, but physically okay. Their mother picked them up and took them home."

He pulled out of the hospital driveway and headed toward the side of town where Kelly lived, with its big old turn-of-the-twentieth-century brick houses and well-kept yards.

"You know where she lives?" I asked.

He glanced at me. "I know where you put the dirty tissues when you sneeze. Of course I know where she lives."

That was probably true. We rode in silence for a few minutes.

"How much do you know about that Tabernacle of the Whatever upstairs from your place?" he asked.

"The Tabernacle of the Inaccurate Conception?" I asked.

"Yes. That's it."

"Well, to begin with, I think the name's a typo, so to speak. I think it's supposed to be the Tabernacle of the *Immaculate* Conception. The sign wasn't made professionally. And the cult members aren't a particularly well-educated lot."

Montgomery narrowed his eyes and glanced at me sideways. "And I suppose you are?"

"No. But I can *read*. And I know the difference between *inaccurate* and *immaculate*."

"How'd you find that out?"

I shifted in the seat, drawing the hoodie closer around my shoulders. "Remember when you and Belkins left me lying in the alley? When he slammed my head against the wall and kneed me in the nuts?"

"Yes."

"This cult member, Isaac, helped me get back to my apartment."

Montgomery raised his fine dark eyebrows. "I didn't realize you needed help."

I shrugged. "I kind of passed out. But Isaac got me up and got me down the stairs to my place."

"What was he doing out in the alley?"

"Turns out they lost their goddess."

"Lost their goddess?"

"Yeah. They had this cat they thought was their goddess. She got out. I think when this guy Xavier was supposed to be watching her. He'd sneak out for a smoke, leaving the door propped open behind him. Isaac was looking for her."

"You know Xavier?"

"Not really. Is he the guy who shot up the school?"

"We're investigating all possibilities."

"Cause Xavier had a kid he was trying to get custody of. And he just got some kind of gun."

"What else do you know about the cult?"

"Father Peter, the leader, is Xavier's father. I don't know that Xavier's as dedicated to the whole Tabernacle thing as the rest of them. He had unsupervised visitation with the kid, but I think the mother was trying to get that changed."

"Do you think that's a good idea?"

"I don't know. If he was really the nutcase who shot up the school, then no. But seems like kids ought to be able to see their father. Supervised, maybe. That's how Kelly's kids are supposed to see their father. But I don't think it would be a good idea to give custody to a crazy like Xavier, even if he wasn't the shooter."

"Do you know why Kelly's kids' visits with their father are supposed to be supervised?"

"He drinks." I didn't mention that Kelly did, too. "He left them in his car one night while he was in a bar, then had a DUI accident with them in the car."

"Back to the goddess. What happened to the cat?"

"She ended up in the stairwell outside my apartment in the sleet the day I went to Mrs. Coleman's wake. She looked miserable, so I let her come into my place."

"Did you think she was a stray?"

"Nah. She was obviously someone's cat. Fat and she had this heavy collar, with rhinestones and things on it."

"Really? A collar with rhinestones?"

"Yeah. Probably because they thought she was a goddess. But she hated the collar, kept scratching at it. So I took it off."

"You still have them?"

"What? The cat? Or the collar?"

"Both."

"Well, Isaac was real happy to see the cat. Turns out she was pregnant. That's why she was so fat. She had two kittens. He thought the kittens were little gods. I helped him carry them back upstairs to the altar, where they had this gold box she was supposed to sleep in."

"Real gold?"

"Gold paint, I think. Then he got kicked out of the cult until he brings back the collar. He took the cat along with him."

"So where is it now?"

"At my place. I put out enough food and water for her for a while. Since Kelly asked me to come over after work, I was thinking I might get, you know, lucky. And I didn't want to have to worry about feeding the cat."

"So where's the collar?"

"I dunno. Probably somewhere in my place. I tossed it on my dresser. Isaac was so happy to get the goddess back; we never thought about putting the collar back on her."

"Nobody ever asked about the collar?"

"Just Isaac, like I said. But he decided not to go back to the cult, so I just let it go."

"So you didn't look for it?"

"Nah. But I didn't really look for it, either. I mean, *he* didn't have anything to do with the collar going missing. Or the cat, for that matter. They wouldn't believe him. Said he'd probably hocked it. To go back to the pawn shop to get it back."

"And I take it he'd done no such thing."

"Nope."

We rode on in silence. After a few minutes, I said, "Somebody was talking about jewelry in the Tabernacle. Was gonna break in to look for it. A bracelet or something."

"Who was that?"

"Aaron." I paused. "Those weren't *rhinestones* in the collar, were they?"

"Good chance not."

"Maybe I better see if I can find it. And get rid of it."

Montgomery glanced at me. "Be careful."

"Maybe give you a call if it turns up?"

"Might be a good idea."

The car's heater was beginning to churn out heat. It felt good and made me sleepy.

"Back to this Tabernacle thing. You think it's really a cult?" Montgomery asked.

"Seemed like it to me. All dressed in those saffron robes. Saying a cat is their goddess. Everybody is supposed to do whatever Father Peter tells them to. Sure isn't any kind of regular religion that I ever heard of."

"How much do you know about their beliefs?"

"Not a whole lot. Seemed like a jumble of religions. The immaculate conception idea is Catholic, of course. And worshipping cats is Egyptian—Isaac told me that. From what he said, it takes in young men who haven't had much of a father figure in their lives. Isaac said he doesn't know who his father is. That's why I didn't realize the 'inaccurate conception' was supposed to be 'immaculate conception' at first."

Montgomery chuckled. "So you think most of them were looking for a father? And Father Peter stepped in to fill the void?"

"Probably. Except for Xavier, of course. Isaac said they were all searching for roots. He said Father Peter was born somewhere around here and had come back to find *his* roots."

"Do you know who Father Peter's parents are?"

"No idea."

"What happened to Xavier's mother?"

"No idea."

"Do you know what Xavier's street name is?"

"No. I didn't know cult members had street names."

"This one does. He's known as Zee. Probably from Xavier."

That got my attention. "Aaron says that Zee was at the Colemans' house when she died."

Montgomery sighed. "And you didn't tell me that?"

"I wasn't even sure Zee actually existed. I thought he might be a figment of Aaron's overactive imagination."

"And what supposedly happened that ended up with Mrs. Coleman dead?"

"The housekeeper—Rosa, her name was, or something—gave her a shove, and she fell down the stairs."

"You weren't going to tell me that, either?"

"Well, I figured you'd have found her and talked to her."

"She hasn't been seen since the day Mrs. Coleman died. She seems to have been an illegal alien. We thought she was afraid she'd get in trouble and be deported. But after what happened today, we'll be looking harder for her."

I shivered. "Xavier was screwing her, wasn't he?"

"Yes."

"She thought he might marry her."

"Sounds likely."

I leaned back against the headrest. Montgomery drove a comfortable car. No surprise there. "What I don't understand was how come Mrs. Coleman would let Xavier hang around. I mean, yeah, Rosa could have let him in the house and all, but why would Mrs. Coleman give him the time of day?"

"What's your theory?"

He was asking me? "Mrs. Coleman had a baby she gave up for adoption. At first I thought Xavier might be that baby. But he's much too young. Maybe she was getting senile or something?"

"Whatever it was, she was writing checks to him. And giving him cash. She said it was pay for doing yard work and painting the garage, but it was much too much for that."

I thought about that for a minute. "They were cheating an old lady."

"Yes. Convinced her that she *owed* them something."

My head felt too heavy, like it would break off and fall into my lap. I forced my eyes open as far as I could.

We were sitting still, parked at the curb in front of Kelly's house. I stirred myself.

"I wonder if she'll want to see me," I said.

"She should. If it wasn't for you, her kids might have been shot."

"If it wasn't for me, her kids wouldn't have been in school at all this morning. And they wouldn't have been where they could've gotten hurt."

"Can't speak to that." Montgomery leaned back in his seat. "You want me to wait while you go see about your jacket? If she doesn't want you to stay, I can give you a ride home."

I looked at him. "You're being awfully helpful."

"And you're being awfully talkative. Not like you. That's helpful to me."

I had been, hadn't I? Babbling on like I didn't know any better. "Probably an effect of the drugs they gave me."

"Maybe we ought to use those drugs whenever we want to interrogate somebody. Especially you."

I smiled. "If it was some kind of truth serum and you could use the results in court, it might not be so bad. Then you'd know for sure I didn't kill Mrs. Coleman."

"Oh, I'm pretty sure by now you didn't kill Mrs. Coleman."

"Really?"

"I think so. But there's still a lot I don't know yet. That's why I needed to find out what you know about the Tabernacle and Xavier and Father Peter."

"What's the Tabernacle got to do with Mrs. Coleman's murder?"

"Not entirely sure yet."

"How about the shooting at the school?"

"What about the shooting at the school?"

"Did that have anything to do with the Tabernacle?"

"Well, the shooter *was* Xavier."

"What did he think he was trying to do?"

"Seems to have just flipped. He was supposed to be in family court for a hearing on the visitation. But he went to the school instead. That's where his kid goes. He claimed that the public school was corrupting the kid and that he had the right to take his son whether the court agreed with him or not."

"Couldn't Father Peter stop him? Where was he?"

"Sitting out in the van, ready to take off with the kid if Xavier got him."

I tried to digest that. "Did he really think they were going to get away with that?"

"Apparently. He's been listening to his own preaching too much. Decided that, like in biblical times, children belong to the father."

"Yet most of his followers have no fathers to speak of."

"Even Father Peter had no idea who his father was. He was adopted. But he did find out who his birth mother was."

"Yeah? Who?"

"Mildred Coleman. She had him before she was married and put him up for adoption. He couldn't forgive her for that. Or for not telling him who his father was."

"He went to see her?" Of course, I'd been tempted to do the same thing. And she wasn't even my biological mother. In the end, I'd waited until she was dead.

"Yes. And Xavier extorted money from her. Told her she owed them."

"So Xavier was Mrs. Coleman's grandson."

Montgomery shifted in his seat. "Yep. And he was demanding more and more from her. Maybe he got too rough with her. Probably didn't mean to *kill* her."

"How about Rosa?"

"We think she panicked when she realized Mrs. Coleman was badly hurt and called 9-1-1. Then she fled. Immigration problems and all."

My sleepy brain was reeling. My head pounded. "So what's going to happen to the Tabernacle?"

"Unless someone else steps up to run it, my guess is that it'll be disbanded."

"What's going to happen to the cat?"

"You want to keep it?"

"Yeah. I guess. If I'm not gonna be locked up."

"I don't see why you would be locked up at this point. I'll see what I can do."

I climbed out of the car and stood shivering on Kelly's porch, Montgomery's hoodie pulled around me. I glanced back at Montgomery, still sitting in his car by the curb. No point putting off seeing Kelly. I pressed the doorbell.

"Who's there?" Kelly called from inside.

"Jesse."

She didn't say anything. I heard the key click in the lock.

"I came to see if I could get my jacket. Is it still in the car? I could just go pick it up."

The door opened. Kelly threw her arms around me. "Jesse!" She collapsed against my chest, crying.

I tried not to flinch away at the pressure on my bandaged arm. I put my unwounded arm around her shoulders and very carefully leaned my face into her hair, kissing the top of her head.

"Come in," she said, straightening up and wiping her eyes. "You look terrible."

"I just came to get my jacket."

"Nonsense. You'll stay here for a few days, until you're better."

"But back at my apartment I got to…"

She tugged my arm. "We can go get whatever you need from your apartment. Later."

"Do you like cats?" I asked.

"Yep. And I've been promising the kids we could get a kitten when this custody mess gets cleared up."

I turned and waved at Montgomery. He started the car.

I followed Kelly into the house. She shut the door behind us.

ABOUT THE AUTHOR

KM Rockwood has a diverse background including working as a laborer in a steel fabrication plant, operating glass melters and related equipment in a fiberglass manufacturing facility, and supervising an inmate work crew in a large medium security state prison. These jobs, as well as work as a special education teacher in an alternative high school and a GED teacher in county detention facilities, provide most of the basis for novels and short stories.

Look for the next books in the Jesse Damon series, including: *The Buried Biker*, *Sendoff for a Snitch*, and *Brothers in Crime*.

www.kmrockwood.com